# THE CATHAWYR

Odan Terridor Trilogy: Book 3

## By Savannah J. Goins

# THE CATHAWYR

Owen Dwir
Sequoia
Castell

Obart
Terrisor
Ibatsius
Arboria

*This book contains brief, vague flashbacks of sexual abuse. Many people who have experienced this in their past have found this story to be cathartic and helpful in their growth and healing, but discretion is advised for readers sensitive to this theme.*

See page 274 for glossary and pronunciations of
places and names.

I broke through the surface and beamed at the ledge, but no one was there.

*He must be a little farther back, hidden in the trees.*

But I paddled closer, and still there wasn't the slightest hint of red anywhere. I pulled myself onto land and climbed up to the ledge, my heart sinking further and further. Where was he? Maybe just invisible?

"Gaedyen?"

Dirt clods freckled the grass in places—the few places grass remained. Was this evidence of a fight? A fight that resulted in Gaedyen being taken away somewhere against his will?

My heart raced. Had Meleena found us? But Gaedyen hadn't smelled her at all on the way here. I knelt and traced a track in the dirt with two fingers. No, not a track. Lots of little tracks together. Made by lots of little feet.

Last time we'd been here, Veri and I had accidentally pissed off all the other Crivabanians. Had they found Gaedyen alone and taken this opportunity to capture him?

Focusing on the disturbed ground again, I followed the pulled-up grass as it turned into tracks.

"I'm coming for you, Gaedyen."

# CHAPTER ONE

"Hey, Fuzzbucket!" I flicked a pebble at Veri. "It's time to get up! Let's go!"

A drowsy, heavy-lidded Crivabanian face emerged from the folds of my discarded sweatshirt, looking half-dead. The dark swoosh of bangs, usually swishing over his forehead, was tousled. One tuft poked out above the rest while his pointed brown ears drooped.

I cocked my head. "Veri, you look ridiculous."

Standing, he smiled sleepily and stretched his little arms toward the sky, his furry gliding membranes flaring out from his wrists over either side. "Thanks, Enzi. I can always count on you for moral support." Yawning, he rubbed his eyes.

I grinned. "Always." A cool wind rustled through the trees around us, but there was no sign of Gaedyen returning from his walk yet. My heart ached for him. Padraig had his faults for sure, but he was the only father-figure Gaedyen had ever known. And he'd just sacrificed himself to take out Tukailaan and save us all.

Veri stumbled stiffly from the folds of worn fabric, running coal-black forepaws over his messy fur to smooth it out a bit.

With a twinge of surprise, I noticed the whites of his eyes were off-color. "Hey, man, are you feeling okay? You actually do look kind of terrible."

"'Ridiculous, terrible.' You embarrass me with your compliments, madam." He yawned again, slouching more deeply than usual.

Crossing my arms, I squinted at him. "You're welcome, sir." Maybe I was just imagining it, but something seemed off. "You fell asleep last night while Gaedyen and I planned our next move. We decided we're going to fly back to Odan Terridor and talk to Soroco, Gaedyen's great aunt, about what to do next."

Someone had to tell Odan Terridor and the other realms about the deaths of Padraig, Aven, and Dyn Meddy, the last remaining Possessors. Well, *official* Possessors anyway. Right now, no one else in all the realms besides us three knew about them or the death of the menace, Tukailaan.

Veri swayed and fell back hard, his long tail keeping him from rolling backward.

I slid on my knees to his side. "Veri?"

He blinked up at me, then shook himself. "Just tired. I'm fine."

"How about I carry the rocks for a while?" Maybe that would lighten his load enough to help.

He shrugged. "Sure. I'll still have Possession of both of them either way." Reaching into the furry pouch over his belly, he removed the ruddy Crivabanian rock—the one that gave him even *more* incredible strength than what he'd already been born with—and placed it in my palm. He yawned again and retrieved the forest-green Adarborian rock, which had granted him the ability to expand in size just in time to stop Tukailaan from crushing me yesterday, and laid it next to the other.

He'd saved my life, but he only had the ability because he'd been the first to touch the Crivabanians' rock after its previous Possessor had passed away. Dyn Meddy, Veri's mentor and friend. Veri was grieving just as much as Gaedyen right now. That was why he was so…not himself.

"Thank you." I frowned, wishing in vain for the right words to comfort him as I shoved the rocks into my pants pocket. They pressed uncomfortably against my leg, barely fitting with the white rock of healing—the one we'd soon be trading to the Cathawyrs for information about my and Gaedyen's fathers—already taking up space there. But better my pocket than Veri's right now, apparently.

I shivered in the cool morning breeze. It had been delightfully warm under Gaedyen's wing, and I missed that heat now. While the ability to turn invisible like a Gwythienian was incredibly cool, it would also have been nice for Possession of their rock to come with Gwythienian-like body heat, too.

Veri stood and stretched again, less wobbly than before.

*Hmm.*

I grabbed the sweatshirt from the ground and pulled it on, wishing my biggest problem was fitting all five rocks in my pocket, instead of the fact that the Gwythienians' purple rock and the Rubandors' cerulean one were currently in some mysterious location known only to the now-deceased Tukailaan. At least he *was* finally dead.

Hoisting the Adarborian bow and quiver that had been a gift from Aven over my head, I sighed and wrinkled my nose. "Ugh, this sweatshirt smells like wild animal now."

"Really, Enzi." Veri climbed onto my shoulder, slipping a bit before catching his grip. "Ooph. You better lay off the flattery or I'm going to start thinking you've got a crush on *me*." He patted my head.

My face warmed and I glanced over my shoulder. No Gaedyen yet. *Whew.* Gaedyen wouldn't need any teasing with what he was going through right now. I needed to get Veri on to another topic before Gaedyen returned. "Dude, did you just miss your footing? Are you okay?"

"I think I'm just sore from yesterday. You know, suddenly having ten times your original amount of strength and turning into a Crivabanian rubber band can do that to a person."

"Hmm." He did have a point.

Veri nudged the quiver just a bit further to the side and settled into the sweatshirt hood. Immediately he went uncharacteristically still.

*Grieving for Dyn Meddy and healing from the fight. Makes sense.*

Leaves rustled more loudly behind me and my cheeks heated again. I turned. Gaedyen's huge dragon form strode through the leafy branches, the sun glinting off his red-brown scales and the moisture in his eyes.

My heart dropped to my toes. He was hurting, of course. What was the right way to comfort him?

He caught my gaze and offered me a tired-eyed smile as he approached. "Are the two of you ready to fly for Odan Terridor?"

I returned his smile, trying to calm my heart rate back down. It seemed too good to be true that *he* loved me, too, after everything. "We're ready. Veri's still wiped out, though."

He stretched his wings and shook them out like an athlete shaking out their arms before a game. "Veri, I'll fly as smoothly as I can so you can rest on the flight."

"Thanks, Gaedyen." Veri mumbled.

Adjusting the neck of the sweatshirt so that Veri's weight didn't choke me, I stepped to Gaedyen's side as he leaned one shoulder down for me to mount. I pulled myself up slowly, careful to avoid jostling Veri. Though of course they were both right. Veri just needed a little more rest.

"Ready?" Gaedyen asked.

"Ready." I leaned forward and pressed my knees against his neck.

Gaedyen leaped forward, slamming his wings down. Soon we were riding the breeze. I smiled at the chill bite of the wind on my face. This was my place. This was where I belonged. In the sky, with Gaedyen. Breathing the fresh air no one else got to breathe.

Veri shifted in my hood. Coughing, I pulled the fabric and the quiver strap away from my throat again. Normally he enjoyed the wind of flight even more than I did, hanging on to me with one paw, relishing the breeze on his face and singing at the top of his lungs with me.

Could all this really just be tiredness from yesterday?

The last edge of a brilliant sunset stretched over the forest where Odan Terridor's entrances were hidden near Mom's and my apartment. The foliage had grown so thick and green that I wondered how Gaedyen would find the cave entrance. But after following the river for a while, his earflaps perked up with recognition and his wingbeats slowed. As we descended, I poked Veri, hoping the additional day of sleep had helped. "Hey! We're landing. Wakey, wakey!"

He swatted my hand away and mumble-growled.

Hmm. Attitude. That *could* be a good sign.

After Gaedyen landed, I slid down one side and stretched my arms.

Veri crawled onto my shoulder.

I watched him from the corner of my eye. "Hey, Fuzzbucket. How're you feeling?"

"Fine. Just a little sore still."

"Hmm." He did at least seem a little steadier on his feet.

Lush foliage sprang from every direction, filling up all the spaces that had been sparce and gray several weeks ago. Last time I'd been here, it was snowing and all the trees were bare. That was when I'd first met Tukailaan in his human form, calling himself *Tony*.

I had been such a scared little girl then. Afraid of everything. It was nice to see that I'd changed since then. Gotten stronger.

I turned to Gaedyen. "So where in Odan Terridor should we look for Soroco?"

"Do you remember when you first woke up in Odan Terridor, in the root tunnels? When you screamed and gave our location away when everyone was on alert for a human scent? It is kind of near there."

I raised an eyebrow. "You know, that wasn't my fault. You scared the crap out of me, so you deserved that."

He winced. "You are not wrong. I am sorry about that."

I squinted in the general direction of the cave again, trying to make it out among the greenery. "So how many Gwythienians want me dead for being a human and having Possession of the Gwythienian's rock? And what about Veri? He's in as much trouble as me now. Twice as much."

Gaedyen stared ahead. "You do not have anything to fear from them now."

"But now that Tukailaan isn't a threat, there's no reason for them to keep us alive. From their perspective, they'd all be better off if both of us…weren't around so one of them could take Possession."

His tired eyes hardened. "Trust me, Enzi. You will be safe."

I pursed my lips, but I did trust his word. "All right." I had the bow too, and now a Gwythienian to bite sticks into rymakri if needed. "Let's go."

Hoisting the strap of the quiver into a more comfortable position over my chest, I followed Gaedyen into the tunnel, Veri by my side.

It was a quicker walk this time. Gaedyen and I were more surefooted, and when my hand found that strange section of wall with all that piled-up rubble, I remembered something Tukailaan had said. There was a trigger of some kind, something that had alerted him when we walked past this section of old, unused tunnel. No alert could reach him now, but if that pile of rubble blocked a tunnel that led to his lair…

"Hey, Gaedyen, what if the other two rocks could be through there? On the other side of this wall where Tukailaan had sensed us pass by in the beginning? He could have hidden them there before coming after us again. It would've been safer than risking dropping them during a fight."

The echoing of his heavy footfalls shrank into the distance as he paused. "It could be a great place to start looking. We can return here after consulting with Soroco."

His footsteps continued, and Veri and I followed. I strained my ears for Veri's soft footsteps. If we lost him in this dark… My hand bumped hard into something soft and furry.

"Ouch." Veri complained.

"Oops." I drew my hand back. "Sorry."

"If you want to babysit me so bad, just hold my hand."

I tentatively waved my hand around at my side. Was he joking or serious? My fingers closed around his small hand, and he pulled me to catch up with Gaedyen.

*Not joking? Veri?*

Mottled blueish light just barely shone through the leafy vine curtain covering the entrance when Veri yawned once again.

"Dude, just come back up here and sleep in my hood. You don't need to be walking around when you're not feeling well."

"I'm fine," he said through another yawn. I rolled my eyes and determined to pick him up and stuff him into my hood the next time he wobbled.

We approached the entrance quietly, not yet ready for our presence to be known. Not before we knew who was out there. Gaedyen stuck his head out first, carefully scanning the area. When he took a step through the vines, I followed him, Veri slogging at my side.

Dense vegetation grew several feet higher than the last time I'd been here. Many of the plants were taller than Gaedyen, creating something like a full-fledged jungle.

Gaedyen went invisible and strode right through the vines and into Odan Terridor with Veri and an invisible me close behind.

The thick stalks and wide leaves of the most common plants were thicker and wider than I remembered. And that faintly blue light that came from nowhere but illuminated everything was also the same, creating a peaceful ambience. It didn't feel anything like being in a cave.

Far above our heads, a twisting jumble of crisscrossing tree roots made up the ceiling of Odan Terridor—and many Gwythienian living spaces.

A distant rushing of water called my attention to the stony wall on the same side of the path as the entrance we'd come through.

*The Vorbiaquam.* The place where I'd found the Adarborians' Lyrik with directions to their realm's entrance, and then had to hide from Padraig while he railed at Gaedyen.

I frowned. Hadn't Padraig complained about Gaedyen coming to the Vorbiaquam all the time, even after being warned away over and over? But he hadn't been going for the Lyrik, because he couldn't remember all of it, and that was why I'd had to go get it in the first place. What had he been going in there for? Looking for his parents?

I wanted to ask him, but it was too soon after Padraig's death to bring him up just out of curiosity.

"We can fly from here. Enzi?" Gaedyen leaned one shoulder down, and I scooped Veri up, tucked him against my side, and slid over Gaedyen's neck. We flew over the dusty section of path where he'd dropped me that first day. I'd been so pissed at him. And to think now we were…

"Hang on!" Gaedyen's voice rumbled.

I pressed Veri into my side and gripped Gaedyen's neck with my knees and my other hand.

He grabbed the edge of an opening into the root ceiling, nearly slung us off with the sudden change in momentum, and then swung up and into the hole.

My heart raced painfully. I slid off him, clutching Veri, and cleared my throat. "How about a clearer warning next time, huh? I was holding on tight, but barely enough to have survived *that*." I tripped over the uneven floor and caught myself on Gaedyen's arm. "Oops. Thanks."

The blueish light from below glowed brightest over the opening, throwing a slight blue-purple hue to his skin. He smiled, then ducked his head to peer out of the hole. He had a nice smile, no matter which of his forms he wore.

Tangled roots made up the floor and ceiling of this place, stretching out as far as I could see. The ceiling height varied from tall enough for Gaedyen to walk through to one place that looked too short for even a hunching Veri to enter. It reminded me of the attic in Jillian's house, where the roof tapered to a point. We played there sometimes when we were younger. Before she ditched me for cooler friends.

A few roots hung from the tangled masses like a loose curl waiting to be tucked back into a braid.

Gaedyen lifted his head, shadows playing over his face. "Here she comes."

"Gaedyen? Is that you?" A female Gwythienian poked her head through the hole and squinted at us, fine wrinkles gathering at the edges of her eyes. Her head bobbed up and down with her wingbeats as she held herself aloft.

"Yes, Soroco. I've returned with Enzi the human, Possessor of our rock, and Veri the Crivabanian, Possessor of the Adarborians' and Crivabanians' rocks." Gaedyen nodded at us. "I fear we bring grave news."

Soroco's huge fingers latched on to the rim as she hoisted herself up and in. She gracefully turned and sat on her haunches across the opening from us. Her faded beige skin had a slightly loose appearance, and her head was more slender and her neck slightly longer than Gaedyen's, but she held herself straight and proud like all Gwythienians do.

"Go on," she said, resignation in her voice. She acknowledged both Veri and I with a polite nod as her tail wrapped around her forelegs.

Gaedyen glanced down, his ear flaps drooping. I laid a hand on his shoulder as he continued. "Padraig is…he is dead."

Soroco's eyes closed as her head and ear flaps mirrored Gaedyen's. "I feared this would happen when he left in such a state. When…when did he pass?"

"Yesterday."

She sighed. "Oh, Padraig. He was an excellent leader, your grandfather, but he never did get his freedom back."

I wiped a stray tear off my cheek. *Interesting choice of words.* But it was true. "None of the Possessors did. They're all dead now. Aven and Dyn Meddy died shortly before Padraig— we weren't able to get to Aven in time to save her from the arkencain wound, and Tukailaan had already murdered Dyn Meddy. And Gwaltmar died a few years ago."

Soroco's eyes flashed from mine to Gaedyen's. "Oh no. Does that mean…?"

"No, Tukailaan did not win." Gaedyen assured her. "Padraig died taking Tukailaan down with him. For that, at least, we can be grateful."

Soroco's eyes slid shut as her body sagged a bit. "That is a relief. How many other rocks do you have in hand?"

Gaedyen nodded to me. "We have the Adarborians', the Crivabanians', and the Cathawyrs'—the rock of healing."

Veri's sleepy, ruffled head emerged over my shoulder, blinking drearily as I produced the first two rocks for Soroco's inspection.

Soroco brightened. "So it *does* exist? You found the rock of healing?"

Gaedyen nodded. "Tukailaan was the last to have the other two, but he did not have them on him when he died. We are planning to ask the Cathawyrs for advice on where to look for them once we take their rock of healing back to them, as we promised."

Soroco's eyes grew so wide that flecks of gold shone in their brown-green color. There was something deeper in her interest. Something important to her about this one.

"Where is it?" she glanced between the three of us.

"Here." I pulled the whitish rock out of my pocket and held my palm up to her.

She squinted at it, then her eyes focused on me. "Are you sure this is the rock of healing?"

I looked at Gaedyen, surprised. "Yes. I mean, Bricriu said it was."

Her face went solemn. "You met Bricriu?"

"Unfortunately," Gaedyen frowned, "and Soroco, Geneva is still alive. Bricriu has been keeping her alive with the rock of healing all along. He is still the Possessor, so it still works right now for her. I am worried about what the Cathawyrs will decide to do with it, but we promised we would return it, and I do not think the Cathawyrs are to be crossed."

"Enzi, may I see it?" She held out her leathery, Gwythienian hand to me. It was about the same size as Gaedyen's, but her wrist and fingers were slimmer and her scaly skin lighter. It was the only other Gwythienian hand I'd ever really seen this close—without fighting for my life.

I placed the rock of healing in her open palm and watched as she examined it. Blue light flickered dimly off its surfaces. She turned it this way and that, bounced it in one palm a couple of times, then held it up to one eye.

Her gaze alighted on us again. "Gaedyen, this is not the rock of healing."

# CHAPTER TWO

My stomach dropped. This hard-won, freaking magic rock was not the actual magic rock we'd thought? The Cathawyrs were supposed to be our next stop. It was time to finally find out what my father had to do with any of this—how I ever came to have the rock in the first place and end up in this world with a crush on a dragon.

"How can you tell?" Veri piped up, his voice slightly hoarse.

She held it out to me. "Compare it to the other two."

Our hands met in the middle of the space between us, the crimson and emerald ones shimmering in my open palm, the pale grayish-white one sitting opaquely in hers.

Soroco eyed them. "This rock is rough. It does not shimmer as if it was just pulled from a river. This is a regular rock. Not the rock of healing."

Gaedyen closed his eyes and inhaled slowly. After exhaling, he eyed Soroco. "I do not think that we should return to the Cathawyrs without the rock. Should we return to Bricriu and Geneva to search for it again?"

My shoulders slumped. Veri grunted and scrambled to keep his perch. "Sorry, Veri. This is so frustrating."

Soroco frowned at the false rock of healing. "I am afraid you are right. We will need the Cathawyrs' magic to transfer Possessorships without the deaths of the current Possessors."

I exchanged gulping glances with Veri. *It would definitely be nice if Possessorship could be transferred without our deaths, please! But how could we convince Kymri to help us now?*

Soroco continued. "If you renege on a promise to them, getting their help could prove exceedingly difficult. I am afraid there is no other choice but to visit Bricriu and Geneva again and find the real rock if they have it, or learn whatever you can of its location so that we are ultimately able to secure the Cathawyrs' assistance."

Gaedyen closed his eyes, probably fearing seeing his mother so sick again. So close and yet still so far away. She had looked sick enough before that she could even die before we returned. She could be dead right now.

I couldn't imagine how hard it had been on Gaedyen to have to leave his mom with the guy who'd tried to kill her once. How would I have handled it if Mom had ever dated? Of course, she knew my father was still alive and living in the nearest psychological institution. Even though she went years without telling me about it—just let me *think* he was dead that whole time.

I waited for the familiar ache of betrayal to claw at my stomach, but it was muted. More like a memory of a feeling I'd had a long time ago. I missed her. I was still pissed at her for keeping Dad from me for all those years. But now...I wanted to see her again.

Soroco sighed, bringing me back to the sapphire light glowing along the edges of intertwining roots. "I wonder what might have been different, if Padraig and Gwaltmar, all those decades ago, would have just kept their own rocks. I should have known they had switched. I cannot believe they are both gone now."

So much would've been different. Would I have ended up the Possessor of the Rubandors' rock instead of the Gwythienians'? Or would the rock never have crossed my path, and I never would have met Gaedyen?

I squeezed his shoulder, glad to be here now, with him, despite whatever difficult task we would need to do next.

I eyed Soroco curiously. "You knew Padraig and Gwaltmar when they were young?"

Soroco smiled, a far-away look coming over her face. "Yes. My friend, Taflicyel, Gaedyen's grandmother, was obsessed with Padraig. She used to spy on him while he practiced Arunca Rymakri. He was quite good throwing rymakri, but she was better. It took many years longer than it should have, but it was thanks to me that they finally decided to commit to each other." She wore a quietly proud smile, despite the tear rolling down one cheek. "They were very happy for the time they had. Your father, Ferrox, was a very loved youngling."

A lump of emotion clogged my throat. *Thank you for getting Gaedyen's grandparents together, Soroco.* I squeezed Gaedyen's shoulder again, grateful for Soroco because without her, he wouldn't have existed, and my life would've been so gray.

Soroco swiped her tear away and straightened. "You must leave immediately to secure the real rock of healing. Then take it to the Cathawyrs as you promised, get any information you can on the whereabouts of the Gwythienian and Rubandor rocks—if they know anything—and ask them about coming to the Possessorship Ceremony to set everything straight. I fear this will be complicated."

Definitely. We had come so far, and we still had so much to do.

Exhaling, she gazed at all three of us. "It will not be an easy journey, Gaedyen." Her eyes softened, tears pooling. "I love your mother, too. I would love to see her again, alive and healthy. But you have to understand the importance of keeping your word to the Cathawyrs, since they are the most magic-wielding in all the realms since the Arkensilvers died off."

"Wait," I interrupted, "the Arkensilvers. Who were they, and what do they have to do with the arkencains?"

Her eyes flashed. "The Arkensilvers were a cruel race. Beautiful, but cruel. They had the bodies of silver foxes—black and silver, sleek and slender. They could draw magic out of something and put it into something else. They often pulled magic from nature and wove it into their weapons. Despite these attributes, they fought amongst themselves and eventually killed themselves off."

Soroco's eyes and teeth gleamed with blue flame. "The arkencain was the cruelest of their inventions. Elongated, sharp projectiles could be shot with a crossbow or used for stabbing—similar to our rymakri. But the magic in them warped to a poison. When pups were training to hunt, they were made to shoot arkencains at their prey, and they were forced to follow the prey around until it died from poison. The farther from the heart the projectile struck, the longer the poison would take. And the longer the pup would go hungry, waiting for its prey to die."

I asked, "Why would anyone be so cruel?"

"It was to force the younglings to improve their aim."

Was that why it took Aven longer to die than Dyn Meddy? Because maybe Tukailaan struck him closer to the heart? A shiver rippled through me, and I leaned against Gaedyen's warm foreleg. We'd been so near one of those horrible things recently.

She continued. "You must avoid such weapons at all costs. Get the real rock of healing, and then fly to the Cathawyrs as quickly as you can. You must understand what it means for the realms not to be able to fix things with a Possessorship Ceremony." Her mouth trembled as twin tears escaped her eyes.

Gaedyen regarded her gravely. "We understand. We will return to Bricriu."

We slept in Soroco's quarters—a bit of the root tunnels near the entrance we'd come through. She shook loose dirt from the ceiling onto the floor and pressed it in between and over the roots. When I asked why, she said it was so Veri and I would be more comfortable since we weren't accustomed to sleeping on the uneven surface of the roots. It still hadn't been very comfortable, but I'd fallen asleep quickly after an exhausting day.

Veri's eyes were more open and awake the next morning, and he finally stopped dragging his feet. He stood a little straighter too. Not quite back to his old self, but better.

He scampered up to my shoulder and perched, gripping fistfuls of fabric as I climbed onto Gaedyen's back.

"Feeling better?" I asked.

He laced his little fingers together and stretched his arms in front of him. "Yeah, I'm fine now. Less sore and tired than yesterday."

"Good." But I frowned. He'd said he was fine earlier when he clearly wasn't. How much could I trust his claim now?

Slinging the Adarborian bow and quiver over my shoulder, I settled on Gaedyen's neck. Veri hopped on behind me and gripped my shirt.

"Ready?" Gaedyen asked.

"Ready!" Veri and I called at the same time. I smiled at him, feeling slightly more confident in his claim of improved health.

A few leaps later, we were airborne.

Closing my eyes, I relished the wind on my face, the heat of the sun. Gaedyen's wings rose and fell beautifully through the wind. The reddish-brown membranes were thin but tough. With the light above us, I couldn't see the veins, but bones and muscles held strong along the front edge and branched toward the back.

Something in my middle contracted. The owner of those beautiful wings *loved* me. Majestic and wild, they carried me through my newfound freedom.

My sweatshirt pulled against my throat and brought my thoughts back to Veri, who'd apparently curled up in the sweatshirt hood again. I coughed, pulling the fabric off my throat. Shuddering, I wondered if Crivabanians could get colds. Or was this sickness more dangerous?

# CHAPTER THREE

Gaedyen's claws dug rivets in the earth as we landed near the grove of trees where Bricriu had been hiding Geneva. The sun warmed my face and reflected off the cool dew on the grass and sparse foliage. Only a handful of trees dotted the plain. I slid off, Veri bouncing awake in my hood.

How nervous was Gaedyen? His mom was somewhere around here, as was the Gwythienian who had stolen her from his father and brainwashed her. The guilt of sacrificing Aven for his mother's life, the life of a criminal and someone nowhere near as important to the world as Aven had been, weighed on him. I'd seen it in his eyes.

What must be going through his head? Of course I couldn't blame him for his decision. I wanted to be there for him, but I wasn't sure how. I took a step toward him and laid a hand on his shoulder. His skin shivered at my touch, but he leaned into it the next instant.

I smiled as Veri climbed out of my hood and glided to the ground.

"Enzi, you and Veri wait here, please. I will scout ahead. I do not want to be taken by surprise again." He flickered and vanished, though I could still feel his warm skin under my palm.

Burning pressure touched my cheek, and I realized he'd planted a light kiss there with his dragon lips. Laying my hand over the spot, I grinned like an idiot, my heart leaping in my chest and making me feel very happy and silly.

I watched the signs of his invisible presence as he strode away to investigate, even though I couldn't see him. His feet still flattened grass, and his bulk still stopped the wind from moving the blades on the opposite sides.

"Gaedyen and Enzi sittin' in a tree, k-i-s-s-i—" Veri giggled somewhere out of swiping range.

I crossed my arms. "Oh, shut up, you Fuzzbucket."

Gaedyen flickered into sight and leaped back to us. "That reminds me…" He stood on his back legs and ripped three boughs loose from a tall tree. Dropping back down to all fours, he bit each of them into rymakri and handed them to me.

"Thank you. And be careful," I whispered as he turned away and disappeared again.

Veri hopped down from the tree and stretched. "Come on, Enzi! Why are we just staying here? We're gonna miss all the action! I can take *anything* a Gwythienian can dish out! Of course, I always *could* handle anything. But now I'm even stronger!"

I raised an eyebrow, glad he was acting so much more normal, but I wasn't one-hundred percent convinced. "Sure, you are, Veri. Come on, I trust Gaedyen. So should you. Let him look around a bit. His mom's around here somewhere."

"You know what would be really funny?" he asked.

"What—"

A crash and a heart-stopping roar filled the air.

"Gaedyen!" I shrieked, taking off toward the sound and pulling a rymakri into position on the bow. Veri soared between branches at my side.

Another tree snapped and fell as a second roar rumbled through the air. They were fighting invisibly. Of course, Bricriu was strong in his ability to turn invisible. I could never forget—I'd sort of fought the Cadoumai myself once.

"Gaedyen!" My feet couldn't move fast enough.

Veri quickly passed me as he grew to three times his size and his strides tripled in length. Should he sit this one out if he was getting over an illness? Shoving my worries aside, I willed myself invisible and pumped my arms as fast as I could to keep up.

A loud smash and crack sounded up ahead, and a gigantic tree tilted, falling toward me. I leaped to the side just in time and felt a whoosh of air as the invisible fight barreled past. Veri leaped toward them and expanded further, landing on a writhing mass I couldn't see. How Veri was planning to help when he was just as blind as I was, I had no idea.

Veri shouted, "Gaedyen, turn visible!"

Gaedyen reappeared, and only Bricriu was still invisible. Veri scrabbled at him and wrenched him off Gaedyen.

An angry roar ripped from Bricriu's throat. It sounded different than his roar last time we fought—more feral.

Veri caught a vicious blow in the stomach and lurched backward.

Gaedyen leaped into the air and came crashing down on Bricriu. In an instant Gaedyen was sitting on him, and Veri had pinned Bricriu's arms to the ground. I brandished a rymakri and closed the distance.

Hoisting it in the air, I brought it crashing down like a baseball bat onto where I guessed his head was. It vibrated but remained intact. Good ole Gwythienian saliva. I wrinkled my nose. What would that mean for kissing Gaedyen? As a Gwythienian or a human? A peck on the cheek was one thing, but more…

Instantly the other Gwythienian came visible, and something about the still, knocked-out face looked wrong.

Veri loomed over the other Gwythienian, examining its face from many different angles. "Uh, guys? This isn't Bricriu."

Its neck was slimmer and longer, its face softer around the edges. Like Soroco. A female? But it couldn't be Geneva. She was near dying just a few days ago.

"Who the heck is that?" Veri wondered as we all leaned in to look.

The mystery Gwythienian's eyes flashed open and she bucked, heaving Gaedyen over her head. The earth shook when he slammed into a tree trunk, and the other Gwythienian was up and racing toward him, hauling Veri and me to the side with her massive tail.

Who was this? Why would another Gwythienian be out here? Bricriu said he'd kill any Gwythienian who came too close to Geneva, and Geneva was an invalid. *Unless…*

She was on Gaedyen in a flash, pinning his arms and legs. Blood dripped from a wound on her side onto Gaedyen's chest. She raised her head and roared at the sky.

She was about to deliver a death bite. Gaedyen couldn't die. I had to stop her.

"He's Ferrox's son!" I screamed, fumbling to nock another rymakri on Aven's bow.

Her open jaws stopped just before snapping over his neck. For another beat she didn't move a muscle, and then she swung her head to stare at me with narrowed eyes.

Gaedyen's chest rose and fell quickly, and with a deep, menacing growl, she returned her attention to him, pressing down even harder.

Her voice was higher pitched than Bricriu's, too, but deeper and raspier than Soroco's. "Who is this Ferrox of whom you speak? His name is…*familiar*, but it is the dimmest of memories."

She didn't know? Maybe she *was* some other female Gwythienian. She looked so much healthier than the Geneva I'd seen only days ago. But with the rock of healing…

"Aren't you Geneva—?" Maybe it was better to leave off the part about her being Ferrox's mate. That might be too much of a shock to her.

She turned her scowl fully on me, her eyes wide with surprise before narrowing down to suspicious slits. "Yes, my name is Geneva. But how can you know me? You are human, are you not?"

I held her gaze. "Yeah, I am."

"Hmm. I have been sick for some time, human, and many things must have changed while I slept. It used to be that humans and Gwythienians were not allowed to interact. We were supposed to keep ourselves hidden from you."

"Well, that hasn't actually changed…it's a long story. No other humans know about you, just me. And *kind of* my dad, but he doesn't count."

Geneva regarded me, then returned her gaze to Gaedyen. His breaths came a bit more slowly now.

"And who are you, Gwythienian who associates with humans and strangely large Crivabanians?" She winced almost imperceptibly, and I glanced at her stomach wound again, fearing she was at a greater risk than most for losing too much blood.

I did a doubletake. The wound's edges appeared to be straining toward each other, and blood no longer flowed from the area. The scarlet trail down her stomach was beginning to dry.

Was she healing that fast because Bricriu had the rock of healing nearby?

This was great as far as her health was concerned, but it made her so much more formidable an opponent, too. We should get her on our side ASAP.

Veri paused in a crouch, by the looks of it preparing to knock into her and toss her off Gaedyen. I caught his eye and gestured for him to wait.

"My name is Gaedyen. I am the grandson of the late Keeper—"

"The *late* Keeper? Padraig is dead? Or is there a new Possessor?"

Gaedyen sighed. "Geneva, there is much you need to be caught up on. I am afraid some of it will come as a great shock to you. But first you must know you are being kept in the dark about these things on purpose."

Her eyes narrowed. "That is impossible. The only other Gwythienian I have seen since awaking has been my committed, Bricriu. He would do me no harm."

I stifled a gasp. *Committed? To Bricriu? Ew!*

Gaedyen's lips tightened to a thin line, but he showed no other sign of repulsion. "Geneva, did he tell you the two of you committed to each other before you became sick, or did you commit once you woke up?"

Her eyes narrowed. "We were committed before I became ill, though I do not know what business that is of yours."

Gaedyen pressed a little more. "Do you remember it yourself?"

"Of course I do! How dare you ask me such a thing? Who are you to come to our place of solitude and ask outrageous questions? I should call him over now." She swung her gaze to one side. "He is feeding in the river nearby—"

"Wait!" I blurted. "Please wait. Gaedyen was telling the truth when he said there was a lot you don't know. Even if you don't believe everything we say, wouldn't you like to hear it anyway, just in case it's important?"

Her frown darkened. "And who are you, human, to know of the Gwythienians and our secrets? To speak to me this way?"

I controlled my face into not glaring and said calmly, "My name is Enzi, and I'm the Possessor of your realm's rock."

Her eyes widened. "Prove this."

I went invisible for several seconds, flicking a few nearby leafy branches to prove I was still standing in the same place and not a threat, and then became visible again.

She stared at me. "How is this possible?"

"We do not know," Gaedyen informed her. "All we know is she must have been the first to touch the rock after its Possessor's death, and it allowed her to Possess the abilities."

"How long has it been since our Keeper died?"

Gaedyen sighed again. It would be tricky to explain it all, considering the part she'd played and apparently didn't remember.

We told her the story of how Gaedyen and I met, how we found Veri and two of the rocks, and how all of the old Possessors were dead. We left out the fact that Veri was a double Possessor. It wasn't something she needed to know, and I didn't want that getting around and putting his life in more danger than it already was.

"And Padraig sanctioned your journey?"

Gaedyen's earflaps drooped. "No. He did not know about it and would not have approved if he had."

"You are indeed a bold one. The son of Ferrox, you say?"

My heart skipped a beat. Was she about to realize who she and Gaedyen were to each other?

"Yes." His voice trembled as he searched her eyes. I wanted to reach out and touch him, to do something like holding hands. Something to let him know I was there for him whatever happened next.

She cocked her head, eyeing the clouds with one eye and squinting the other. "That name is so familiar."

I exhaled. So she hadn't figured it out yet. Maybe that was best for now.

"It is as though we were good friends once, but I can't see the memories. As though I am aware they are there but am blind to them. I would like to meet him. When could that be arranged?

I feel some kind of…positive feeling associated with him, and I would like to understand it."

I looked at Gaedyen. Was it just me or were his eyes a little moist? My arms ached to hug him.

Gaedyen cleared his throat. "I am afraid that is not possible. He passed away several years ago."

Devastation passed over her face as she fell back on her haunches, her taut muscles going limp.

I peeked at her stomach wound again. Where a ragged gash had oozed copious amounts of blood a few minutes ago, now a puckered seam of skin looked as if it had been healed ages ago. Definitely not someone I wanted Gaedyen fighting any further.

She opened her mouth, closed it, and opened it again. "I am not sure why that news affects me so gravely. Did I know him well?"

"Yes, you did." Gaedyen swallowed.

"What happened to him?"

Gaedyen hesitated, glancing at me.

Stomping her foot, Geneva hissed, "We do not have long. Tell me what happened to Ferrox."

I raised my eyebrows at her sudden demand. "He was killed in the act of stealing the rocks from the Keeper's hiding place. That's when all the rocks were lost."

Her brow furrowed, even as a silent tear rolled down her cheek. "And what does that have to do with me?"

Gaedyen hesitated, then, "You helped him steal them."

She frowned at the ground, then glowered at Gaedyen. "But why would I do that?"

"I think the two of you wanted to take over the Keepership, maybe all the Possessorships as well. To be powerful. To rule our realm and the ones beyond."

"How can I know you are telling me the truth? You could be lying."

I crossed my arms. "Because you're starting to remember, aren't you?" I asked.

Her huge bright eyes glared at me. "Perhaps. But Bricriu has not told me any of this. He said we were committed to each other years ago, and I remember that even though you tell me it is not true. Why should I believe you over him?"

She remembered her committing ceremony? Maybe she was thinking of Ferrox, not Bricriu. Maybe she couldn't quite picture the right face.

"Are you sure?" I asked. "Do you remember seeing Bricriu's face that day?"

She scoffed. "What, do you propose I am committed, but not to him?"

We stared at her, neither of us answering.

She swallowed, a flicker of fear and vulnerability in her eyes. "Ferrox? I am committed to the thief?"

She glowered at Gaedyen again. "How could I have done such a thing?" Her earflaps drooped, then flared up as her eyes narrowed. She leaped off Gaedyen and backed away. "Bricriu is coming. It would be best if you stayed away. It will not go well for you if Bricriu found you too near our home."

Gaedyen rolled to his feet and stood on all fours, concern creasing his brow. "Are you in danger from him?"

I frowned. Would he beat her for hiding something from him? Would it be even worse if he knew she'd spoken to us?

"No, no of course not. He treats me kindly, but he is protective of me. Since I have been ill."

Gaedyen lowered his head. "We understand. Go and be safe. We will return…soon."

Backing away, she nodded at him, then me. She cast a quizzical look at Veri, then turned and leaped gracefully into the sky after a mere two flaps of her slender red wings. They were the exact same shade as Gaedyen's.

# CHAPTER FOUR

"Since we can't go to the Cathawyrs without the real rock of healing," I pointed out as Gaedyen started a fire, "I think we have a better chance of convincing Geneva to choose our side if we let her think about things for a few days. Maybe start paying attention to inconsistencies that must be there if Bricriu's been lying to her all this time."

I brushed off a boulder and sat on it, resting my elbows on my knees and my chin in my hands. "If she knows where Bricriu keeps the real rock, maybe we could even talk her into stealing it for us once she's stopped blindly trusting him. Once we get around to breaking the news that her life might be permanently tied to the rock." I dropped my face in my hands. "There's always the route of convincing her that her life force won't be able to sustain her far away from the rock—which is probably true— and so she'd have to come with us. But that could backfire and convince her not to help us either."

Gaedyen nodded. "I think we should start with giving her a few days to think through things. That is the best plan. Then she may want to give us the rock and maybe even leave with us on her own, once she understands how deceived she has been at Bricriu's hand." He added a few small sticks to the fledgling flame. Orange glowed over his face and in his eyes. "We should go back to Odan Terridor for a few days and see what we can find behind that pile of rubble. If he really did have a lair back there—well, it seems unlikely he would give away the location of the two missing rocks so easily, but it is the only lead we have left."

Veri eyed him, popping another berry into his mouth. "Makes sense to me."

"That settles it, then." Gaedyen smiled at me, a tired but pleasant expression on his regal face. "Ready for sleep?"

My heart thrummed with the knowledge that he wanted me close to him. It wasn't a cold night, but I relished the thought of sleeping near his warmth. I needed that. I'd missed it so much in Sequoia Cadryl.

I got up and crossed over to him, pulling my sweatshirt off for Veri to sleep in. Gaedyen's face went blank. I spun to face the other way—was something behind me? I didn't see anything. Raising an eyebrow at Gaedyen, I asked, "What's that look for?"

Stooping, I handed the sweatshirt to a hyper Veri, who dove under it. A moment later, his smiling face emerged with the voluminous hood drooping over his head and his little brown arms stretching through the too-big sleeves.

I laughed. "You goofball."

He grinned back, eyes bright.

*Funny. He seems in better health after all the fighting. Is he back to normal?*

I turned to Gaedyen. "Is everything okay?"

He shook himself. "Yes, of course. Sorry, just a random thought. Nothing really."

Lifting a wing, he looked away a little too quickly for me to be sure it was nothing.

It was a little chilly without the jacket. I settled into my spot between his side and his wing. Smiling, I breathed in his scent.

What was he hiding from me? I frowned. I didn't like people hiding things from me. It was one thing to lie to an enemy, but lying to your closest friend? Or your only family? Like my mom, who'd hidden the fact my dad was actually alive after all those years. And come to think of it, Gaedyen had lied to me too. Multiple times. About big things.

Something in my stomach dropped. He *had* lied to me a lot. He'd lied about Shimbators, that Shaun was really him in human form, about lots of things. How much could I trust him? What if he was lying about more things? What if he was lying about how he felt?

No, he wouldn't do that…

But he had before, hadn't he?

I was breathing too fast, like I did when waking from a nightmare. A tear left a moist trail down my cheek before I swiped it away.

So what was he lying about when he said that look wasn't a big deal? I'd thought about how Veri would need my sweatshirt more than I would, so I'd taken it off and handed it to him…

The change in his expression had happened right when I pulled off the sweatshirt.

*Oh, crap!* He'd turned away, hiding his face. Had he been thinking I was just going to take all my clothes off, right there? Ew!

Except…was he relieved or disappointed I *hadn't*?

I mean, in front of Veri? Of course not! Clothes were safe. Since Caleb had…had hurt me and taken my innocence from me ten years ago, I'd avoided looking at myself. I'd showered with the lights off, intentionally neglected to replace the shattered mirror in my bedroom…no, I would *not* be taking off my clothes in front of anyone.

But all that aside, had he been disappointed? Or relieved?

Part of me wished he'd been disappointed. I wanted him to like how I looked, to want to see me. I wanted to be comfortable

with him that way. But then there was what that entailed…
no matter how he felt about my appearance, I couldn't go any
further with it. I couldn't handle that. And he knew that, right?
I'd told him about that before I had any idea how he felt.

How much of a problem would that be for him? How long
could we last without that aspect of a relationship? It was a relief
he was stuck in Gwythienian form, for now, at least. I didn't
know how to handle a relationship with him in human form. At
least at this point, it couldn't be bothering him too much. Was
all that less of a thing with Gwythienians than with humans?

But still. *Hmm…Ugh! I wish I knew!* The thought of him
being relieved made my stomach ache. I wanted to be beautiful,
even though it was scary to be noticed. I wanted him to think I
was pretty.

In love with him, scared of the physical aspects of a
relationship, and worried about trust. What a mess.

With those troubling thoughts filling my head, I lay awake
for a very long time.


*The kittens yowled, then suddenly their crying was cut off. Caleb
came back into view, the knife even bloodier now.*

*No, no! I had to get away…but my legs were so sore, so stretched
the wrong way, I struggled to move.*

*Then he was on top of me again. "Another sound out of you, and I
will slice you again."*

*I couldn't hold in the sobs. Terror paralyzed me. I didn't know
what to do. I needed to get away.*

*Behind his black-haired head, the sun shone through the open
loft window. But there was something there, something blocking the
light. A shape, like a dragon…*

*"Gaedyen!" I screamed. He was here! He would save me!*

*"I said, be quiet!" Caleb waved the knife at me. Would Gaedyen
make it before he cut me again? I strained to look out the window.
He was here! He might make it…*

*His face came into view, and our eyes met. I was embarrassed, I didn't want him to see this. But I could get past that if he could get me out of here. But his face held no recognition.*

*And then he was gone, flying over the barn, past me. Away from me. When I needed him.*

*He'd left me. Again.*

*There was nothing but Caleb.*

"Enzi? Enzi wake up!"

A large, Gwythienian hand pressed against my back, shaking me awake.

"What?" I blinked in the moonlight, disoriented. His wing was gone, and he was looking down at me, shadows of branches and leaves hovering over his concerned mouth and confused eyebrow ridges.

"Everything is okay, Enzi. It was a nightmare, but it was not real."

I spotted Veri peeking out from my sweatshirt, sleepy but wide eyed. I'd woken both of them. Breathing hard, I ran my fingers through my hair and dropped my head in my hands. Would I never get rid of these nightmares?

Gaedyen lowered his voice to a soft whisper. "What happened? Do you want to talk about it?"

"No." I rubbed my eyes, finding them wet. Crap. "No, it's fine. Sorry I woke you." I rolled over toward his side, away from his eyes.

He was still for a moment, then he whispered, "I love you, Enzi. I do not know how to help, but I want to." And then he gently caressed my cheek with the edge of his wing.

That gesture warmed my heart. Confused as I was about everything, I knew I loved him too. That was a sure thing. I stroked the ridged scales of his side once, then rested my palm against him. A rumble came from somewhere inside, drawing a smile from me.

Whatever there may be to worry about later, this was a good moment. I wouldn't let my fears ruin this. I snuggled closer, resting my other palm against his skin, too. He rumbled once more just as I drifted off to sleep.

"Remember the first time we were here?" Gaedyen asked, holding up leafy vines for me to duck under.

We'd flown the rest of the way back to Odan Terridor in the morning and now were heading for the tunnel with the blocked off branch. Hopefully it would lead to Tukailaan's lair and the missing two rocks.

"Yeah. You swiped your tail at me and sent me skidding into this tunnel I hadn't been able to see through the vines. I have scars to prove it."

I had other scars too, from worse memories. But no need to think of those right now. Scars from adventuring with Gaedyen were different. Reminders of our story and good memories.

"I did not mean to hurt you. I did it to protect you from Padraig when he was in a rage about your scent and catching me in the Vorbiaquam, remember?"

"Yeah, I do. It was a pretty bad fight."

"Yes, it was," Gaedyen agreed. "And walking through the tunnel first made you uncomfortable, so you stepped on my face to get around behind me and make me do the trailblazing."

I chuckled and let my fingers trail along the rough, rocky cave wall, not bothered in the least by being in the lead this time, or by having Gaedyen right behind me. Now he was a comfort rather than an unfamiliar, disconcerting presence.

The tunnel narrowed, and I had to crouch a little to get through. "You doing okay back there?"

"Yeah, I am! Thanks for remembering I exist!" Veri chortled, his voice growing closer as he scampered over or around Gaedyen to get to me.

"Sorry, Veri." I held out my arm, a motion he could probably see in the dark even though I couldn't.

He hopped onto my shoulder and gripped my shirt with his toes. "Only messing with you, Enzi. Now where's this rubble mess I get to smash?"

"I think it's a little farther on. Gaedyen, do you remember?"

I didn't hear his footsteps anymore.

I spun around. "Gaedyen?"

"Oh, yes. What?"

I sagged in relief, then frowned at his absentminded response. "What's with you?"

"That scent. Of Tukailaan. Old, but so strangely reminiscent of yours. It strikes me as odd, though I knew to expect it and have met him myself now. Such a strange similarity."

Sniffing came from all around me as Veri leaned this way and that, still gripping my shirt with his toes. "Oh, that *is* weird. I'd noticed something funny, but I didn't realize how strong the similarity was until you mentioned it."

Gaedyen's breath came from just behind me, and I started forward again, wondering why Tukailaan and I *smelled* similar. Concerned and a little creeped out.

"Yes," Gaedyen agreed. "It is notable, but it smells old. I do not detect anything recent. Mine and Enzi's scents from when we last passed through nearly overpower Tukailaan's. Do you detect anything I'm missing, Veri?"

"Nope."

My heart dropped. "Which means he didn't come back here with the rocks. They aren't here and we're wasting our time, aren't we?"

"Not necessarily," Gaedyen said slowly, considering. "It only means he did not come in through this entrance. Once we get to whatever lays beyond, we will be able to determine if any other entrances lead to…wherever it is."

"I think I found it!" Veri shouted, nearly choking me with my shirt's collar.

"Watch the throat!" I croaked, pulling the shirt away from my neck and sidestepping toward what Veri reached for.

"Sorry!" Veri squealed. "But this is it, isn't it?"

My shoulder found a sharp edge in the otherwise smooth wall, and I winced, tracing my fingers lightly over the other jagged bits of rubble.

"Yes," Gaedyen and I said at the same time.

"This is it," I confirmed as Veri hopped off my shoulders, probably to scour the pile for loose pieces. "This is the entrance to Tukailaan's lair—in theory."

Feeling the rubble smashed into the wall, I tried to grip one of the rocks. It was too heavy and too crammed in there, so I felt for a smaller one. It was more jagged, better for gripping. I tugged hard. A resounding crash sounded all around me as rocks and rubble tumbled to the ground, pummeling my feet.

Light came with the crash, illuminating our surroundings.

"Ouch!" I jumped out of the way.

"What the heck did you do?" Veri scampered up to my shoulder, out of harm's way.

"Is everyone okay?" Gaedyen's voice carried over the echo of the tiny avalanche.

Veri shouted, "Yeah, we're good. Enzi got a little over-zealous with the rubble pile, I guess."

"Well, keep doing that," Gaedyen said. "It cleared out a whole layer of rubble and it looks like there are several more to go."

I took a step toward the mess and peered into the hole. Yep. A lot more crap was wedged back there. One rock the size of

Texas took up most of the space. Dim beams of light filtered in through the remaining rubble.

"Oh, great," I complained. "How in the world are we ever going to get through all that? We might as well chip away at the tunnel itself for all the good trying to move *that* thing will do us."

A small weight left my shoulder as Veri hopped onto the pile. "I got this."

I launched after him. "Wait, Veri, be careful! You're sick. You don't need to go messing with that thing."

"Pfft! I'm fine. I feel great. I could move a mountain! This puny little thing's no big deal."

I eyed the rock again. "It's hardly *puny*. If it was hollow, I could fit a hundred of you in there. And I'm guessing it's not hollow."

He ignored me, marching over the debris toward the monster rock. As he inspected it, he grew several inches to check out the top of it.

I rolled my eyes. "Show off."

Grinning, he tested several places on the mostly smooth surface, grabbing protruding rocks and yanking on fingerholds. The boulder didn't budge.

"Hmm…what if…?"

Placing his larger-than-usual palms on the rock, he braced his feet and pushed. This time, the rock slid just the teeniest bit.

Veri hopped around to face us, looking surprisingly healthy considering how wilted he'd seemed recently. "The good news is the rock will move! The bad news is I can't move it with pulling, only pushing. And I don't know what's on the other side. But the only way we're getting in there is by pushing the rock out of our way."

I started to panic. "Wait, what if it's supporting the ceiling? Veri, it could fall down on you, and we might not be able to find you through all that. You could die!"

"Pfft!" He rolled his eyes, waving my concerns away. "The roof looks secure. I just don't know what this rock might crush once it's out of here."

Gaedyen stepped forward, but Veri cut him off before he could speak. "Don't even think about it, dude. You'll barely fit through here once I get it cleared out. Only I can do this, so I'm going to."

I didn't like it, but we needed to check if the rocks could be here, and Veri was miraculously healthy enough to give this a try. I wished I had a rope to tie around him so I could pull him out if the ceiling collapsed. But if this was what he wanted to do, there was no changing his mind.

He marched in and braced himself to push out the rock. I watched, cringing a little, as his whole body shook with the effort. Then the rock moved. Only a fraction of an inch, but it moved. Then another teeny bit. Then a little more.

It scraped and squealed across the floor, sending little shards of stone all over Veri's toes. I kept a close eye on the ceiling, watching through the dust for any cracks. So far, so good. He'd moved it about a foot.

"Whew!" Veri dropped to his butt on the stone floor. "That is *heavy.*"

"Thank you, Captain Obvious." I rolled my eyes. "How are you feeling?"

"I feel great!" He jumped to his feet again, the shortest break ever taken.

"Why don't you rest a little longer? We're not in that huge of a hurry."

"What are you, my mom?" He smirked and braced himself to push again. Nearly two feet later, he dropped to the ground. "Oh, man!" He jumped up seconds later and started hopping around, shaking out his wrists and ankles.

I arched my eyebrow. "Veri, you look ridiculous." But honestly, I was glad to see him so happy, even if I was confused by the sudden change.

In no time he was back at the rock pushing some more. He'd gone over three more feet when he backflipped away from the rock and said, "It can't be much longer!" Hopping out of the hole, he scampered up to my shoulder. "Really, Enzi, I feel great! Better than ever. I could push this rock all the way to Sequoia Cadryl if I had to! It would take a while, but I *totally* could."

He was zooming back through the hole to the rock before I could comment.

It was like he'd drunk too much caffeine or something. What had happened? How did he go from sick and dragging to healthy, fit, and energized? Even *hyper?*

The sound of crumbling rock met my ears, and blinding light filled the tunnel. "Veri?" Blinking against the shocking brightness, I dove into the new tunnel, searching for him through the blinding dust. "Veri! Are you okay?"

The tunnel shook as a resounding boom echoed off the walls. "Veri?" I shrieked.

And then he was right in my face. "I got it! It's out of our way. Totally out of the way, completely gone. Come on, I'll show you!"

"Wait, Veri, what was that sound? Be careful!"

He pulled my hand too hard, and I fell, scraping my knees on the tunnel floor. "Dude! Turn down the energy over there."

"Oh, sorry! Just hurry up and come see this."

I got to my feet. "Gaedyen? Are you coming?"

"I am right behind you." I didn't envy his size right then. It would suck to try to fit through this little tunnel with a Gwythienian body. A human body would be much easier. Had he tried to morph again? If he had, I was kind of glad it hadn't worked. It was too soon for that right now.

I stepped onto a dirt floor, covered in dead plants, and focused on the ground as my eyes adjusted to the brightness. "Whoa. What is this place?"

Shielding my eyes with a hand, I blinked upward. Mirrors?

The ceiling was a jagged mess of mismatch mirrors at all different angles. Some encased in wooden frames, some broken pieces and shards fastened together in disorganized messes.

The room itself was vast but uneven. As if it had been hollowed out by someone in a hurry. There were many levels of wonky platforms, each one lined with stones, full of dirt and covered in wilted, crackly plants. Flowers? A huge stony… *something* in the middle of the dirt floor looked like it might have been a fountain once.

The platformed walls each angled toward the floor and far wall, at the bottom of which was a small archway in the stone, barely large enough for a Gwythienian to slouch through. Carefully, I stepped down the platforms, which felt like awkwardly wide steps in a huge staircase, making my way to the floor and trying not to crush dead plants.

Gaedyen stood behind me, still taking it all in. Veri bounded after me, to my shoulder, and then to the crumbling fountain in the middle of the room. "What *is* this thing?"

He turned in circles on the top of it, balancing on one foot and slapping the other against it as if to test its strength.

I pointed. "Look at the little troughs that lead from it. They go to the first layers of shelves. Maybe a watering system of some kind? Though it would be hard to get the water up there…"

"Hmm. Interesting." Veri leaped from it toward the opening at the far wall.

"Hey wait for me!" I shouted. "Coming, Gaedyen?" I turned long enough to see him open his beautiful wings, balancing as he tiptoed around the dead plants after me.

Following Veri through the entrance, I squinted at the darkness in this new room. My head ached with the constant lighting changes. I reached out mummy-style to feel what was in front of me. I felt nothing but air, then suddenly a cold, flat surface. I ran my hand over it, trying to decipher what it was. My finger found a corner edge, then, "Ouch!"

I yanked my hand back, losing my balance and pushing the flat thing to catch myself. It spun, and I caught myself on the stone floor, holding one throbbing finger.

Light blazed around me, illuminating the archway tunnel. I was momentarily blinded again. I looked down at my finger—bleeding a bit but fine—then at the thing that had cut me. Another mirror. I'd cut my finger on its edge, and when I moved it, it caught light from another one and reflected it to several other mirrors.

Using my uninjured hand, I pushed myself up and stepped farther into the room.

Was that a regular human bed in the corner? And a baby cradle next to it? Three little shelf-crevices were dug out of the wall above the bed. On one of them sat a folded quilt. The middle was empty, and the top held a small book. I picked it up and blew off a layer of dust, revealing bright letters: Baby's First Words.

*What?* Confused, I crossed the small room toward the box to look into it.

A soft, pink blanket was coated in a thick layer of dust. And a little purple rattle.

*Humans with a baby? In Tukailaan's lair?*

Veri hopped onto the—cradle?—and looked up at me. "Is this one of those things humans put their young in, since you guys aren't cool enough to come with pouches?"

I would've smiled at him if I wasn't so confused. "Yeah, Veri. One of those things."

"Weird place for it."

"Hey Gaedyen, are you seeing this?" I turned to find him already wedged through the tunnel, straining his neck to see into the room.

"Yes."

I turned back to the cradle, hands on my hips. Why would Tukailaan have human things in his lair? Soft, baby things? Did he kidnap them? It doesn't look like he tortured them—which is what I would have expected. That was what he'd been denied the keepership for doing years ago. But layers of flowers and warm fuzzy blankets hardly seemed torturous. What in the world was this?

I shook my head. "Any ideas why all this *family* stuff is here?"

Gaedyen spoke from behind me. "Tukailaan had a daughter with the human woman who Meleena killed, did he not?"

"Yeah, he did. Do you think she lived here?" I asked.

Veri piped up. "No, don't you remember? He'd wanted to keep his human family, but young Bricriu killed the woman, and the baby survived. Since Tukailaan was stuck in Gwythienian form, he took the baby to an orphanage to be taken care of until he could turn human again."

"But he wasn't ever able to. Until so many decades later that she was already an old woman."

Gaedyen glanced at the landscape of long-dried flowers. "So this was meant to be a home for his daughter? That explains all the pinks and flowers."

"Wow," I said. "So did he hide the rocks here, or was he too heartbroken to return since he wasn't able to be a father to his daughter?" I leaned out of the room and surveyed the bigger area again. "I don't see another entrance."

Gaedyen met my gaze. "He noticed when we passed by just a few weeks ago. So he must have been here to notice that, right? He could have come back to hide the rocks a little later."

I nodded. "Let's get searching then. Veri, could you look around the flower beds?" Hopefully that would keep him from exerting himself too much. "Gaedyen, maybe you could check for any loose stones he might've buried them under?"

They both nodded and turned to get started.

"I'll go through all these human things." I knelt in front of the trunk and pushed the lid open. Dust poofed and sank toward the floor. I pulled out some fabric. A shirt? No, a dress. With a yellowed collar and long skirt, like something from a different era. Eighteen-hundreds, maybe? Fashion history wasn't my strong point.

I dug through a few more faded dresses and found a square piece of paper at the bottom of the trunk. It had an address under the name *Susan Mathews*. Flipping it over I found a black-and-white photograph…of *me?*

# CHAPTER FIVE

ell, almost me. Me if I'd lived a hundred years ago and been several sizes smaller. Every time I ran into Tukailaan the past several weeks, he always said something about how I looked like someone. This must be her. But who was this Susan person?

The light reflecting throughout the room faded and darkened from a yellow-orange to a deep purple. It was getting late, and we hadn't found anything else useful. Just some really confusing things and a whole lot of regular, non-magical rocks.

"What do you say to spending the night in the quarters where I grew up?" Gaedyen crouched on his haunches amid the dried brown flowers, eyes half lidded with exhaustion.

"Yeah, I'd like that." I wanted a break from this sad place, but I also wanted to see more of Odan Terridor. To see where Gaedyen grew up. "But look at this first."

He eyed the photograph and cocked a brow. "She looks a lot like you. Hmm."

I flipped the photo around and showed Gaedyen the other side. "This address is only a few counties over from mine. Maybe it's worth checking out? On the slim chance the rocks could be there. Or someone could know something."

Peering at the address, he nodded. "I agree on both counts. But for tonight, how about we relax and get some sleep?"

The aching soreness in my limbs from flying and fighting reminded me how much I needed more rest. "I'm so in."

He smiled. "Okay then. We will go to my old home."

I smiled at him, his smile lighting me up inside. "That sounds great."

Veri swooped onto my shoulder, gripping my T-shirt sleeve firmly between his flexible toes. "Yeah, I got nothing over there, either. I don't need to rest, but I do need to get out of this boring place."

I pushed off the floor, and something shifted in the trunk. Reaching into a dark corner, I found a small cloth pouch with small, rock-sized things rolling around inside.

I ripped it open and dumped the contents into my hand.

Gaedyen and Veri gasped as I held out…seven purple stones.

None of which were the Gwythienian rock.

"Shoot!" I stared at them, wondering where they'd come from and why we had to be disappointed again.

Gaedyen's earflaps drooped, and Veri rolled his eyes. "Aw, man!"

My heart sank. We were so close! I poured the rocks back into the pouch and dropped it into the trunk. Why the heck did he have those in there?

Scowling at the pouch, I stooped to pick it up again. I peered inside and found the roundest looking one. Pulling it out, I shoved it into my pocket. Just in case.

We crawled back through the tunnel, through the dense vegetation, and over the creek we'd flown past the first time I'd been in Odan Terridor. The root tunnels made up the ceiling overhead, and I wondered if that was where we were going.

Before long, Gaedyen lowered a shoulder for me to mount, and I swung a leg over his back, Veri hopping over my arm to stand on my shoulder. It was a relief to see him so happy and healthy and full of life. So like his normal self. I hoped this meant he was over that bug or whatever it was.

We flew briefly, just enough to reach an entrance to the root tunnels again. We nearly got tossed off Gaedyen when he latched on to one of the openings to sling us up into the tunnels.

The feeling of stumbling over a sprawling pile of potatoes was becoming a familiar one.

"This way." Gaedyen led us deeper, blueish light fading with the distance from the opening. I tripped at least three times, and Veri let out a couple of grunts as well.

"In here. Watch out for the wall."

I felt for the wall and ran my fingers lightly over the rough texture.

Gaedyen drew a blue lantern from a crevice in the roots and led me through the entrance to his old home.

Flickering azure light glinted off the root walls of a room just big enough for him to fit in and turn around. The way the roots intertwined together created a couple of makeshift shelves on one side. On one of the shelves sat a small stone knife, which appeared to be his only possession.

"This is where you slept while you were growing up?" I asked.

"Yes. Slept and spent a lot of my free time. Until I learned Arunca Rymakri. And other than looking for my parents in the Vorbiaquam."

"That was why you went to the Vorbiaquam so much— looking for Ferrox and Geneva?"

He nodded.

"How does it work?"

"Because of the waterfall walls, it is a place where even those who are not Cadoumai, or those who are weak in the Gwythienian gifts of invisibility and seeing through water, can find what they are looking for in its ripples."

"Really? How?"

"I believe it has something to do with the way the water reflects on itself, with the walls and the floor both being moving water."

"But you are a Cadoumai," I reminded him.

"Yes, but I did not always know that. As I thought up many reasons for my parents leaving me, I assumed I must be weak in the gifts—an embarrassment. It was not until much later I became aware of the potential for strength I had within me, if I would only put in the work to shape it."

I touched his shoulder, smoothing my hand over the muscle there. "I'm sorry you felt that way, Gaedyen."

He covered my hand with his. "I know you did not have an easy hatchling-hood either."

His touch over the back of my hand touched something else inside my chest, sending warmth through me. I stepped away to keep my focus on his words. "So you spent a lot of time in here because the other little Gwythienians were jerks?"

He gazed at the wall with a sad smile. "Sometimes. Not always, though. Their parents gave them the idea I was dangerous. They were merely taking the advice of their trusted elders to stay away from bad blood."

I snorted and started to say something in his defense, but he continued. "But it was not their parents' fault either, was it? They wanted their offspring to be safe. Knowing what my parents were capable of was understandably a concern. I am not mad at those who rejected me because of them. Not anymore. But I have no desire to ever spend time around them. I've spent a great deal of time imagining what my future would entail, once this adventure is over, and I realized I am not sure I want to spend the rest of my life here."

His eyes followed me as I walked around the room, running my fingers over the root walls. "What do you think of that, Enzi? Where do you want to spend your future?"

A snore came from Veri, who'd crawled between some roots somewhere and passed out.

"I'm not sure. Though I'd like it better if you were there, wherever it turns out to be." My throat dried out. Why was it so hard to say things like that? Would it make him uncomfortable? I mean, I knew he cared for me, but it didn't necessarily follow that he wanted to be with me *forever.*

I risked a sidelong look his way and found that tender smile on his face. Even his eyes were smiling. Relieved, I sighed and smiled back.

"I am glad of that. Would…would you please come here?"

My heart thrilled at the words. He wanted me closer to him. Tentatively, he stretched out a huge, reddish-brown Gwythienian hand, and I took it. His fingers closed over mine, their rough surface rubbing against my skin. He pulled me toward him, slowly wrapping his arm around me. I wrapped my arms around his neck, burying my face there. He bent his head slightly, touching the top of my head with his chin.

His bent arm covered most of my back, his huge hand stretching around my shoulder and just under my arm. "I love you, Enzi," he whispered.

My heart flip-flopped. "I love you, too."

"This is okay?"

"You mean the hug?"

"Yes. I do not want to make you uncomfortable." He started loosening his grip, pulling away from me. "I am sorry if this was too forward of me—"

*No! Don't move! I need you here!* I cut him off. "No, no, it's fine. It's really nice. I'm not uncomfortable at all. I like this."

He exhaled, sounding relieved. "Good." I heard the smile in his voice as his arm held me a little tighter.

Leaning in to him, I relished his warmth and closeness.

"Enzi, can I ask you something?"

"Of course." My stomach flipped again with anticipation and shyness.

"It is just, well…forgive me if this is too forward to ask… you see, ever since you told me you reciprocate my feelings and accept me as a Shimbator, I have desperately wanted to show you how much I love you, how important you are to me. I want to make you happy, but I do not know how. I am afraid of doing something that will scare you away, something that will remind you of…of how you got your scars."

I opened my eyes, fighting the images dripping into my mind.

"I am so terrified of making you rethink your feelings for me, I am paralyzed. I have wanted to hold you like this, but I was afraid. I am relieved to know this is okay, but please, tell me more things that are okay, if there are any. I need to know."

My heart melted. So that was why he'd seemed a little distant. What a relief!

"Enzi? Did I say too much? I apologize. I am no good at this."

I sighed against him, thoroughly in love with every bit of him. "Oh, Gaedyen. You're wonderful."

I sensed his drooping earflaps lift a bit, but he didn't say anything. It was my turn to explain things.

"This is definitely okay. I love this."

His other arm came around me, pulling me closer. I didn't know how he had the strength to hold himself up with just his back legs at this angle. He must have abs of steel.

As his fingers settled over my waist, a thrill rippled through me when one of them lightly touched the exposed skin of my hip. Apparently my shirt had lifted when I reached up to hug him.

The contact was gone in a moment—maybe he was afraid I wouldn't like that. But he was wrong. Feeling his skin against mine was nice. He held me for a few moments longer, until his abdomen was shaking with the strain. He dropped one arm, propping himself up in the cramped space, but continued to hold me tightly with the other.

"And touching my skin was okay, too. I liked that."

His head moved against mine, as if he was cocking it in surprise. "Really?"

"Yes." I wanted him to touch my skin again, but I was too shy to get the words out.

"I will remember that."

"What else were you wondering?"

"Is it okay to give you things?"

"To give me things? Like presents?" I tilted my head.

"Yes. Among my people, giving gifts to each other is a mating ritual. I mean," he spluttered, "a pre-committing ritual. Like a courtship."

I smiled. "That sounds nice. But I don't know what to give you. What kinds of things would Gwythienians normally give to each other?"

Of course, the whole committing thing had crossed my mind, but it gave me a little thrill when he said it. A thrill of joy at being accepted, and a thrill of nerves at the long-termness of it. I'd have to think about that some more.

"Anything."

I giggled. "Oh, good. That narrows it down."

Blue light flickered on the shadowed root walls all around as he laughed softly. "I mean there are no rules. The gifts are meant to show affection and attention to details. For example, if you are interested in a Gwythienian, and you give her a lemon as a tasty treat because *you* like lemons and assume that *all* Gwythienians like lemons, but it turns out that she actually *hates* lemons, it would be a sign to both of you and to other Gwythienians that you do not know each other well enough to consider committing yet. But giving a gift they will like and is perceived as valuable, whether anyone else understands or not, that is a sign you are compatible. I was afraid gifts might not be taken well, that you may see them as too forward, perhaps too early…"

"No, I would be happy to exchange gifts." I wracked my brain, trying to think of what to get him. I frowned when my mind went blank. "I'm not sure what to get, though. I'm not good at thinking of the right gift."

A familiar stab of guilt poked my gut as I remembered the many birthdays and Mothers' Days I'd failed to get something really nice for Mom. Of course, we couldn't afford much anyway, but I never knew what to get her. How did I choose the right gift for someone who'd done so much for me? It was overwhelming. And it was happening again.

"It is my turn, so do not worry about this now."

"Your turn? You mean the guys give the first gift?"

"No, Enzi." He smiled. "The tradition can be started by either. But you have already given me a gift."

I leaned away from him to look at his face with one eyebrow raised.

He smiled at me. "Remember? The satchel you made for me, to carry sticks to bite into Rymakri. That was a most useful gift."

"Oh yeah." I smiled, relieved to have given a gift so well once in my life.

"I have so many ideas for things to give you, I do not know which to pick first."

"Wait, we give each other *multiple* gifts?"

He chuckled. "We do not have to give the same number of gifts. As I said, there are no strict rules."

I would have to think about that. I couldn't let him out-gift me. "Okay. Anything else you were wondering about?"

He hesitated, then, "Only one, in particular. But I admit I am so nervous about asking, I am not sure I can."

Hiding my face against his neck again, I cringed a bit inwardly. But my curiosity was peaked. "Uh-oh. That bad?"

"The problem is, I do not know." His voice rumbled louder with my ear against his throat.

I squeezed his neck a little tighter. "Go ahead and ask. I promise not to freak out."

But I was *totally* freaking out.

If he was going to ask about…if I would be comfortable with…*that*, I wouldn't be. Not yet. Maybe not ever. We wouldn't be able to last forever if I couldn't, but I didn't think I ever could. I didn't want to see him that way, without the sweetness, the considerateness. It terrified me. But I didn't want to reject him, either. What if he left me? That would be awful. At least he was still stuck in Gwythienian form for now. That would buy me some time. But oh, crap. What if he'd figured out how to morph again? What if he was about to turn into Shawn—I mean, his human form?

"I…wanted to ask if…well, it seemed okay on that island, sort of…"

I frowned. "The island? I'm not sure what you're saying." My voice was muffled against the scales of his neck.

"Is…is it okay if I…if I…kiss you?"

Relief rushed through me like his racing heart that beat against my cheek. He really was nervous. It was so sweet and adorable. And he was just asking about kissing! Nothing more. I had kissed him on the cheek on the island. And I'd been afraid I'd freaked him out…

"When I kissed you on the island, I ran away because I thought you were disgusted with me. But if you weren't, then why'd you go all stiff?"

"I froze because I had never felt so many things at once. I felt elation that you seemed to have feelings for me, something I had believed impossible until that moment. An instant later, I felt ashamed for thinking you had meant it that way—you must have meant it differently than my heart had taken it. And my chest ached with disappointment."

I wanted to say something, but I wasn't sure what.

"But then you were gone. And when you came back, you were invisible, and your voice sounded thick with tears. I wanted to comfort you, but I did not know how. I did not even know what I had done to make you cry. It was all so terribly frustrating, and when I tried to ask, you got angry with me."

I winced. "I'm sorry about that, Gaedyen." His fingers tightened around me slightly when I said his name. "I felt like an idiot for letting my feelings show. I didn't think it was possible for you to feel the same thing, but when we laughed together… it was just such a perfect moment, I forgot my boundaries and couldn't help myself. I cried because I thought I might have put a wedge in our friendship. And I got angry because I was angry with myself, but I couldn't explain it without telling you how I felt—which I also couldn't do."

"I see. So what was it like for you, kissing a scaly dragon face? I supposed if there was to be kissing between us, you would rather kiss me in human form?"

My stomach roiled, twisting in nervous knots as I searched for the right words. I'd never kissed anyone before. Never a human, anyway. I wasn't sure what I thought about it.

"That bad?" He laughed nervously, probably trying to keep it light. But he sounded concerned. It pulled me back to his train of thought.

"No, no. I mean, actually I don't really remember. I was so embarrassed afterward, I don't remember how it actually felt." I frowned, annoyed at myself for having ruined the experience of my first kiss so completely.

He chuckled. "If you decide that kissing is okay, well, I hope I will be able to make it nicer for you than 'unmemorable.'" His arm loosened. He was doubting himself, getting nervous again. "Perhaps it would be best to forget it for now and talk of something else. We can revisit this once I can turn human again. You do not need to answer now. There is no pressure—"

That was enough of that. I loved him, and here I was letting him talk himself into a nervous tizzy just because I was struggling to sort things out. I let go of him and stepped back, grabbing either side of his jaw instead and pulling his face toward mine.

My lips touched his, and he froze again, but it didn't stop me this time.

How was a human supposed to make out with a dragon? I had no idea. I'd never done this before. The most experience I had was seeing humans make out in school or on TV. I was clueless. But somehow in this moment, I didn't care.

And judging by the rumbling vibration that emanated from him, neither did he.

As I pressed my lips against his, I ran my hands over his face, enjoying the texture and contours of it. I felt his strong jaw, the smooth ridges on either side that spread into his ear flaps, the raised portion covering the backs of his eyes. His eyelids were closed. His face was warm and smooth, nice to feel.

At last I backed up a step, breaking the kiss but still holding his face in my hands. I hadn't noticed how heavily he was breathing. The rumbling stopped, and I could just see the glimmer of light flicker off his eyes as he opened them. He stared at me, his eyes wide.

"Enzi." A thrilling tremor went through me as he rasped my name.

I smiled. "Yes?"

"There are not words…I do not think I can effectively communicate—"

Grinning, I pulled him to me and cut him off. I kissed him and caressed his face again. He took a deep breath and sighed, whispering my name. His huge hand found my waist again and squeezed gently. And now I understood he was trying to tell me how much he liked it, how much he loved me.

I shivered, wanting to be close to him. I couldn't kiss his lips and wrap my arms around his neck like when we'd hugged at the same time, so at last I broke the kiss and nestled into his neck. He brought both arms around me and pressed me against him.

"Oh, Enzi."

I'd never relished the sound of my name so much.

# CHAPTER SIX

When Veri woke and found us sitting quietly together and smiling at each other, he gave us the eyebrow and a mischievous grin. He knew something was up. I couldn't help smiling back as I rolled my eyes at him.

Crawling out from where I'd slept snugly between Gaedyen and his wing, I smiled at the bumpy floor he'd carefully shielded me from last night. He'd kissed my forehead and situated his tail and his leg so that I rested on them instead of the roots. Stretching and yawning, I realized something. I'd slept peacefully that night without any visits from a phantom Caleb.

Gaedyen pushed himself to his feet and stretched the back leg that had been injured in the first fight with Bricriu several weeks ago. It hadn't ever gone quite back to normal, even with Dyn Meddy's healing back in Sequoia Cadryl. He'd had to shift forms again too quickly—probably before enough time had passed for it to heal properly. "It has not been long enough yet for us to return to Geneva. We should try looking for Susan. Or at least clues about her that could lead us to the rocks."

After leaving Odan Terridor, we flew invisibly over trees and backroads, then streets and houses and buildings. Finally, after trees had begun diluting the urbanity again, we at last reached the street in the address from the photograph.

Despite his teasing grins, Veri's eyes looked a little off-color again, and his pointy ears hung wrong. Too tired and droopy. I didn't like it. He shouldn't be traveling in that condition. But as nice as Soroco was, there was enough tension between the Gwythienians and the Crivabanians that I wasn't going to leave him in Odan Terridor alone.

The faded main road stretched on with little ranch-style houses every few hundred feet along it. We flew low, watching the numbers on the mailboxes for the right one. Finally Gaedyen glided to a stop and back-tracked on foot, eyeing a homemade wooden mailbox with painted numbers so faded we could barely make them out.

Sliding off Gaedyen with a protective hand keeping Veri from diving out of my sweatshirt hood, I squinted at them. "Yep. That's them." I looked down the driveway and squinted harder. "But where's the house?"

The weedy gravel driveway ended on a lot of overgrown grass and no house. But there was some kind of ramshackle outbuilding further back behind some trees and overgrown shrubs. I stepped towards it and tripped, scraping my hands on the gravel to catch myself before landing face-first.

"Enzi! Are you okay?" Gaedyen was by my side in a flash, offering an invisible hand to help me up.

"Yeah, thanks." I smiled at where I thought his face probably was and bent to beat the dirt off the knees of my pants.

Veri yawned, pointing at my boots. "That looks like… something."

I glanced down. A long, raised line stretched several feet in either direction before making a ninety-degree turn and continuing on perpendicularly. Several similar lines were ahead of us.

"Gaedyen, look at this." I said. "An old house foundation? Maybe this is where Susan lived."

"Maybe. But what about that crumbling building over there?" Gaedyen swiped a hand over the ground, stirring up dust toward the outbuilding.

I shrugged. "Maybe a shed or barn or something?"

"Perhaps."

We stepped over the foundation line, careful not to trip, heading toward the other building. Veri sluggishly clambered down my leg and meandered behind us, perhaps to do his own investigating? Once we were better concealed within the shadows of the trees, Gaedyen appeared at my side. I smiled to myself, glad to be able to see him.

The building was mottled coal-gray with long-rotten wood boards. It was an awkward sort of rectangle, and we stood on the long end facing a homemade-looking wooden door missing a couple of boards.

It obviously wasn't a typical house, but I wondered whether I should knock. I mean, of course no one lived there, but just in case…I lifted a hand and rapped three times with my knuckles. The knocks echoed through the building and back out through the holes where the missing planks should be.

"You're *knocking?*" Veri leaned around an overturned metal bucket, giving me the eyebrow again.

I rolled my eyes. "Uh, yeah. I mean, just in case."

Veri snickered.

"Well, it can't hurt."

He smirked and crossed his arms. "No one answered. Shocker. Maybe you should try again. Looks like the ghosts didn't hear you."

*Little jerk.* Glaring at him, I pushed on the door gently, hoping the whole thing wouldn't collapse.

I peered inside. A shaft of light fell through the rafters, casting shining lines on the sawdust-covered floor. I froze, staring at the lines of light. My vision blurred as my heart thumped louder and louder in my ears. It looked just like… wooziness overcame me, and I stumbled. The need to run clawed at me as my skin overheated and my vision tunneled. I turned in slow motion to find Gaedyen or Veri and couldn't see them. Where had they gone?

Had I only been imagining them this whole time? Was it all just a dream, just a fantasy to get me away from Caleb? Was he all that was real?

Gaedyen was there, eyes wide. "Enzi! What is wrong? What did you see?" He steadied me, leaning around me to peer inside the door.

I stumbled toward him, collapsing on his arm. Breathing heavily, I tried to steady my frantic breaths.

"What did you see, Enzi? I do not see anything."

"Me either." Veri launched himself inside to see what upset me. "There's nothing here."

I willed myself to stop shaking as Gaedyen pulled me closer, wrapping his arm around me and cradling my head.

"What did you see, Enzi?"

"It was the lines…of light…on the sawdust. It just took me by surprise. reminded me of…*him*. It just freaked me out a little. But I'm okay." I tried to push myself up, not wanting to look like a dramatic baby.

But he just held me tighter, stiffening as he realized who I was talking about.

"Enzi. You do not have to go in there again. Stay here. Veri can take a look on his own. Enzi?" Gaedyen whispered my name, stroking my hair with his long fingers. "I am so sorry. But you are okay. I am here, Veri is here. *He* is *not*." His voice grew sterner with the last sentence, as if he'd like to break every one of Caleb's bones.

Eyes closed, I finally stopped shaking. I wiped a tear from my cheek, hating that it had such an effect on me. "I'm okay, Gaedyen. It's not a big deal. It just caught me off guard."

"There is still no need to go in there. Veri will look. I can, too, if you would like."

I sighed, not wanting to see the lines in the dust again, knowing I needed to face them. "It's okay, Gaedyen. I can handle it. I need to look around. Veri isn't himself and could miss something, and you might not fit everywhere that needs to be searched."

For several moments he was silent, maybe trying to come up with some way to get me out of it. "I wish I could shield the rays of light from your sight."

I smiled, squeezing his hand where mine rested over his. "Thanks, Gaedyen. I really appreciate your trying, but I need to face it and get past it. I can't let stuff like that affect me for the rest of my life."

"If you insist." He slowly drew his arm away from around me. He frowned and lightly brushed one finger pad across my cheek. "You were crying."

Facing away from him, I sniffed and scrubbed a hand over my stupid face. "Just a little. I'm okay now. Let's go."

I stepped toward the building again, Gaedyen in tow, and leaned through the doorway. I fell back into his face as Veri catapulted out, aimed right at me.

"Woah! Hi! Hey, you guys need to come see this thing. I don't know what it is."

Heart pounding, I resisted the sudden urge to throw him across the field. "Okay, show us." Why was he suddenly so cheerful after being so dull this morning? Was it a morning thing?

We followed him past the broken door. Lines glinted from the floor, thousands of dusty bits floating in their rays. I lifted my eyes from them, keeping them hooked on Veri. He bounded forward out of this small room and into the next.

"Veri?" I called. Why was he suddenly so perky?

We followed him, Gaedyen tearing through the broken doorway to get through. I winced at the shattered boards and glanced up at the holey ceiling. Would this thing hold?

Already across the room, I ducked through the next collapsing doorway to follow Veri.

Perfect squares of light covered the ground, evenly spaced. Dust moats swam through the beams.

I shielded my eyes from the bright light that contrasted with the darker corners and faced the roof of this new room. It looked like dozens of windows had been cut out and evenly spaced, covering the whole ceiling. I took another step as Veri shouted, "Ouch!"

Something chinked under my shoe, and I lifted my foot to check what it was. "Veri? Are you all right? I think I just stepped on some glass. Watch your step, Gaedyen."

Veri growled, "Yeah, I'm all right. I stepped on some glass too, but I don't get to wear shoes."

I squinted at his foot. "Are you bleeding?"

"Barely. It will stop in a second."

Relieved he wasn't hurt badly, I set my foot carefully in a glass-free spot. "You know, Veri, if you want shoes, I can buy you some in the toddler section."

"Pfft." He waved my teasing away, leaping to the wall and hanging on it. "What do you think this is?"

I glanced at the broken glass I'd stepped on. Similar shimmery bits glimmered on the floor throughout the room. Slender tables stood against the walls, full of flower pots and dry dirt. A few crackly-looking, dried stalks stuck up from them, and a few withered brown vines hung dry and limp from places they didn't appear to belong.

*Wilted plants...lots of windows...* Both connections hit me at once. "Guys, I think it was a greenhouse. An old-fashioned one. Kind of like Tukailaan's lair. With all those plants and the mirrors lined up to reflect the sun."

Veri shrugged. "Maybe. Though you humans should quit trying to keep plants inside. See what it does to them?" He gestured to the long-dead plants.

Gaedyen was still regarding the strange roof. "How interesting. Was this Susan perhaps a gardener?"

I crossed my arms and eyed the ceiling again. "That's a good question. So did she plant those flowers in Tukailaan's lair? Maybe something to do while being held prisoner or something?"

Gaedyen nodded. "Maybe. Veri, would you check out the next room? I will inspect what I can from here. Enzi, would you like to search the outside of this building?"

"Will do." Smiling at Gaedyen's care to have me search outside, I nudged a fallen rafter from my path and glared at the light on the floor. *You don't get to have that kind of effect on me anymore.*

Gaedyen watched me as I stepped past him toward the yard, as if he expected me to freak out again. He was out the door a mere two seconds after me.

"Really, Gaedyen. I'm okay."

"All right, if you insist." After a few minutes of looking around, he said, "Enzi, look at this."

I stood and stepped toward him. "What did you find?"

He faced a handful of gravestones. A graveyard? But they were too close together to be adults...were they children?

I peered at the closest one, squinting at the name. "*Bones?* Someone's name was *Bones?*"

"They all have strange names. *Bones, Runner, Brownie.*" Gaedyen peered at the rocks.

I brushed some dirt off Brownie's name. "Weird. But yeah, those don't sound like human names. And the stones are spaced too closely for humans."

"Maybe Susan had some pet dogs?" Gaedyen suggested.

"Maybe. Any of the dirt look disturbed?" Not that a most beloved dog's grave would make a good place to hide magical rocks.

"No. I already checked," Gaedyen said, standing on his tiptoes to survey the rest of the yard.

"Bummer."

Veri glided to my side and leaped up to my shoulder. "What'd you find?"

"Dog graves, apparently. No rocks though. Maybe this was a dumb idea."

Veri squinted past me. "What's that one on the end? It looks…does that say *Susan*?"

Gaedyen turned, and I hurried down the line of graves to find that gravestone. It just said *Susan*, no last name, and it was much more roughly carved. "Oh my gosh, you guys. What if this is the human woman Tukailaan claimed to have married, who Meleena killed? What if Tukailaan buried her and then used his Gwythienian hands to carve her name?"

"Are you implying that Gwythienian hands are sloppy?" Gaedyen asked with a quirky grin.

I avoided his eyes, trying not to smile too big in front of Veri. He would give us such a hard time. "*No*, I'm not. I'm saying if you were used to your human hands and suddenly had Gwythienian hands, it might be hard to do some of the things you'd done before."

"Mm." Gaedyen rumbled a laugh.

Veri scampered over to Susan's grave, still looking suspicious. "I don't know, guys. I've got a feeling about this." He laid a little black paw over the grass, lightly brushing the strands. "I think something's here. Help me."

I winced at the idea of digging up a grave. How far down was he planning to go?

Gaedyen took a couple of steps to help Veri dig, but then he froze, his eyes darting toward the sky.

"What's wrong, Gaedyen?" I asked, crouching over the spot Veri had started digging.

"Probably nothing," he murmured, head swinging to survey our surroundings.

"Okay…" He was often alert like this. Paranoid, even. I refocused on digging.

"Holy moley!" Veri cried as light glinted off something about a foot deep in the hole.

"No way," I said, watching as his small hand grasped something. He drew out a dirty blue stone—the Rubandors' rock?—and dropped it into my hand. Peering back into the dirt, he withdrew the Gwythienian's purple rock, still on my necklace chain, his eyes wide.

"Oh my gosh, Gaedyen. Look!" I cried.

He glanced down at us, his face shocked. "Enzi! You touched the unpossessed rock!"

I dropped it immediately, staring in horror at what I'd done. But I hadn't felt anything.

And Veri had handed it to me.

"Oh crap! Veri, did you feel anything when you touched it?"

He shrugged. "Just excitement, I guess. I didn't notice anything else."

I frowned. "Well it *is* dirty. Maybe the dirt kept his fingers from actually touching it."

"I certainly hope so." Gaedyen watched the Rubandors' rock, his eyes glazing. He was thinking of Padraig, I was sure.

"Gaedyen!" Veri shouted, leaping to his feet and growing to three times his size. "Do you hear that?"

Gaedyen was already glaring at the sky with a snarl ripping through his lips. "Grab the rocks carefully. We need to fly."

I shoved the Gwythienian's rock and its broken necklace chain into my sweatshirt pocket, then pulled the sleeve over my hand and grabbed the blue rock.

The sun glinted off something else under the dirt. "Veri, is something else in there?" I reached toward the hole just as the sound of rushing wind met my ears.

Gaedyen sidestepped me and hurled Veri and me back. We rolled over the other graves, my elbow slamming against one of the stone markers.

"Ow!" Spitting dirt, I pushed myself up and glared at Gaedyen. "What the heck, Gaedyen—oh crap."

Behind him stood an even larger Gwythienian, her skin faded and slightly wrinkled like Soroco's, but more of a purplish-beige. She grinned a slanted leer down at Gaedyen.

Her eyes slid to me and the smile faded. "I will never understand a Shimbator's strange attraction to human women. How embarrassing."

I frowned. "Excuse m—"

"It seems Tukailaan did bury certain items here after all." She sighed at Gaedyen, sounding bored.

I clenched the Rubandors' rock in my sleeved hand and felt the chain of the other hanging from my pocket. But what had the other thing I'd seen been? Was there another rock?

"We have not found anything of Tukailaan's." Gaedyen ground out, his muscles tensing as he tried to sound calm.

Her brow rose in surprise. "Oh, no? You only found the rocks, then?"

I frowned, then my stomach dropped as dread roiled in to fill its place. *The arkencain!*

The new Gwythienian's eyes flashed to me, then narrowed as her grin returned.

"I—"

She cut me off with a roar and wavered into invisibility.

There was a puff of dirt from the hole we'd dug, then a thump. Gaedyen roared in pain, his head swinging as if struck.

A moment later she reappeared, standing on top of Gaedyen and holding a shimmering black arkencain to his throat.

"No! Wait!" I screamed, terror overwhelming me. She couldn't strike Gaedyen with that—it would be a death sentence! It was simply too horrible.

The female Gwythienian sneered at me. "Only the weak could feel anything for humans. For this you deserve to die, Gaedyen. I should kill you right now." She twirled the arkencain between her long fingers, smiling at Veri and me.

I raised my hands in surrender. "Wait! Please."

Her eyes fell on my hand clenched around the blue rock, and her expression morphed into rage.

"You have found them! And you already touched them? Do not swallow it, human! Or I swear I will give all of you a slow, painful death by a slice from this arkencain!" She raised the stone blade toward the sky, then brandished it at me. "Do you understand me, human? Do not dare swallow them."

I gulped, trying to conceal my confusion. Why would that be the first thing to come to her mind? But I had distracted her, and I needed to keep it going.

"I'll swallow both if you don't get off of Gaedyen right now. Step away from him!"

She scowled at me. "If you swallow them, I stab the tip of his tail. A slow and painful death, but one you may be able to prevent by *removing* the poisoned portion of his tail." Her smile grew. "Of course, you would have to guess between erring on the side of cutting off as little as possible and risking not getting all the poison, or cutting off more than needed and hampering his ability to fly for the rest of his life." She dropped the grin and her cold eyes grew more frigid as she placed the arkencain against his neck. "If you continue to test my patience, I will stab him closer to the heart, and he will be dying before you realize it has happened."

My mind raced to figure out how I could make this end well, but terror made it impossible to focus.

"Place them on the ground and back away. Move too quickly or give any hint you plan to do something else, and I stab this Shimbator fraud, and you can watch him die painfully for as long as it takes. Understand?" Sunlight glinted off the sharp teeth she bared at me.

I glanced at Gaedyen, who shook his head, then back at this intruder. Who was she? How did she know we would be here? "If I set them on the ground and back away, you could stab him and grab the rocks before I could do anything about it. Give me a better option."

Her glower darkened. But she couldn't stab him, because she knew I could still swallow the rocks, though what *that* meant, I had no idea.

"All right. You will set them down, I will step off the Shimbator. Then you will step away from the rocks, and I will leave with them. You will leave with your lives. Unless you try to follow me."

"Deal." I placed the rocks on the ground, keeping my eyes on her the whole time. Then I straightened and waited for her to step off Gaedyen.

She removed one foot, then glared at me until I took one step back from the rocks. *If only we'd been a few minutes sooner!*

Eventually she was off him and circling toward the rocks as I circled toward Gaedyen.

Finally, she pounced on the rocks and leaped into the sky, the loud whooshing of her huge wings blowing by us.

I ran to Gaedyen and knelt to inspect his tail and ensure it hadn't been nicked. "Are you okay?"

"I have some scratches from when she pounced on me, but none are from the arkencain. So I think I am in pretty good shape, all things considered. Besides my bruised pride." He lifted his head and got to his feet, shaking out his back legs and stretching his neck. "But we have a new problem."

I threw my hands in the air. "Yeah. Like finally finding the other rocks just in time for someone to snatch them."

"It is worse than that." Gaedyen sighed. "That Gwythienian is Tukailaan's ex-mate and Bricriu's mother, Meleena. Who is supposed to be dead."

# CHAPTER SEVEN

We trudged home, defeated, to let Soroco know what had happened. Even after that, the day was only half over, so we decided to travel toward Geneva and Bricriu again, to see what we could find out about Meleena's habits and hiding places. And mostly because Gaedyen felt anxious about Geneva's wellbeing.

When we stopped for the night, Veri was too tired to forage for himself. Gaedyen and I left him by the fire in my sweatshirt and went in search of food for all of us.

On our way back to camp with full bellies and some berries for Veri, Gaedyen slowed to a halt. "Enzi?"

"Yes?" There had been a sort of electricity between us ever since yesterday, even in spite of the major disappointment of losing the rocks once again. But I couldn't help smiling at my name on his lips.

"We didn't quite finish our conversation yesterday, about what things are okay."

"Oh?" Yes, we did get a bit distracted. "Go ahead, ask away." I was already planning to say yes.

He was silent for several steps. "Would it be okay if I… surprised you with a kiss sometimes? You see, right now I want to kiss you so terribly much, even though I am in the wrong form for you to really enjoy it, I am about to explode and I simply cannot focus on searching for food."

My heart thrilled at his words, at the knowledge that I was wanted, and that I was about to make him happy. I looked back at where he'd stopped, a straight, expressionless mask covering his face.

I put my hands on my hips and stared at him. Grinning, I said, "Yes, Gaedyen. You should definitely surprise me with a kiss sometimes."

His face thawed out immediately as his ear flaps went up again. He stood straighter and smiled back. "Good."

I kept staring at him. "Well? Where's my kiss?"

He smirked and sauntered past me. "I said, 'surprise you with a kiss.' If I did it right now, it would not be a surprise, would it?"

I snorted, my eyebrows lifting as I watched him walk ahead. "Well, okay then."

I dropped my hands from my hips and lifted one foot to step forward when I was thrown backward. "Gaedyen?" I flailed my arms, trying to catch my balance.

But he was there, holding my waist, kissing me. I was pinned between him and a tree several feet off the ground. But the bark didn't scrape my back. His huge arms and hands wrapped around my waist and shoulders, between me and the tree.

He placed tingling kisses on my lips and my cheeks, even one on my neck. Several moments later, he paused, leaning his head against the tree above me and facing me. His eyes were closed as he heaved breaths. His neck muscles flexed and contracted as he breathed, and the sight of them heated my insides even further. I closed my eyes for a moment.

When I looked up again, he was looking down on me. "You are so beautiful."

My heart melted all over again. I felt like laughing and crying and dancing. Mostly like kissing him some more. He thought I was beautiful. All the times I worried about my scars, all the times Jillian and Carlie ridiculed me, none of it mattered. Gaedyen thought I was beautiful.

I put a hand flat against his neck muscles, feeling them move beneath my palm. "So are you."

His lips found mine again.

We were flying toward Bricriu's territory the next day when Gaedyen's earflaps whipped into hyper-attentive mode and Veri peeked out of my hood to peer at the sky around us. Thin whisps of clouds blustered around us.

"We're not alone," Veri said in my ear.

I pulled out the Adarborian bow and nocked a makeshift rymakri, scanning the clouds around us.

Then Geneva appeared from within the mist, soaring through the air a few yards away, keeping pace with us. Gaedyen lurched away at first, but when she gestured for us to follow her, he nodded and swerved to get behind her. Veri leaned over my shoulder and we shared a worried look.

Geneva led us a few minutes away, then landed among thick trees, her tail and wings delimbing a few of them in her quick descent.

We landed a safe distance away, Gaedyen's earflaps snapping around in the heavy breeze. Geneva bounded toward us before I could dismount and began pacing before us. "I am certain Bricriu has been lying to me," she huffed, her brow creased. "I am unsure what is true and what is false, but I feel drawn to this Ferrox, though he is dead. But his name angered Bricriu. I can tell something is not the same between us. He is acting strangely. Strangely enough that I am concerned for your safety here. We must be quick. The hard winds might carry your scents to him despite the extra distance."

Letting the bow rest in my lap, I asked, "Do you want your memories back? To understand about Ferrox?"

Geneva eyed me, her frown deepening, then nodded. "Yes. I want to understand."

Gaedyen watched her. "You are prepared for many memories to be painful?"

She hesitated, then stood a little straighter. "I am not sure. But I want to try."

Gaedyen nodded. "Then you should come with us to the Cathawyrs. Kymri, their leader, promised us she would answer our questions about our pasts if we return the rock of healing. I cannot guarantee it, but there is a good chance she will be able to return your memories if you help us get the rock for her. Even if she is unable to help, we can answer a lot for you on the way. Will you come?"

She grimaced at the ground. "I…I want to go with you. There are things I need to know, and I will not learn them here."

I held in a relieved sigh. I had no idea if she'd go with us, and we needed her help to get the rock back. "Good. But you should know, the rock could be tied to your health. Returning it to the Cathawyrs…it could come at a cost to you."

She nodded. "I need to understand."

I blinked slowly, relieved that she still wanted to help us. "We should prepare to leave immediately once we've found the rock. Do you know where he keeps—"

A deep, furious roar cut me off.

Geneva's eyes went tight. "That is Bricriu. I should have headed you off sooner. He must have caught your scent. I should go to him—calm him down. You must leave and fly far away. Perhaps we will meet again someday and then I can meet the Cathawyrs and understand."

"No." I wasn't going to let her do that to herself—deny herself the answers she wanted to please a controlling, brainwashing monster. "How long before he figures out you know more than he thought and starts mistreating you for it? You should leave with us now."

Gaedyen nodded, his gaze still locked on Geneva's bright, sad eyes.

She blinked away a tear, shaking her head. "But…"

Veri urged over my shoulder, "Come on, Geneva. You may never have another chance."

Bricriu barreled into our midst before she could answer, faster than any of us expected. He came in from the sun, so we didn't have warning. Landing between us and Geneva, he roared long and furious in Gaedyen's face. When he finally paused for breath, a giant vein pulsed beneath the finer scales of his forehead. His eyes bulged, and his skin pulled tighter over his bones than last time I saw him. Was *he* sick now?

"I told you to stay away! What are you doing here, bothering my committed and filling her head with disturbing ideas? Leave at once!" Tiny red veins crisscrossed over his yellow-tinged eyes, and spittle flew from his raging maw.

He stared each of us down. When none of us moved to go, he roared again, taking a step closer.

Veri popped out of my hood onto my shoulder and whispered, "Turn invisible!" then darted up Gaedyen's neck, probably to whisper the same thing. Gaedyen blinked out of sight, and I followed suit. Gaedyen tilted one shoulder down and I slid to the ground as quietly as I could, bow raised once more as Veri danced on tiptoes around me.

Bricriu roared again, but it sounded weaker. He stuck out with a sharp-clawed foreleg, taking a swipe at Gaedyen. But Gaedyen had already swerved. Bricriu wavered, off balance, and his tail knocked into a tree. The ground shook as Bricriu's bulk crashed against it.

So he was still strong, even if he appeared weaker than before.

I snatched at Veri's hand and jumped out of the way, pulling him with me, just as Bricriu's clawed hand came flying through the space where we'd been standing.

And then Veri was growing in front of me, his size multiplied many times. He leaped at Bricriu, expanding even more and wrapping his arms around Bricriu's forelimbs, pinning them in front of him.

Bricriu roared again, and Veri bellowed with him, throwing him back. The two rolled over each other, then Bricriu's head met an invisible force that held him still and kept his mouth shut.

"Where. Is. The. Rock?" Gaedyen's voice roiled around Bricriu, his head becoming visible inches from Bricriu's face. "Well?"

Bricriu gasped twice. "It…it is…." He laughed. And kept laughing.

Gaedyen shook him. "Look at me! Where did you hide the rock of healing? We will not hurt Geneva, but we must have the rock."

I held that makeshift rymakri trained on Bricriu's face. If he tried anything toward Gaedyen…

Bricriu only laughed harder. Gaedyen glanced at me, one brow raised. I frowned. Whatever he found funny was surely bad news for us.

"Good luck finding it!" he wheezed.

"Where will we find it?" Gaedyen snarled.

"You will never find it."

"Yes, we will! If we have to uproot every tree in these woods, dig up feet of soil…"

Bricriu chuckled darkly again. "Ah, but it is not in the trees or the soil. It is in *her*!" He pointed a scaly, clawed forefinger at

Geneva and cackled again, his outstretched arm falling limply to the ground.

Gaedyen and I both shot a glance at her. I expected her to turn on us, if she had the stone all along and had chosen not to tell us. But she stepped back, mouth open and eyes as confused as mine. *In* her?

Gaedyen shook him again. "What do you mean, 'in her'?"

Bricriu coughed, his head lolling back. "I mean I made her swallow it. Without her knowing, of course. I knew something strange was in the works, and I wanted her to be protected. Now she will be the first one to touch it after I die, no matter what anyone does."

Was that why Meleena had ranted about not swallowing the rock? Had she known Bricriu had made Geneva swallow this one?

"I know you will not kill her to get it out, because of who you think she is to you. But even if you wanted to, it would be impossible. I ground it to a powder, and she swallowed it all. It is not a rock anymore. This way, she is safe no matter what."

I stared at Geneva. The corners of her mouth turned down in confusion, her brows knit.

"When did you do this, Bricriu?" she asked.

"I hid it in your food. I watched you eat it—the powdered rock of healing. It needed to be done. It was clearly the right thing to do and something I should have done decades ago. You started healing so much faster. Now if they kill me, you will be the next Possessor. It *wants* to be Possessed by you. I—I can tell. Now no one can take it from you, my sweet. It will stay inside you forever. It will always be yours. Like my heart." His voice grew raspy, and he coughed again.

I struggled to hold in a gag. His *sweet?* Ugh!

Gaedyen rolled his eyes. "Oh, would you stop talking to her like that!"

But Bricriu didn't respond. He stared past us, mesmerized.

Geneva leaned in, concerned but wary. "Bricriu?"

Was he having a fit? It would be terribly convenient if he would just…go ahead and die right now…

A cold, female chuckle rippled from behind us as another Gwythienian became visible a few yards away. "I thought you had done something like that, you fool of a son."

The dappled shadows of the leaves above danced over another Gwythienian as she emerged from a thick grove of trees. *Meleena*.

# CHAPTER EIGHT

It was definitely the same female Gwythienian from the ruins of Susan's greenhouse. She was just as huge and had the same gleam of menace in her eye.

I glanced at Gaedyen. He flashed a concerned look at me and returned his somber gaze to her. I wanted him anywhere but near Meleena. She'd nearly struck him with an arkencain, and of course she'd still have it on her.

Grabbing Veri's hand, I stepped into the trees, nodding at Gaedyen to do the same just before I turned invisible. Meleena knew we were here, but she was distracted. Might as well put some space between her and us while they did whatever they were going to do.

"Mother," Bricriu hissed, his eyes going wide with a crazed expression. "I knew I was not crazy!" Bricriu straightened with a demented grin and bright eyes. "I have sensed you on every other breeze, felt your presence tingling in the back of my mind more and more. I see I was right to do what I did." He leered at Meleena, insanity emanating from him in waves.

Meleena approached slowly, less gracefully than before. Her legs were stiff, and the bags under her eyes more pronounced.

"How could such an idiot of a Gwythienian come from my own body?"

Harsh words from a mother, though I agreed that he *was* crazy.

"If you would have left things as they were, I would not have needed to come here and take the rock. You have only succeeded in sealing your beloved's fate."

Bricriu's insane smile vanished as he stumbled in front of Geneva, standing between her and Meleena. Snarling, he let out a fierce roar. "You will not *dare* to harm my Geneva."

Meleena smirked. "Or what? You will kill me? When you have weakened your own body even more than mine by your actions?"

Bricriu tried to stifle a cough but couldn't hide the hoarse sound.

"In case you have not managed to figure it out yet, *son*, the rock of healing acts a little differently than the others."

His eyes narrowed. "What do you mean?"

"You cannot even guess?" She rolled her eyes and began to circle us. "The rock of healing has a flaw. It can be possessed by more than one at a time."

Understanding dawned across Bricriu's face, overshadowed by terror.

"Yes, Bricriu, when you killed me to steal my rock, somehow enough magic was left in me to return life to my bones. When I tried to heal a scratch out of habit, I was surprised it worked, albeit slower than before. I followed your trail and discovered why you needed it—to save the life of the female you love and nearly murdered."

Bricriu's ear flaps drooped, then went flat against his head.

"I realized that while it worked for you, it also worked for me, though at a reduced rate. But the closer I stayed near you and the rock, the healthier and younger I felt. So I stayed just out of range, leeching from your dearest love the power you had fought so hard to snatch from me for her."

"You evil—" he snarled, but Geneva laid a slim Gwythienian hand on his shoulders. He froze instantly at her touch, resuming his protective stance near her and refocusing his snarl on Meleena.

She continued. "Several weeks ago, the power suddenly slipped away without explanation. I knew you were unfortunately alive, and I knew you had given these intruders a fake rock—"

"How did you know these things without being close enough for me to sense your presence?" Bricriu barked.

She spoke on right over him, "—so I came to see what had befallen my rock of healing."

We all watched her, waiting for what she would say, holding our breaths.

"And I was confused. I could sense it, to some extent, but it was not like before. My connection to it had faded further. But the small sense I still clung to seemed to emanate from Geneva. When she suddenly made a substantial recovery, and you ceased your habit of checking on the rock multiple times a day—"

"How did you know about *that*?" he snarled.

"—I guessed at what you had done. A foolish thing indeed, since it brought your greatest fear out from the shadows, and it has been draining your strength as well."

Bricriu swayed, then leaned on Geneva. Gaedyen's nostrils flared at Bricriu's touch on his mother, but Geneva held Bricriu up without flinching.

Meleena smiled "Yes, you have been feeling weaker and weaker since Geneva's sudden recovery, but you did not want to admit to yourself the two could be related. But they are. And I warn you, Bricriu, I have absolutely no intention of giving any ground on this. It is a pity that Tukailaan had to die before I was able to realize his ambitions and make him watch, but so it is." She sauntered around them, Bricriu stumbling to keep himself between Geneva and his mother.

"And now you and Geneva must die, and I must touch Geneva as if she were the rock itself as the life drains from her body so I may gain back my former abilities. I will be young and fit and beautiful again. And then I shall take the remaining stones for myself and make all the realms pay for the suffering they thrust upon me!"

Bricriu's sly smile returned. "And how do you plan to do that, when Geneva will easily heal herself and I am still—to some extent—a Possessor?"

Meleena nodded at Bricriu. "It would indeed be difficult, if I planned to kill you with tooth and claw." Suddenly she was brandishing the arkencain, light glinting off its smooth, onyx surface. "But I have a more effective weapon."

Bricriu's smile vanished and he stretched a wing out between Geneva and Meleena as both his and Geneva's eyes grew wide.

Geneva leaned around Bricriu's protective stance. "Is that a weapon of the Arkensilvers?"

"Indeed, it is, young Geneva," Meleena purred, then leaped toward them, swiping the arkencain.

A sharp squelch came from Bricriu's chest, and he grunted, his hand grasping Meleena's around the weapon. "Fly, Geneva, fly!" he rasped.

Geneva's head whipped back and forth from Bricriu to Meleena, apparently unable to decide what to do.

Bricriu sank to the ground, his other hand coming up to rest on the weapon as it tore through his chest.

"I brought your wretched hide into the world, Bricriu, and you tried to kill me, the one who gave you life. So now I am taking you out—"

In a flash, Bricriu screwed up his face, ripped the arkencain out of his chest with an agonized howl, and shoved it into Meleena's neck.

She roared, staggering back from Bricriu, who stood a little straighter, still supported by Geneva. He held one clenched fist against his bleeding wound.

Bricriu sneered. "I have borne your poisonous influence my entire wretched life. I will not let you kill the one bright thing that ever made it worth living!"

He dove at her, but she evaded him, wrenching the weapon out of her neck. "Oh yes, I will."

She leaped for Geneva, and Gaedyen soared out of our hiding place and raced to her aid.

"Gaedyen, no!" I shouted at the same time Meleena spun to face him.

She growled and brandished the arkencain at Gaedyen.

"No!" Geneva, who'd watched in terror since Meleena had shown up, suddenly found her voice. She jumped out from behind Bricriu's sagging form and pounced on Meleena, latching on to her neck with her powerful jaws.

I aimed my nocked rymakri at Meleena, but Gaedyen and Geneva were too close. Meleena rose onto her back legs, bucking Geneva off, and Gaedyen took the opportunity to shove a rymakri into Meleena's stomach.

She roared again. Losing her balance, she toppled over Bricriu. He opened his eyes, saw the arkencain in her hand, and strained toward it with his teeth.

Gaedyen bounded to Geneva as Meleena rolled off Bricriu. Meleena shook herself as if dizzy, then focused on Gaedyen and Geneva. She dropped into a hunting crouch, raised her wings, and leaped into the air just as Bricriu swung his head to the side, catching her thigh with the arkencain and tearing a long gash through her flesh.

Blood gushed from her leg much faster than from her neck.

*Must have hit the artery! I never thought I'd say this, but good swing, Bricriu!*

She roared at Bricriu and pivoted toward him, ready to finish him off. But then her ear flaps swung to Geneva as she pushed Gaedyen away and begged him to save himself.

I raced through the trees toward Gaedyen, my bow in hand and Veri tearing through the branches nearby, trying to reach Gaedyen so he could take Geneva's advice.

But Meleena needed the healing abilities more urgently than Bricriu's death. She turned and stalked toward them, already ahead of Veri and me.

Bricriu roared, flinging himself lopsidedly through the air onto Meleena's back. With another hoarse cough, he crawled toward Meleena's head and raised the arkencain.

Meleena bucked him off, swiping at him with her tail as he spun through the air. She swiped the arkencain from him and plunged it into his side as he hit the ground hard.

I gasped. Bricriu's lips stretched to the side as he growled at Meleena and shoved himself back to his feet.

"Geneva!" Gaedyen hissed.

Her shocked eyes rose from Bricriu's still body to Gaedyen's pleading eyes.

He howled, "We have to go, now!"

I hauled myself onto his back and clutched Veri's now-huge hand to pull him on behind me, as Gaedyen raced forward, gesturing for Geneva to follow us.

Gaedyen's hand stretched toward Geneva. "Geneva, please, come now, while Meleena's distracted and before she heals from being near the rock in you!"

# CHAPTER NINE

When we landed hours later, Gaedyen eyed Geneva with concern. Meleena had landed a couple of bloody swipes across Geneva's back legs before Gaedyen realized we were leaving her as the only target by staying invisible ourselves. Geneva wasn't Cadoumai, so she couldn't hide like we could.

But thanks to Bricriu's shocking actions regarding the rock of healing, the pink scar tissue was barely even noticeable now.

Geneva breathed heavily, stumbling onto her side and looking nearly to tears. "I was wrong to leave Bricriu. He *was* a little crazy. And too protective of me. But he *did* love me. Of that I am certain. I did not have enough time to discover whether I loved him back."

Gaedyen sighed. "You loved Ferrox, once."

Sliding off his back, I elbowed him hard in the side. *Not the time.*

She blinked, setting tears loose in a race down both sides of her face. "And the confusion around that is a portion of my problem." She sighed. "We still should have buried Bricriu."

Veri and I shot a glance at each other. Was he really dead? Meleena had been alive enough to put up a chase, but where was she now?

Geneva covered her face with one slender Gwythienian hand. "And if we must return the rock to the Cathawyr, how are we going to remove it from me to do that? What if it is bound to stay inside me forever?"

Veri stretched and yawned. "Maybe the Cathawyr will have a way to coax the dust out and bind it into rock again with some kind of magic."

Gaedyen paced. "It is more dangerous now, though. For you. How do we know it can be removed safely? She could rip it out of you and cause damage, for all we know."

Geneva eyed Gaedyen. "Why do you care so much whether I live or die?"

Gaedyen's gaze dropped to the ground. Geneva blinked, slowly taking in his reaction. "Oh. Oh, my." She turned to me. "You said he is Ferrox's son." She turned back to Gaedyen. "And you told me I loved Ferrox once. Did…did I have a child with Ferrox?" Her voice trembled. "Are you…mine?"

Gaedyen met her gaze. Then nodded.

Her lips trembled as more tears flowed. "I am so sorry, Gaedyen. I do not know what I did…I do not even remember discovering I had an egg to lay. Something is wrong with me and my memories, and I fear you have had to suffer for it for a very long time. Can you ever forgive me?"

Gaedyen stepped toward her and lightly placed his large Gwythienian hand on her shoulder. "I do forgive you. I will no longer hold it against you. You are my mother, and I am your son. Let us be family now."

Then the sobbing really started. She sure deserved the chance to cry after everything she'd gone through and all the information she'd learned today. She'd lost two loves but also gained a surprise nearly-adult son. It must be quite an emotional day.

Even Veri wiped a tear off his face. Then he dramatically scrubbed under his nose and wiped that on the collar of my shirt.

"Ew!" I whispered, swatting his little hand away.

He snickered and hopped nimbly from my shoulders to a leafy branch.

After Geneva calmed down a little, I asked, "Have you ever met Meleena before, Geneva? Did you know who she was when you saw her?"

"Bricriu never spoke of his parents, which makes sense now. Whatever was wrong with Bricriu, it must have been because of her. The horrible things she said to him." Geneva met Gaedyen's eyes. "I missed out on so much of your life, and that I deeply regret. But I would never treat you like Meleena treated Bricriu."

Gaedyen nodded and offered her a small smile, but kept silent.

Geneva continued. "If I remember the stories correctly, she was the most beautiful female in Odan Terridor when Tukailaan was about to become Possessor. According to the stories, she seduced a very willing Tukailaan and then used her influence over him to disguise her…disgusting secret. She likes to eat humans. She would round them up and eat them whenever she could, even though it was a jailable offense."

I shivered, the images that revelation had brought up when I'd first heard it coming to mind.

"Tukailaan, enamored with her beauty and delighted to brag about his conquest of her, gave into her pleading and became like her. A young female Gwythienian discovered them at it in the human realm and warned Padraig. When he caught them, he had to inform his father.

"Batran—your great grandfather and the Keeper at the time—threw Tukailaan in the dungeon alongside Meleena. But Tukailaan had played in the dungeons as a youngling and knew how to escape the cells. He freed himself, but blaming Meleena for his misfortune, left her behind. She was furious, especially when she discovered she was going to lay an egg. Or so the stories go. And the stories seem to have had it right."

I frowned. "Why does she hate humans so much?"

Geneva regarded me. "You do know where humans come from, right?"

I stared at her. "Um…I'm not sure. Where *do* humans come from?"

"In the beginning, all of the races had the ability to shift from their animal form to a human form. The word Shimbator, which now means having the ability to change into a human, used to just mean a *person*. It was a term that applied to anyone, no matter their native realm."

"*That's* where humans come from?" It seemed a little farfetched to me. I glanced at Gaedyen at the mention of Shimbators. Did Geneva know he was one?

"Yes. As the various races explored and expanded, some of one type fell in love with and married those of other types. However, the offspring of these couples could only exist as human. Their parents' genetics were only compatible in that single form. Sometimes the children of Cadoumai retained vague abilities as humans, but even those were soon bred out of the new human race."

Veri's voice tickled my ear. "Hear that, Enzi? We might be long-lost cousins! Maybe that's why you're so easy to tease."

"Shh!" I hissed, rolling my eyes at him.

He hung upside down from a nearby limb, then swung toward a lower one and grabbed it with both hands as he let go with his feet, narrowly missing me.

"Be serious for two seconds, *please*." I glared at him, gesturing toward the newly discovered mother and son.

"Pfft! Where's the fun in that?" He grinned and dodged another playful smack.

Geneva continued over our bickering, and I didn't want to miss it. "A rare few members of every race lacked the ability to turn human. This was undesirable before the races began intermarrying, but soon those who lacked the ability became more sought-after as mates because their offspring couldn't become stuck in a human form or produce human-only children. Over the decades, the ability to shift into a human form became something undesirable. So those who had the ability hid it, as if it became known, they would be less likely to find someone to commit to them. It was mostly bred out of all the realms, but some were better at hiding it than others, so there may be some Shimbators still today."

So she didn't know. I pointedly kept my eyes on her and off Gaedyen. If he wanted to tell her, that was his choice. I wouldn't give away his secret.

That was a really wild story, though. I'd been thinking these other creatures had lived on the outskirts of humankind all along, but they'd been here long before us? It helped make more sense why Gaedyen had tried to hide it from me. Culturally, it was looked down upon. He still shouldn't have lied to me, but how could I blame him, knowing this? And knowing the feelings he had for me? What would I have done?

# CHAPTER TEN

*I* woke in the middle of the night, thinking of him. I brushed a hand over his side, exploring. Finding the edge of his wing, I caressed the taut skin there. He rumbled with appreciation. I hoped that meant he was awake.

"Gaedyen?" I whispered.

His wing lifted off me, and his whole body shifted a little as he turned his head. "Yes, my love?"

Smiling, I pushed myself up and crawled out of my spot next to him. He watched me closely, earflaps raised. "Is everything—"

I shushed him with a hand against his lips. Then I reached up and, cupping a hand in front of his earflap, whispered, "Come on."

His wide eyes shone in the moonlight, never leaving mine as he quietly stood. I shot a glance at Geneva, then Veri, confirming they were both still asleep, then stepped deeper into the woods.

Despite the drastic differences in our weights, my footsteps crushed leaves and twigs more loudly than his.

"Did you have a nightmare? Do you need to talk?"

I paused, then turned toward him. His eyes were full of loving concern. He was worried. "Gaedyen, everything is fine. More than fine." I stepped toward him. "Stop worrying so much."

"Okay…then why did we come out here?"

I cocked an eyebrow at him, grinning. "Why do you think?"

"I…I am not sure…"

"Well let me spell it out for you then, Gaedyen. I am desperately in love with you, and it's been way too long since we've kissed."

Had I really just said that? Judging by how his face lit up, I must have. Well, it was true. I couldn't help giggling. This wasn't like me at all. But it felt nice.

In the blink of an eye he picked me up, and before I knew it, he was on his back on the forest floor and I was straddling his chest. He planted a quick kiss on my cheek, then leaned back and watched me. I sat at a slightly awkward angle, but with his huge arms supporting me, it was unexpectedly comfortable.

I was a bit surprised at myself for not feeling an ounce of weirdness at straddling him like that. But the truth was, I liked it. It felt good. Warm. I worried it would remind me of Caleb, but it didn't really. I was safe, near someone I wanted to be close to.

His large, warm fingers gently brushed against my back, soothing me and stirring up thrilling tingles on my skin. I traced the lines and contours of his face, savoring the feel of those smaller scales against my fingers. But I was struck with the knowledge that something else would make it feel nicer. I wanted to feel his skin on my skin.

But did I dare take my shirt off?

Nope. I definitely did not. I was beginning to believe he loved me as I was, so it wasn't that. I just didn't know how to go about it. That was too much for tonight. But still, my whole body reveled in each stroke of his fingers over my T-shirt.

Screw the T-shirt.

I wasn't brave enough to take it off, but I could manage hiking it up a bit, couldn't I?

Shaking slightly, I leaned up to kiss him while pulling my hands away. He slowed when my hands left his face, but he didn't stop. I reached back, heart pounding, and pulled the back of my shirt up a few inches. Cool air caressed my back as Gaedyen's fingers swept down, then paused when they found bare skin.

"Oh, sorry, Enzi. That was an accident, I did not mean—"

Once again I cut him off with a kiss as I nervously held my shirt in place a few inches higher than it should be. Three of his fingers trembled against my spine, sliding down as I leaned closer to him.

For a moment he was completely still, then ever so softly, he brushed his hand over my back. So slow. Tremendously slow. And *wonderful.*

The pads on his fingers were slightly rough but gentle and warm. They left tingling trails behind them as they lightly swept over my back.

I couldn't explore him the same way from so high on his chest, so I broke the kiss and ducked under his chin to hug his neck, letting my hands travel past his jawline down his neck, over his incredibly muscled shoulders and forearms…

The rumbling changed, growing deeper and fiercer, almost like a growl. But I wasn't afraid. I knew this person, this one person in the world, wouldn't hurt me.

I smiled, enjoying the way he purred.

The motion of the fingers on my back transitioned from up and down to tracing little circles all over, causing more tingles. I accidentally slid a little to one side, and his other hand steadied me. I tried not to think of how all the flab was gathered there with the way I was curved over him. But if he noticed, he didn't seem to mind.

"Enzi. Enzi." His hands slid around so that each was gripping my waist.

He held me up as he rolled to his side, laying me down with my back against his chest. He wrapped one arm under me and one over. That one bent at the elbow by my legs, putting his hand near my chest. I grabbed a hold of his hand with both of mine and hugged it to me, relishing the place where my shirt was still pulled up, allowing the corded muscles of his arm to lightly touch my skin each time I breathed.

He placed a wing over me too, and I brushed my fingers over the velvet texture of the edge. He sighed against me, and I smiled some more.

His hands stilled. When they remained still for several seconds, I asked, "Gaedyen? Is something wrong?"

"No. I just remembered something…this is how I held you when we fell outside Sequoia Cadryl. When you passed out after Tukailaan attacked you, he stole the necklace and then threw you. Of course I let him go and attempted to save you. There was no time to slow down, so I pulled you against me just before you hit the ground. I only had time to cushion your fall."

"And that's how you injured your shoulder and damaged your Shimbator mark?"

"Yes." His fingers brushed lightly over my forearm, completely melting me.

"Gaedyen, thank you for saving my life. I'm sorry it cost you so much, and for being rude in Sequoia Cadryl. I really appreciate you risking so much to save me."

"I would do it again, anytime."

I smiled, though guilt clouded my good mood. "Thank you, Gaedyen."

"Of course. Can I ask you a question?"

"Sure. What?"

"Enzi, how in all the realms did you fall for me? It almost seems too presumptuous a question to ask, but…I really can't imagine."

I lightly slapped his wing. "It's not so weird that a boring human girl would be attracted to a gorgeous, powerful dragon, is it? What *is* hard to believe is that the dragon could fall for the boring human girl."

He kissed my hair. "Enzi, you have never been boring once since I have known you. You love music, and with such a passion! You leaped into training with the rymakri, you were willing to come on this journey with a complete stranger, a monster no less. You love to cook, even though I may not understand all your cooking methods." He chuckled.

I grinned, remembering the octopus I'd attempted to cook on the way to Maisius Arborii. He'd preferred the meat raw and had choked and coughed all over the fire after trying a cooked piece.

"Yeah." I chuckled, sliding my hand over his wrist.

He sighed, laying his head lightly on mine. "You are a very interesting person, Enzi."

"Huh. I've never thought of myself as interesting before."

"You certainly are."

He thought I was interesting. How...*interesting*.

"You have no idea how glad I am that we have broken the ice a bit over what is okay for me to do for you, with you...I did not know what I was missing. I am very glad to know now."

The giddy feeling stirred inside me again. "Me too."

"There is something I would like to ask you, but it has to do with your scars. If you do not feel comfortable hearing it now, though, of course that is fine."

I paused, anxious not to think of that right now. Of the scars he'd surely felt beneath his fingers as he touched my skin. I'd forgotten for the moment that my skin wasn't silky-smooth. His touch had soothed those thoughts right out of my mind. They were back now, dirty and nauseating as they always would be.

"What's your question?" My voice sounded colder than I meant for it to.

"Well, did you ever realize what my original plan to gain your affection was?"

I frowned. "What? What does that have to do with my scars?"

"I am getting to that."

"Okay." I brushed a strand of hair away from my face. "No, I don't know what your original plan was. I didn't know you had a plan."

"When I first realized I was in love with you—I tried to deny it for a long time, certain you wouldn't reciprocate my feelings—I knew the only chance I could have with you was to manage to get you to fall in love with my human form. Except, I did *not* like hearing you call me Shaun. It was just the first mash of syllables I could throw together that time I stopped those girls from stealing your necklace. I craved hearing you call me by my real name, but I did not think you could accept someone who had two forms. If Shaun was the only way I could be with you, the only way I could express my love for you, then so be it."

What did that have to do with my scars? My heart raced as I worried where he was going with this.

"So I tried to keep Shimbators a secret from you, and I tried to be a fun human to be around as Shaun, always terrified that you would figure it out. Especially after waking in Sequoia Cadryl. I meant all the things I said there though, in my human form. Everything."

I thought of the kind things he'd said about coming on the journey to help people I didn't know, and smiled.

"All that leading up to this: Enzi, I love you. I love holding you and kissing you, knowing I am able to make you feel loved, hearing you say my real name and accepting me for who it means I am. I love every bit of that. But I can only do so much as a Gwythienian. I think I will be able to show you better how impossibly in love I am with you in human form. My hands will fit around you better, my face will be smaller so I can really hug you and kiss you at the same time. I want that very much."

I thought of the human body I'd known as Shaun—Gaedyen's human form. He was the kind of attractive that would never have acknowledged my existence at school, and who I would have stuttered around and run from if he ever had. I quite honestly couldn't imagine him wanting to kiss me. It would definitely be something to get used to.

"But I know you may not. Or, maybe you would. I guess what I am trying to say is, which way do you like me better? And more specifically, do you think all these things we have been able to do are only okay because of my Gwythienian form? That the same things would make you uncomfortable if I were human?"

I squirmed. I did *not* want to talk about this. I didn't know the answer anymore. I fell in love with him in this form. I'd noticed how attractive his human form was for sure, but when it came to this…it would be different.

If he were in human form, I would lose my excuse for avoiding going to certain lengths. I didn't want to hurt him, but I couldn't do that. He deserved someone who could. I could never be enough, for either form. But at least with him as a Gwythienian, it wasn't my fault. If he were human, it would be.

At the same time, though, he had given me butterflies. He was attractive. And yet he was still Gaedyen underneath. Still the soul I loved, though he looked different. I'd felt a pull toward him in Sequoia Cadryl, that was true. But still.

"I like this form better. And, Gaedyen, I do feel very loved. You make me feel beautiful and amazing. This—I love this." I stroked his wrist with my fingertips. "You don't need to change anything for me."

"I am glad, Enzi. But what if I did change, because *I* wanted to. What if I were a human more than a Gwythienian? Could I still touch you? Still kiss you? Or would that be too much a reminder of the past?"

He should just never turn human again, and we could easily avoid that issue. "I don't know, Gaedyen. I don't know how close I could get without triggering problems. It's easier this way—and I really like it. Don't you?"

"Yes! Yes, I do. I cannot begin to describe how incredible this is." He gently brushed a hand over my hair, and I closed my eyes, luxuriating in the feeling. "Thank you for answering, Enzi. I hope I was not too forward in asking."

I shrugged. "It's okay. We should be able to ask each other questions, to talk about things. Since we're already on that topic, you're saying it was because you were afraid I would only like you in human form and not Gwythienian form? That was why you lied about being a Shimbator? Why you lied to me about growing up as a human in Odan Terridor?"

He hesitated, exhaling slowly. "I was terrified of losing my only chance with you if you knew Shaun and I were the same. It is not desirable to be able to change forms among my kind, as Geneva explained earlier. I did not want you to write me off because of that. And when I was in human form, I did everything I could to tell things as truthfully as possible. I knew I was already in deep, and I knew how much it devastated you when your mom lied. I did not want to do that to you, but I already had, and the cost of undoing it would likely be you. I was not willing to lose you so easily.

"I told stories that really did happen to me and left out obviously Gwythienian parts. Do you not remember me saying there were some things I would rather not say because they could hurt you? I was talking about if you ever found out about me being a Shimbator. I wanted to be as truthful as possible to avoid breaking your trust any more than I already had. I am so dreadfully sorry that I lied to you, Enzi. I did the best I could to fix it at the time. Can you ever forgive me?"

His worried eyes met mine, and I couldn't help but smile to ease his fears. "Yes. I can. And I do, Gaedyen. But it does make it harder to trust you completely now."

His hand stilled over my hair, and he went silent for a long moment. "How can I win back your trust?"

"I don't know."

"Please, Enzi, this is very important to me. I do not want you to be unable to trust me. I want to be more than that to you."

I sighed. "I don't know, Gaedyen. Maybe it's just something that will come with time."

"Then I will be on the lookout for every opportunity."

Smiling, I kissed his wrist. "Goodnight, Gaedyen."

"Goodnight, Enzi." His whisper ruffled my hair. "I love you."

"I love you, too."

# CHAPTER ELEVEN

We sneaked back to camp and I was lying next to him with his wing covering me before anyone else woke up.

When I woke at sunrise, Geneva was strolling back into camp with a mouthful of rabbits for breakfast.

I watched her with the one eye that Gaedyen's wing had uncovered when it slipped as he slept. She sat one rabbit on a pile of sticks and then divided the others into two piles. Was the stick one for me to roast for myself? And the two piles… she had three in each with one rabbit left. She placed the fourth on one stack and then stepped around to start on the pile of three.

I smiled. She was giving Gaedyen the bigger pile, wasn't she? It was nice to have a motherly figure helping us with things like that. But frowned as she scarfed down the first carcass. Her brooding eyes stared off at nothing as she swallowed. Several still seconds passed before she seemed to suddenly remember the remaining rabbits in her pile. She eyed them. And kept eyeing them.

It had to be hard for her, barely knowing who she was or what her life had been like. I couldn't imagine waking up and finding out I had a son who was nearly an adult. How weird would that be?

Gaedyen's warm wing lifted and I tilted my head back, grinning as his smile melted into a yawn. "Good morning, Enzi."

"Good morning, Gaedyen." His name morphed into my own yawn as I stretched my arms, then rolled over to push myself up.

"I brought food for the two of you." Geneva called. "Veri left to forage for his kind of food. Before he left, he told me you liked to, um, cook your meat, Enzi. So I gathered firewood for you. Gaedyen, your food is there." She jerked her head toward the four rabbits.

Gaedyen rose as well and stepped toward Geneva, his earflaps standing straight up. "That was very thoughtful. Thank you…" He trailed off, probably wondering whether he should call her Geneva or Mom now.

"Enzi! I gashed my ankle," Veri whimpered, limping through the trees.

"How the heck did you do that?" I asked, sprinting to meet him where he'd plopped down in the leaf litter.

"I fell out of a tree, and the branch I broke fell with me and landed on my ankle. I know, I'm very talented." He rolled his eyes. "But I haven't seen any blemdinger beetles or celomary root since leaving Sequoia Cadryl, so I don't know what to do about it."

He slumped on the ground, looking much more defeated than usual.

*He fell out of a tree? He just doesn't do that. What makes him constantly swing back and forth from healthily obnoxious to weirdly subdued?*

"May I see?" Geneva asked from across the woodpile.

"Sure." Veri swung his legs the other way as Geneva rounded the fire and approached us.

"I do not understand the full implications of what Bricriu did when he caused me to eat the powdered rock of healing, but I have accidentally healed myself a few times since waking up. I was unsure what was happening, but of course now I understand. Maybe I can use my new knowledge to heal your wound?"

Veri shrugged, blinking wearily. "Worth a try."

Geneva got down on her belly and covered Veri's foot and ankle with her slender Gwythienian hands. She closed her eyes and concentrated.

Nothing happened.

Gaedyen approached and stood behind me, lightly resting his head on top of mine.

I reached up and touched his cheek absently, focused on Geneva.

Several minutes later, she lifted her hands.

I leaned forward as far as I could. "How does it feel, Veri?"

Eyeing his ankle, he flexed and rotated it slowly. "A little better. Looks like it stopped bleeding, too."

Geneva frowned. "It looks exactly the same to me."

"It really does feel a little less painful, though," Veri assured her. "Maybe try again for a little longer?"

"Yes, I will." Turning her eyes on me, she said, "Maybe you should get that fire started for your breakfast? It would probably be best to be on our way as soon as possible."

I nodded and stood as she replaced her hands over Veri's injury and closed her eyes.

We soared among the mountain peaks that day. At dusk, we landed on the biggest rocky crag we could find. It was a small place for two Gwythienians to fit, but we managed.

In the warmth between Gaedyen and Geneva, I started sweating in my sweatshirt. I pulled it off and wrapped it around a shivering Veri in my lap. Geneva's healing hands had restored his ankle almost back to normal, but his ears had still drooped for most of the flight and he'd spent the day curled up in my hood.

His shivering finally came to a stop as the sweatshirt warmed him, and at last he breathed steadily. That little Fuzzbucket had been there for me through so much. And he might be the only person in the whole world who'd never lied to me even once.

I just wished he would tell me what was up with him, though. Or did he not know either?

Maybe more time with Geneva would help him heal. She'd healed his ankle. Mostly. Was it such slow going because she didn't know what she was doing, or because it was harder to heal someone other than the healer's self?

Or was it because Geneva was only one of multiple Possessors, all dividing the ability between themselves? Did that mean Bricriu and Meleena were still alive?

"Gaedyen," Geneva said, her voice rumbling through me where my arm was pressed against her side, "will you please tell me how Ferrox died, and how I ended up with Bricriu?"

Gaedyen winced, but met her eyes and nodded. "You and Ferrox schemed to steal the rocks. No one ever figured out why, but it is presumed it was for power. You left together with them and got into a fight and the story goes that you killed each other. But they never found your body."

"But they found Ferrox's? He is definitely dead?"

"Yes. I am sorry. And it was on the night my egg was laid that you and Ferrox fled Odan Terridor, planning to take over power of the realms. Padraig raised me."

I noted how he left out the part about being secluded and ignored by others for his parents' actions. That was nice of him.

She already looked so ashamed and horrified, any more of her past wrongs might be more than she could bear.

"Did I…kill Ferrox?"

"No. Bricriu told us that he and Tukailaan, his father, were lying in wait for Ferrox. Bricriu wanted…wanted you for himself, so he attacked the first Gwythienian out of Odan Terridor that night thinking that it was Ferrox. But it was you. And it seems he has been caring for you ever since."

"But how did Ferrox and I find where the rocks were hidden? No one is supposed to know except the Keeper."

"That I do not know. If Padraig knew, he never revealed it to me."

She looked down at her feet, troubled. "I wonder what happened to make me such a horrible, selfish person. I do not remember being so. It grieves me that I caused such distress to so many people and all four of the realms, down to my own son. If the realms knew I was alive, they would kill me for sure."

Gaedyen's eyes hardened. "We will keep your identity a secret. I think the Cathawyr already knows who you are, but no one else need discover it. We will keep you safe."

*As safe as can be expected when you have a valuable power stuck inside your body and everyone and their second cousin hates you*, I thought.

Geneva lifted the edge of the sweatshirt to inspect Veri's ankle. The skin had begun winding itself back together earlier. A lot of reddish flesh was still visible, but dark pink was making an appearance around the edges.

"It does look a lot better. You're really helping him." I smiled at Geneva, hoping that healing Veri would make her feel a little better after hearing all the negatives about her past.

Veri stretched and rolled over to face Geneva. He wiggled his toes and rotated his ankle. "Yeah. It feels so much better. And I think the healing is helping with the headaches and stuff I've been getting. Thanks, Geneva." He grinned at her.

She returned his smile. "You are welcome, little one."

We reached the peak of the Cathawyrs' mountain shortly after sunrise the next morning, me flying on Gaedyen's back and Veri on Geneva's. Being near her seemed to keep Veri feeling healthier and more comfortable, so she'd offered to carry him.

The same three Cathawyrs met us as before. These three had broader features than tigers or jaguars. And they had huge spots patterned like giraffe spots.

The wind whistled past the shear mountain edges as they led us into Kymri's cave. I walked between Gaedyen and Geneva, Veri remaining on Geneva's back.

Standing in a beam of light leaking through the ceiling, Kymri surveyed us, her bright sapphire eyes blazing from her moon-white face. Her coat of the same blinding whiteness glowed as she stood facing us on all fours.

The Cathawyr leader was just as straight to business as ever. "Have you brought me the stone?"

She spoke to Gaedyen, so he replied. "Yes…in a manner of speaking. I am afraid giving it to you will be rather difficult."

Kymri's eyes roved over each of us, narrowing on Geneva. "Please explain."

Gaedyen continued. "The last Possessor may be dead, but he crushed the rock into powder and forced my mother," he gestured to Geneva, "to swallow it, in an attempt to ensure she would become the next Possessor at the time of his death. He claimed it cannot be removed. Do you know if this is true?"

Kymri frowned. "This is quite a development. I do not know, Gwythienian. I have yet to encounter such a thing. I will think on it and consult my sisters."

Gaedyen bowed his head in respect. "Very well. Kymri, we bargained information about our fathers in exchange for the rock. We three faced great peril in order to do the closest thing to delivering it to you that we could."

Kymri's eyes darkened. "And you expect to be given all you asked for despite bringing me a ground-up rock metabolized into another being's body?" Her voice was even, but her eyes sparked.

"How about another bargain?" Geneva's voice quivered a bit, but her face was impassive.

"Geneva, please let us handle this matter." Gaedyen shot her a look of concern, maybe as worried as I was about what she might do when she was already feeling so guilty.

Kymri's striking ocean eyes regarded Geneva. "Another bargain, rockbearer? What did you have in mind?"

"In exchange for the information we seek, I will place my life in your hands. I will remain here indefinitely and use my new powers as you need them. Until you are able to extract them from me, if that is possible."

"Geneva, you can't just throw your life away. You just got it back!" I protested.

Geneva kept her eyes on the Cathawyr. "But you said it yourself, Enzi. Everyone else in the world hates me, and anyone who learned I was still alive would seek my death. I could live peacefully here. I have always liked the mountains, and these mountains are much more glorious than the ones near Odan Terridor. I have no place in a world where I was once a different person. I could be happy here—become someone I can be proud of. And this way, Kymri has access to the powers she seeks, and we all get the information we long for."

Kymri regarded Geneva, then nodded. "I accept your bargain."

"Geneva!" Gaedyen hissed. "Can we discuss this privately first, *please*?"

My heart raced. What had we just gotten ourselves into? Gaedyen had only just met his mother! They'd barely had a handful of conversations. She couldn't just move away so soon.

Kymri turned her bright blue eyes to me. "Enzi. The answer to everyone's questions begins with you."

My eyebrow rose. "With me? But Gaedyen and I want to know about our fathers. Everything should start with them, not me. Right?"

Kymri shook her head once as she bent to lay on her stomach across her boulder. "It goes further back than that, Enzi. But not through your father's blood. All that has happened here is because of your mother's."

# CHAPTER TWELVE

*I* stared at her. My mother's blood? But it was my father in the Crivabanians' story…?

"Let me explain." Kymri closed her eyes and took a deep breath. When she opened them again, they were wilder than ever. "Tukailaan wanted to be the next Keeper, but because of his many poor decisions, the Keeper at that time chose Padraig instead and threw Tukailaan and Meleena in the dungeon as punishment for their crimes against humans. Tukailaan bitterly blamed Meleena and Padraig for the punishment he didn't believe he deserved. He was able to break out, and as he escaped through the human realm, he experienced his first transformation into a human form. Until then, he had not known he was a Shimbator."

Geneva gasped. "I did not know he was a Shimbator either!"

I glanced at Gaedyen. One big eye slid to meet my gaze, then he returned his stoic attention to Kymri.

Kymri nodded at Geneva and continued. "He was alone. In an unfamiliar place. In a body that was not even the same species. On top of just losing everything he had worked for all those years. Disoriented, scared. It was in that condition the lovely young human, a gardener and seller of flowers named Susan Mathews, found him.”

*She grew flowers. So that building was a greenhouse?*

“She took him to her house. Bathed him. Clothed him. Fed him. Cared for him like he had never been cared for before. He fell hard for her, though he hated his human body and longed to be Gwythienian again. She fell for him too, and they were married. Soon she became pregnant.”

“Oh my gosh! What kind of child did they have? Was Tukailaan still genetically a Gwythienian?” I wrinkled my nose, imaging a deformed half-dragon, half-human creature.

I glanced at Gaedyen, expecting him to share my disgust, but to my surprise, his ear flaps drooped ever so slightly, and he avoided meeting my eyes.

My stomach dropped to my toes. Had I hurt his feelings? *Oh my gosh, he doesn't want kids, does he? Is that what that look was about? Oh shoot.*

His face was blank again in an instant, and Kymri continued as if I hadn't spoken.

“One day, they were unfortunate enough to encounter Meleena and Bricriu in the woods, two Gwythienians Tukailaan had treated poorly. The Gwythienians attacked Tukailaan and his wife, and she died, leaving their newborn daughter to his care alone. But he changed into Gwythienian form to fight and did not know how to change back.

“Fearing for the child's life, he did the only thing he could do. He chose to leave her at an orphanage until he was able to return in human form to take her back. He reached through the window, laid her in the moonlight, and promised to come back as soon as he could. Then he flew away into the night.”

Kymri smiled sadly as she met my eyes. “That girl grew up and lived her life, but she had secrets. Tumors grew over her shoulders where wings might attach on a bird, and she saw things. Monsters peering at her in the bathtub, from a glass of water, and even through the cat's bowl. Generations passed and your mother, Lisa, was born, and she feared the water as many before her had. She saw things she didn't understand. And then you came along, and one of the stones found its way to you. It worked for you, because you have Gwythienian blood running through your veins. It was diluted enough that you never developed the ability to see through water without the rock like your ancestors could, but it was not too thin to allow you to gain Possession of the Gwythienian's rock when you touched it after its previous Possessor's death."

My heart pounded in my ears. "Wait. You're saying that *I'm* a descendant of *Tukailaan?*" I must've missed something.

"Yes. Through your mother's ancestry. Not your father's. His part in this story is much more accidental and different from what you might expect."

I stared at Gaedyen. "Does…does this make you and me, like, cousins or something?" Grimacing, I considered Tukailaan's relation to Gaedyen. He was Gaedyen's grandfather's brother, and my…great, great, great-to-something-degree grandfather. Would that be…a problem?

Kymri's pale, slender tail flicked by her feet. "You are both descendants of Batran, the greatest Keeper the four realms ever had. This is something to be proud of."

Gaedyen shifted. "So that is why Tukailaan's scent and yours confused me so much. They smelled like family."

And why I looked like that picture of Susan. Why Tukailaan kept saying I looked familiar. But *family?* Gaedyen and I were related? Distantly, but still…

Wincing, I worried how this could affect everything.

Kymri's eyes rested on Veri. "I am afraid there is more. Veritamyk, you are unwell, I see. Tell me how you feel."

Veri dipped his head in respect. "I don't know. I'm just tired on and off. Sometimes I feel really good but most of the time I don't feel that great. But I'm still able to fight really well, so I don't know what the problem is."

"You have a guess though, do you not?"

When he slid off Geneva's neck with a silent shrug, Kymri lifted a fine, whiskered brow.

"Well, I supposed it could be a problem with Possessing three rocks at once." He traced patterns with a toe on the ground in front of him, avoiding everyone's eyes. "But I'm sure I'll get used to it, right? There's no need to take away the rocks. I'm strong enough."

"While you certainly are a strong creature, no one is meant to Possess three rocks at once. It weakens you. It may give you a jolt of energy in the moment to use your Possession, such as in a fight, but the cost is great. You cannot go on like this much longer."

"Nah, I can handle it."

"No, your body cannot. Veritamyk, you cannot continue this way. No rock is meant to be Possessed by the Possessor of another. Only one can be Possessed at a time. The power is too much for one body."

He faced her, determination in his eyes. "I am *fine!* I just need to get used to it is all." Covering his mouth, he coughed into his hand.

"Do not be a fool, Crivabanian. Your symptoms will only increase. This will kill you well before your time. Besides, the Adarborians will want their rock back. As will the Rubandors and the Gwythienians." She nodded at me. "You must acquire the other rocks, a Keepership ceremony must be scheduled, and each realm must choose their new Possessor. Only under those circumstances can Possession be removed and bestowed upon someone else."

What? "I have to give mine up too?" I didn't want to do that! I was only just getting the hang of it.

"Yes. If you want the realms to cooperate. And if you want your friend to live. Even aside from how Veritamyk views the situation, there are the other realms to consider. It is unfair to keep their rocks from them, once they are finally found. Do you not agree?"

*Oh, crap. So I'm going to lose the good things I have in common with Gaedyen, and now I'm related to him, too?*

I pursed my lips, not liking how this meeting was going at all. "Wait, back to history. So what happened that day that had to do with both our fathers? Tell the rest of that story."

Kymri nodded. "That story, Mackenzi, is an important one to be sure. But you must wait to hear it."

"What?" I gestured toward Geneva. "But she just bargained her life for us!"

"I do not keep it from you now out of anger or to punish you. This is a story that must be told to a wider audience, and at the right time, in order for it to have the necessary effect. You must accept my decision, and take heart in the knowledge that you will hear the whole story soon. Many stand to benefit from its telling. So you must wait a little longer, and trust me to keep my promise to Geneva and to you."

We all stood silently, glaring at the floor. I crossed my arms, sure Gaedyen was just as pissed as I was at Kymri's pulling a loophole like this. How could we know she would ever tell us?

Kymri's sapphire eyes nearly glowed from her pale fur. "Listen closely. It is imperative you plan a Keepership Ceremony and convince all the realms to attend. Veritamyk, your life depends on it. Claim to have all the rocks in hand to convince each realm to send dignitaries and their chosen future Possessors."

"But we *don't* have all the rocks in hand," I said.

"You will by the time of the ceremony. You have my word. Remember, Veritamyk's life depends on this. And they will only come if they believe their rocks will finally be returned."

*No pressure or anything.*

"Once they have all agreed to the date, you must prepare Odan Terridor. Talk to someone from the old days to learn what must be done. Then receive the other realms and treat them respectfully when they arrive. Get to know their selections for Possessors. This is the time to be polite and win friends. You will have to deal with these political figures for the next several decades. Then you must find a place to keep the rocks safe, a new Keeper's hiding place."

Gaedyen eyed her. "Why am I supposed to find the Keeper's new hiding place? Is that not the Keeper's job?"

"Of course it is the job of the Keeper."

He cocked his head. "Surely you do not expect me to become Keeper."

Of course she couldn't expect that. After how they had treated him his whole life? Not only were they wrongly prejudiced against him, but they didn't deserve to have him serve them all with so much responsibility. He deserved to be free.

Kymri nodded. "It seems likely. They will have their chance to choose, but I feel confident they will vote for you. No one is more well-suited for the job. You are young, to be sure, but mature beyond your years. I am sorry for the upbringing that caused that, but it is a good thing to have now. Besides, you have earned this. You sought the Possessor of the only rock you could find, you journeyed far and wide to find them, and you found them when no one else could. You could not have done it without your friends, true, but a Keeper must be Gwythienian."

Eyes wide, I stared at Gaedyen, wondering what he would make of that.

"They will never vote for me, Kymri. I am the lowest of the low in my home realm."

*Only because of their wrong assumptions.*

Kymri eyed him. "I would not be so sure about that, Gaedyen."

"I do not feel ready to be a Keeper. I am not even sure I want to be."

"You don't have to be, Gaedyen." I finally found my voice. "They don't deserve you."

Ignoring me, Kymri went on. "It was the not feeling ready that made Padraig so good a Keeper. And it is for that reason I know you are the best selection. Whether you are ready or not, well, you will rise to the challenge."

Gaedyen stared at Kymri quizzically, as if he wasn't sure what to think of her declaration.

*She better quit trying to pressure him into something that huge that he doesn't want to do.*

"That is enough for one day, younglings. You all should rest. Geneva, rest with them. You and I will discuss your arrangements tomorrow."

My heart sped up uncomfortably at the thought of Gaedyen tied to his realm forever, possessing the rock himself and no longer needing me. No longer having time for me. Why was Kymri so set on this ridiculous idea?

# CHAPTER THIRTEEN

One of the three welcoming Cathawyrs showed us to a couple of caves with stacks of neatly folded blankets for sleeping. I leaned against Gaedyen's side and took a deep breath, struggling to wrap my mind around all we'd just learned. The air was warm and just a bit musty. But the blankets I'd spread on the ground made the rocky surface more bearable.

They didn't have any guest caves big enough for both Gwythienians to fit comfortably, so they'd shown Geneva to another several paces away from this one. Veri had followed her automatically, drawn to her comforting manner and healing abilities to keep his illness at bay.

So his sickness was from Possessing too many rocks at once.

It was a relief to finally have it explained and some plan to fix it. Though I wasn't a fan of us both losing Possession of our rocks.

But the sleeping arrangements had left me alone with Gaedyen, which I didn't mind at all. I tilted my head back onto his shoulder, wondering how to creatively get him kissing me again, when I remembered another revelation from the night.

"So I'm related to Tukailaan."

Gaedyen exhaled loudly. "As am I."

"Which means, even though we're different species…we're related to each other?" I glanced at him, wondering how he would take that.

"You heard the story of how humans came from the original Shimbators. They are a blend of all the species in a way, just in a different form. So we are not strictly different species."

"Does that bother you? That we are like…sort of related?"

He answered immediately. "No. Batran is my great grandfather. Because of the immensely longer lifespans of Gwythienians, he is your ancient ancestor to many degrees. So we are not closely related by any means."

I wrinkled my nose. "So it doesn't really count then, right? I mean, it's *super* diluted."

"I agree. But does it bother you?"

"No, I don't think so. It's so distant. I was really more afraid it would bother you. Or your people, if they found out."

"Good. As long as it does not bother you, I do not give a single shed scale what any of them think. I will not be their Keeper, and they will have no say over my choices. They have had enough of a greatly detrimental effect on my life. No more."

"I'm just glad to know *why* the rock worked for me when it shouldn't have. You know? I always wondered—wracked my brain wondering. It's a relief to know it was something in my blood. Kind of cool, actually."

"Well, I'm not relieved about anything!" Veri's brown swoosh of bangs preceded him through the shadowed doorway. "Now I have to give up Possession of *all three rocks!* I haven't had any of them nearly long enough to find out what I can do with them. I've barely even tried anything with the Rubandors' rock. I don't want to lose them so soon!"

He would have to lose his Possessorships, too. *That stinks. Ugh. I really don't want to give mine up either. Maybe there's some other way…* "Yeah it stinks for both of us."

Veri looked down. "Yeah. I'm sorry, Enzi. I don't want to be the reason you lose yours, too."

"It's all right. I'd rather have you safe and healthy than be able to turn invisible at will. Even though that is pretty cool. But hey, maybe we'll think of something else."

He brightened. "You think there could be another way?"

I shrugged, enjoying the rough feel of my T-shirt sliding against Gaedyen's side scales with the movement. There probably wasn't, but I didn't have the heart to completely disappoint him right now. "Maybe."

"I'll start thinking." He squinted and perched his chin on his fist like a scholar in deep thought.

I laughed. "Okay. Good luck."

There was an awkward pause, then a mischievous grin enveloped Veri's face. "Well then." He swept my sweatshirt from my lap, then dramatically turned and sauntered toward the door, draping my sweatshirt over his back like a cape. "I'll leave *you two*"—he glanced back and waggled his eyebrows—"*alone.*"

With a flourish of his *cape*, he disappeared into the night.

I rolled my eyes, but glanced shyly at Gaedyen out the corner of one eye.

He was glancing out one eye at me, too.

I giggled like an idiot, and a laugh rumbled deep in his chest. His wing curved around me. It was warm and solid and part of him. I lightly ran my fingertips over the bend in his wing.

"I do wish there was another way to fix things—without taking yours and Veri's Possessions. But I do not see how else it can be done," he whispered, his soft words ruffling my hair.

I sighed. "Yeah, same. How soon will the Keepership meeting take place?"

"Normally they were planned a year in advance, at least. With circumstances as they are, we might be able to pull it off in a few weeks. We will need some serious convincing skills, though. We must be subtle and persuasive at the same time. Otherwise the other realms will probably try to drag it out into a power play."

He sighed. "Kymri is right, though. We must find all the rocks for this to work. Which means we will have to go hunting for Meleena. Find a way to steal the rocks from her if she is still alive. That would be difficult to say the least. But if she is dead, finding the rocks could be completely impossible. And we will have to tell everyone we have them all, in order to convince the other realms to select a Possessor and prepare to travel to Odan Terridor right away. And if we do not find them between now and then, well. You can imagine how we will look when we are discovered."

I closed my eyes against the headache I could feel coming on. "Yeah. I wish I didn't have to lose it, though. It's been a part of me for so long now, and it gives me something in common with you. I don't want to let it go."

"I know. I wish there was some way to let you keep it. But according to Kymri, it's the only way to save Veri's life."

I shrugged against his side. "It makes sense. The other realms really should get their rocks back. It's not fair to keep the rocks from them."

Gaedyen was silent for a few moments. "How could Kymri think I am supposed to be the Keeper? They have always reviled me, disliked me, mistrusted me. I do not *want* to spend the better part of my life leading the very people who despised me since the day I hatched. Why should I sacrifice so much for them?"

So he wasn't as sure as he'd tried to sound earlier. I understood his sentiment, but it still felt inconsistent with some things he'd said before. "Didn't you say that you were willing to die for all the realms?"

He huffed. "That is a great many more people than just the Gwythienians. And though they may have heard of me and certainly hated my parents, it was not from the other realms I received rejection and misery for so many years. I do not hate my people. But I do not wish to spend all my time with them, dealing with their problems." He sighed with frustration this time. "Does that make me a bad person?"

I laid a hand over his scales. "No. Not at all. I wouldn't want to be the president of the student body at school, dealing with all those Carlies and Jillians every day. I think I understand." So he would get my rock. I would have to give it up, but I would be giving it to *him*. There wasn't anyone else I would rather have it, if I had to let it go.

"Enzi, if I were to become Keeper…it would mean spending a lot more time in this form. And if shifting is difficult now because of my injuries…" He eyed me and I glanced away. "How would you feel about that? If I was human less often than Gwythienian?"

I hesitated, not wanting this to come back up and not wanting to admit my fears. "Well…" I took the easy—and kind of noble-sounding—way out of that one. "Gaedyen, it's your decision. Your body. I love you, no matter which form you wear." *And I wouldn't mind not having to address the issue of further relationship aspects.*

He brushed my neck with the curve of his wing and then wrapped it around me a little tighter. "I love you," he whispered.

"I love you too, Gaedyen." I nestled as close as I could to him, reveling in his warmth, and fell asleep to dreams of flying through the clouds with him.

Gaedyen eyed Kymri, looking doubtful. "If you insist on keeping Geneva and Veri here for the time being, then how can we be assured they will arrive at the appropriate time for the ceremony? We will already be untruthful about having all the rocks when we invite the dignitaries. If we are also missing the possessor of three of the four rocks, that will be a really difficult situation to rectify in the event we do not find the rocks in time."

Kymri regarded him. "Do you doubt me so much, Gaedyen? Of course I have considered this. First, you must trust I will get the rocks there in time. Second, we will agree on a date for the ceremony before you leave so that I may be sure to get Geneva and Veri there in time."

I crossed my arms. "How can you be sure to get the rocks from Meleena on time? If she's dead, how will you find where she left them? And if she's alive and has them on her, will you fight her?"

"Because I have seen where she keeps them."

I tried to keep a blank expression in place. "What? How?"

Kymri smiled. "The Gwythienian ability to gaze into other places through water—my sisters and I have a similar ability, but through certain stones instead. We had two, once. But Meleena stole my best one when she stole the rock of healing and the life of its last Possessor, Caranyla. It is through watching the happenings of the world within its depth that she has seen so much she should not have. It is through the less cooperative stone I still have that I have managed to miss many important things. But I did manage to see where she put them when she took them from you. Some of my kind are already on their way to recover them."

"That's how you knew getting the rock of healing back would be difficult for Gaedyen—because you knew Bricriu was using it to heal Geneva?"

"Yes. I knew Bricriu had it and had been using it for years on Geneva, trying to heal her from the wounds he gave her. But because of the imperfections of the seeing stone I have, I did not see him ground it to dust and administer it to her."

"Did you see Tukailaan's lair near Odan Terridor? Did he put those flowers and baby things there for…for his human daughter?"

Kymri closed her eyes and nodded. "He did indeed. When Susan was killed and he was bound to his Gwythienian form, he found his way back and made preparations to bring his daughter there, once he'd managed to change again. Though he was prone to extreme selfishness and delusions, there is no denying he was a creature capable of great love for his wife and daughter."

It was weird to think of Tukailaan having a baby and caring about its wellbeing.

"Rest assured, I guarantee the arrival of the rocks and Geneva and Veri on time," Kymri said. "You will have enough to deal with to get the dignitaries all there."

Veri stood and slammed his fists on his hips. "You can't expect me to stay here with all the powers while you guys get to go have all the fun!"

"I cannot force you to stay, Veritamyk. But as Geneva has already promised to do so, if you leave, it will be without her healing powers that have been helping you. She's the reason you feel confident enough to even make these claims."

Veri frowned at Kymri, then glanced at Geneva. With a petulant look, he crossed his arms and sank into a pout.

Kymri looked at us from Veri. "I think one month from now would be the ideal date. Are there any objections?"

My mouth fell open. "One month? You expect us to get all that done in a month?"

"Would you rather risk young Veritamyk's life?"

I glared at Kymri. "We'll find a way." Laying a hand on Gaedyen's shoulder, I looked up at him. "Right?"

He nodded. "We will find a way."

She looked from my eyes to Gaedyen's. "As for you, young Gaedyen, you have another decision to make."

Gaedyen's brows rose. "And what is that, Kymri?"

"Your grave wound. Through your Shimbator mark. The ruining of a mark like that was sometimes done by those who wished to hide their Shimbator nature long ago. Ruin the mark, lose the ability. Dyn Meddy gave yours its best chance of healing, but I fear you lost that when you risked changing forms again before it had fully repaired itself."

Gaedyen's earflaps drooped slightly, avoiding my eyes. "So I am condemned to this form forever?"

*Condemned* seemed to be kind of a strong word. I wouldn't have minded being stuck in a dragon form. He could fly, for crying out loud. And he was bigger than all the humans!

"No. You have one more chance to change, if you so desire. But understand, Gaedyen, that your mark will never work again. This is not something Geneva's newfound powers extend to. Choose the form of a human or that of a Gwythienian, and be content with that form forever."

Gaedyen looked at me, a struggle in his eyes. I stared back, waiting for him to choose. This was *so* not a choice I could make for him. I didn't even know for sure what I wanted. Yes, I was more comfortable with his Gwythienian form now, but maybe with a little time I could feel comfortable around his human form, too. Would I mind giving up the chance to find out?

He straightened and focused on Kymri again. "I make this request, Kymri Cathawyr. I wish to choose human form."

Geneva threw a Gwythienian hand over her gasp. Kymri nodded agreement. Veri examined his foreclaws with a smirk, as if he'd called it before and now basked in his correctness.

My heart raced as I kept my face as serene as possible, a mask over the many whirling feelings.

"But I need this body a little longer. Not only to organize the ceremony and invite the other realms, but also for a personal reason. I must do a few important things before changing. Once I have completed those, I wish to be human. Is it possible for me to leave as I am and return for you to change me once everything else is in order?"

"Yes, though you need not make the journey back. I can give you the ability to make one final change now. You must be disciplined enough not to use it until the proper time. Are you sure you are prepared to give up your wings, Gwythienian?"

"I am willing to sacrifice them for something much more valuable."

"Gaedyen," I said, "you don't have to give up everything you are for me. I want you to be yourself."

He turned soft, loving eyes on me. "I am my best self when with you. I am fully aware this does not bind you to me. But I choose you and the chance for a life with you, if you decide that is what you want, too."

I opened my mouth to answer, though I didn't know what I was going to say. But he'd already turned around to address Kymri again.

But of course I'd never decide against him! He was all I'd ever wanted. No one else would ever be able to understand me like he did. No one else had ever traveled with and learned so much about me, taught me so much about this world.

There would never be anyone else for me.

"We will fly immediately to Odan Terridor and help Soroco begin preparations for the Ceremony. While that is underway, Enzi and I will take care of some family business."

I frowned. *Family business? Like, because we're distantly related?* I winced again.

"Once that is done, we will visit the other realms to beg them to join us for the ceremony. After the ceremony, I will change my form forever."

Kymri nodded again. "So let it be, Gaedyen. Though, this does not excuse you for Keepership if your people choose you. You are still the same Gwythienian at heart, no matter your form, and you could make just as excellent a Keeper."

Gaedyen's face remained impassive as he nodded noncommittally.

She stood and shook out her snowy coat. "It is time for you to go. Your task is of the utmost importance. May your rymakri stay sharp and your aim be ever true."

# CHAPTER FOURTEEN

"*E*nzi, is…is there something about my human form you dislike?" Gaedyen focused on the quietly popping fire in front of us. He had to be tired after a day of hard flying back to Odan Terridor.

But this, again? Why did he have to keep bringing it up?

"I don't dislike your human form at all, Gaedyen." I rolled my eyes, wary of where this was going but trying not to show it.

"No, you do not *dislike* it. But there is something about it, some aspect I do not understand, that you do not like about it. You disagree with my choice to change to human form permanently."

I sighed. "No, it's not that. Not exactly."

"Then please tell me what it is, Enzi. I thought it would make you happy, but it appears only to make you sad. I do not want to make you sad."

"It's just…" I sighed. *Why did I think this was a good idea? I shouldn't be telling him this. It makes me look weak and helpless. I don't want to be pitied!*

I scrubbed my hands over my face, struggling to find the words. "I'm afraid—well—if you're stuck being human, you'll eventually get bored of…of me. There are a whole lot of other human girls in the world you haven't met yet, and, well, most of them are way sexier than I am."

He smiled at me. "Oh, is that all?" He closed his eyes and chuckled, laying his head on top of mine. "Enzi, you do not need to worry about that."

"But you're so *hot!* You are what's called 'out of my league,' and that means I don't deserve to be with you. If you go through with this, well, I'll have a lot of competition."

He shifted to meet my eyes as his eyes softened, and a tender look came over his face, melting me so much I just couldn't handle it. "Oh, Enzi." He sighed. "There is something you need to know, about when I went to Ofwen Dwir. Something I kept to myself when I told you the story."

I eyed him, curious.

"When I reached the wall around the realm, it did not take me long to find the entrance. But the opening was so small. An adult Rubandor certainly could not get through it, and neither could I. So I shifted to human form in order to fit through. That was shortly after the time I accidentally came upon you bathing in the hot springs—I am sure you remember."

I winced and glanced away. "Yeah. I sure do."

"Well, this was the first time I transitioned between forms since that incident." He looked at me with wary expectation, as if I was supposed to fill in the rest.

When he didn't continue, I asked, "Okay, so what?"

"It was the first time I was a human after, well, seeing…all… of you."

I looked down, anywhere but his eyes. "Oh."

"When I saw you—through Gwythienian eyes—I knew you were lovely. But when my human mind grasped the memory…" His voice trailed off, and he exhaled deeply.

"What do you mean?" It sounded almost as if he liked what he'd seen, as if it had some kind of sensual effect on him.

But of course that couldn't be it. I'd built up some muscle, but I was still nothing like Carlie or Jillian. And I was scarred all over. Besides that, my face wasn't anything special. It was just me.

Gaedyen pulled his head back to look at me, covering his eyes with a huge Gwythienian hand, and sighed, "Are you really going to make me spell it out for you, Enzi?"

I shrugged and lifted my eyebrows. Apparently he needed help to see I wasn't following.

"Remembering how you looked that way, natural and not hidden, well…it made me feel something. I was enthralled by your beauty, and I wanted to see it again. I wanted to be with you and see you, to watch you move and to know you from all angles. I wanted you. I still do. I have not told you so plainly before because I did not want to make you uncomfortable… because of the past. But I am choosing to tell you now because you seem to be unaware of how attractive you are." He cleared his throat. "Does that make sense?"

I blushed way past crimson. "Really?"

Of course the only thing I could think to reply with was to question him. He'd called me out on that tendency in Sequoia Cadryl when I only knew his human form as *Shaun*. I wanted to believe him, but how? It just didn't seem possible for me, Enzi Montgomery, to have that effect on someone. To be…attractive?

"Yes, really. Why is it so hard for you to believe? You are beautiful, Enzi."

"And you actually…wanted me? Like…like, um, as in…"

He rolled his eyes. "Yes, Enzi. As in that. I am sorry if it makes you uncomfortable. I was afraid it would and did not want to tell you because of that. But you seemed to need to know."

"Thank you for telling me now, Gaedyen. And for not telling me before out of concern for me. That was considerate of you." I smiled and rubbed his arm. "I *want* to believe you. But for so many years I've been ugly and disliked and bullied, it's too good to be true that *you*, of all people, feel that way about me. And how ironic is it that I'm so scared of exactly what I want!" I dropped my face into my hands.

He covered my trembling hand with his. "Enzi, stop doubting yourself. Know that you are beautiful. Know that I love you. Those are truths that have been so for too long for you not to know them. But you do not need to be afraid. Know also that I will wait as long as you need. I will wait for you, I will not pressure you into anything you are not comfortable with. I would kill the bastard who gave you that fear, if I could. But *he* is at fault, not you. Believe me, you have all the time in the world to sort out your feelings and change your mind."

Then his voice grew soft. "Enzi, you do not need to be afraid of me. No one desires your wellbeing and comfort as much as I do. Not even you."

I wrapped my arms around his neck. I couldn't meet his eyes. I didn't want him to see the tears there. There were no words to describe how wonderful he was and how much better his words made me feel. So I just hugged him.

"Enzi?" He wrapped a huge hand around my back. His skin was deliciously warm.

"Yes?"

"Would it be possible…that is…can I kiss you?"

I smiled, enjoying the moment and enjoying his warmth. Then I pulled away enough to kiss him. His other arm came around my back, huge and warm.

"Gaedyen?"

"Mm?"

"You're supposed to be surprising me with kisses, aren't you? You don't need to ask my permission to kiss me anymore."

"Mm." His smile sounded in the way his voice rumbled in his chest. And he kissed me again. And he thought I was beautiful.

Some time later, I lay curled against his side, his wing covering me and his head resting on the ground, turned toward me as far as it could be. The one eye I could see was closed, but I could tell he was still awake by his breathing.

"Gaedyen?" I whispered.

His eye opened as his earflap flicked back to me. "Yes?"

I shifted to face him better, propping myself up with one arm. "So I get why you need to stay Gwythienian for the Possessorship Ceremony and all that, but what is this 'family business' you mentioned? And why do you need to be in Gwythienian form for it?"

He chuckled. "Wait, Enzi, Please? Let me answer those questions before you fire more at me." His smile reached his eye in a really nice way, softening his expression.

I grinned back. "Okay, yeah. Let's start with those."

"You told me your father was put in a psychiatric ward for raving about being attacked by dragons, that they are coming back to take the rock he lost from him. And while we are not certain, we think it might have been my father who gave him that fear. But what if we could *relieve* your father of that intense fear?"

My eyebrows raised. "That could be really helpful, but how?"

"You told me he repeatedly asked you to help him return the stone to the dragons, right?"

"Yeah…"

"Well, I am a dragon. That is, not strictly speaking, but I look the same as the creatures he would know as dragons. And we will either find the real rock, or we can use one that looks like it. You can tell him you have found the rock, give it to him, and bring him to some place where he can give it to me. If that is what he thinks he must do to be safe, maybe that would ease his fear and start healing his mind. Maybe he could be close to the man he was once. Maybe he could live with your mother again, should she desire it.”

My heart melted, and thickness welled up in my throat. *This guy. What have I ever done to deserve the most kind and considerate soul in the world?*

“Wow. That’s an amazing idea. If I could bring Dad back to Mom, that would give her the companionship and support she always wanted and deserved but never got. And to see them happy together would be really special. Maybe that would ease some of the anger she has toward me for disappearing so much.” I grinned, blinking away a light mist from my eyes. “I think it’s a fantastic idea.”

He smiled. “I am delighted you like the plan.”

“I do, but the question is, how will I get to him? It was a real struggle last time I tried. And once I do, how will I get him to you?”

“You are more familiar with the layout of the place than I am. We can both think about it later today while we fly and see what we come up with. But for now, it will still be dark for a few hours and we would both benefit from some sleep.”

I nestled into his side, sliding a little further under the warmth of his wing. “Yes. Good night, Gaedyen. Love you.”

When he answered, I could hear the smile in his voice. “I love you, too.”

Gaedyen shook water droplets off his glistening Gwythienian body as he rose from the lake outside the entrance of Odan Terridor. “We need to find Soroco and consult with her about whom to make arrangements with for the ceremony.”

Gaedyen's voice interrupted my thoughts about getting Dad out of the hospital for an afternoon in the near future. If only there weren't so many people and security measures everywhere. I left that frustrating half-plan for the moment to listen to Gaedyen instead.

"We will need to meet with the fisheries, and at least one of the malwoden farmers."

I wrinkled my nose at the idea of the giant snails Gwythienians apparently liked to eat so much. There were actual farm-loads of them?

"And we will need to find appropriate housing for each of the specific realm's needs…I wonder where the delegates from other realms stayed when they were last here? Maybe we can use the same places…particularly for the Rubandors, who must remain partially submerged at all times." He trailed off, a frustration wrinkle forming between his eyes.

I shook water from my hands and followed him toward the tunnel entrance. "That sounds like a lot to think through. How much can we rely on Soroco, though? She's already been holding things together since Padraig's death, hasn't she? We might need to avoid putting too much else on her plate."

"Yes, of course. You are right." He scrubbed a hand over his huge face. "This is going to be complicated."

My voice echoed around us as we strode through the cave-like entrance. "I don't know how I can help, Gaedyen, but just let me know what I can do and I'm there."

He smiled at me. I could just make it out in the fading light from the front of the cave.

"Thank you, Enzi. I appreciate that. This is what I think we should do. We will try to get twice as many names as we need from Soroco. Then you and I will interview them and chose the best suited for the preparations. This way we will not be asking Soroco to make any decisions, just to recommend the best Gwythienians she knows for each task, then we will do the rest."

I nodded. "Sounds reasonable to me. Do you think my being human will cause any problems?"

"They will of course all be prejudiced. But none of them have been to any of the other realms, I believe. We were the first to travel to any of them in decades. So you have that advantage. Mainly, I need you to help me keep my head about things."

I tripped over the rubble from when we broke into Tukailaan's lair, and Gaedyen caught me before I could land on my face. "Thanks. But what exactly do you mean?"

"I want the best for my people and all the realms, but I cannot trust them because of how they treated me. I do not want to work with them. I have accepted that I must—my only choice is to deal with them while planning the ceremony, but I struggle with the necessity of it. And while I disagree with Kymri's assessment of my Keeper qualifications, I still dread the possibility of being bound to serve them all forever. I would appreciate your help remembering why I am here. Your presence and support are a comfort to me."

I smiled. "I'll do the best I can."

He exhaled heavily just as I caught a glimpse of azure light ahead. "Okay. Now to track down Soroco."

# CHAPTER FIFTEEN

"Good luck to you both." Soroco gazed seriously at us from the soft, sapphire light of the root tunnels, her wise eyes appraising after she gave us a list of names of fishery and malwoden farmers to meet with. "You will do well. Now I must be off to deal with other matters."

With a raised-eyebrow glance at each other, Gaedyen and I waved goodbye and dropped through the nearest opening. Gaedyen's wings unfurled and steadied us over the tops of the thick foliage below. He banked to one side and headed in the opposite direction from the way we had come. The warm wind of Odan Terridor's underground atmosphere blew through my hair as my head whipped around in every direction, hoping not to miss anything.

A long row of black dots sat in the distance. As we approached, I could finally see that it was actually a tall, stone wall running as far as I could see in either direction, with a different cave entrance looming every few feet.

Gaedyen hit the ground and I leaned forward with the impact. Eyeing the huge cavern entrance, I wondered how he could tell which was the right one.

"We will visit the malwoden farms first today," Gaedyen said. "I hope they are already well-stocked, since we do not have much time for them to begin breeding extra stock for the ceremony. They will have to hold back some of what they would usually sell to breed extras." He glanced back at me with a knowing smile. It would be interesting to visit the strange snail farms. How any society could survive primarily on *snails*, I couldn't imagine. But I was certainly curious. If a bit grossed-out.

I slid from his back and stretched my arms over my head. "Is this the right place?"

"This is the one. If you remember, we would have taken a route similar to this several months ago during our escape, had you not screamed and given us away." He playfully bumped into me, knocking me to the side.

Smirking, I slammed back into him. My efforts had no effect, of course. But never let it be said that I didn't try. "Actually, you jumped out of nowhere and scared the crap out of me. So it's more your fault than mine."

He bumped into me again and I smacked him back, knowing better than to try actually moving him.

*Turd.*

Gaedyen entered the dark hole in the wall and I followed him, our footsteps echoing all around us. As the path widened after a few minutes, water sprung up and flowed on either side, as if appearing from underground streams.

The path was wide enough for three Gwythienians to walk side by side. The floor stayed the same, but the ceiling and the section of water on the right kept expanding. The blueish light had faded when we entered the tunnel, and now what light there was—coming from who knew where—was more of a greenish color.

A menacing gate stood before us, stretching from the stone floor to the rocky ceiling. Gaedyen called out a name that sounded like *nutshell*, and a Gwythienian appeared in the distance and approached us.

He peered through the gate, smirking at Gaedyen. "Oho, the infamous Gaedyen himself. You *have* been stirring up a few things."

I frowned. Was it really necessary to start out so confrontational?

"Hello, Nurshiel," Gaedyen said stiffly. "You are the head malwoden keeper now?"

He nodded down at himself. "As you see. What do you want? I have no time for thieves' sons…"

I opened my mouth to reprimand him for his rudeness to the Keeper's heir, but he turned his glare on me before I could speak.

"…or humans. Tell me, Gaedyen, what in all the realms is a human doing here? Do we not have laws preventing their intrusion?"

Gaedyen clenched his teeth but kept a fairly professional tone. "Our Keeper is dead, as I am sure you know. And without having a chosen Keeper to take his place, the laws are a bit flimsy at present. Besides that, Enzi is the Possessor of our realm's rock, and she assisted Padraig in taking Tukailaan down. I suggest you treat her with respect."

My eyebrows rose in surprise, but I stuffed them back down immediately. It wouldn't do to show my surprise. I needed to own it. So I disappeared for a moment and reappeared leaning on the gate on Gaedyen's other side.

Nurshiel's eyes widened. He looked between Gaedyen and me. "And why have you chosen to honor me with your presence today?"

"Let us in, and we'll explain," I said with my arms folded and face as stoic as possible.

"Why should I?"

"Nurshiel, we really don't have time for this." I placed my hand on the gate, as if I expected him to open it as requested.

"Are you also unaware of the deaths of Aven, Gwaltmar, and Dyn Meddy?"

Nurshiel's eyes flashed to Gaedyen. "Is this true?"

Gaedyen nodded gravely.

Eyes wide, Nurshiel hesitantly stepped out of the way. Unlocking the gate, he pulled it open and bowed slightly to us. "I will hear what you have to say."

"Excellent." Gaedyen waited for me to enter first, then followed just before Nurshiel shut the gate.

Nurshiel walked ahead of us, leading us deeper into the cave. "I was not aware of the deaths of the remaining Possessors." He glanced back, narrowing his eyes at me.

My being a human and knowing so much more than he did about his own world was clearly bothering him. I hid a smile. *Good.*

We rounded a corner, and wow, were there a lot of those malwoden—giant snail things—in the next room! Puddles of water speckled the stone floor. Malwoden congregated around the puddles, and slow streams of water dripped down the wall.

There were some malwoden as small as regular snails, but many had shells four feet high or somewhere in between. The stone glistened with thousands of their shimmering slime trails.

I held back my grimace. Gaedyen had actually eaten these things? "As it stands," I locked eyes with Nurshiel, "the last generation of Possessors are dead. All four are already Possessed by others, not all of whom would be approved of by their rock's realm. Those of us who currently have Possession have agreed to give it up in the name of the greater good." *You're welcome.*

"And so," Gaedyen picked up, "there is great risk to the realms if the Keepership Ceremony is delayed. We have set a date for the ceremony, and Enzi and I will leave shortly to invite dignitaries from the other realms to take part. We will need a steady food source for our guests, and you are one of our main suppliers." He glanced into the room full of snails.

"And you want me to start breeding extra stock? Is the Odan Terridor government going to give me money to outfit this venture?"

Gaedyen frowned. "Have you not been listening? There currently *is* no government. I have no access to funds for you. Besides, it will hardly cost you anything to do this. You farm on Odan Terridor land, not your own. Your herd belongs to the people. You are their caretaker, not their owner. There are plenty of acres left unfarmed to the west. Expand your herds. If you need more help tending them, I will search the younglings for a suitable apprentice for you—you need only ask. But we must have enough food for the ceremony."

Nurshiel regarded Gaedyen for a long moment. "I will require two apprentices."

*Really?* He just had to be difficult, didn't he?

Gaedyen nodded. "Very well. I will bring them to you within the week. Is there any sort of organization for the food producers?"

"Organization?"

"I thought not. We will need to organize one in order to manage everything in so short a time. I will get back to you."

Nurshiel scowled. "Very well."

Gaedyen peered into the snail room again. "I hope you have significantly more stock than this."

Nurshiel bristled. "At present I have twenty caverns of similar size full of breeding malwoden and their young."

"Excellent." Gaedyen nodded. "We will need five more thriving colonies in the next several weeks. And best to shoot for ten, depending on how many representatives come from the other realms."

Nurshiel spluttered, but Gaedyen interrupted him. "This is not a random whim. These are the facts. If you cannot produce what we need, I will find someone who can to replace you."

"You—you are just—you cannot replace me!"

"See that you prioritize the best interests of our people so that I do not have to."

We left through the gate and headed back down the tunnel. Before reaching the opening of the tunnel, we turned down another. I heard the sound of water flowing and, for a second, thought we might be nearing the Vorbiaquam. But there was only one entrance, and it was much shorter than this.

"Where are we going now?"

"To the docks," Gaedyen answered.

The tunnel widened into a huge cavern as the sound of rushing water grew louder.

"Part of the river we followed to the coast feeds in here. Remember me telling you about the fish farmers? How they breed fish to feed the snails? They also keep small colonies of more palatable species. We need them to expand as well, in order to assist with feeding the guests."

Here the light grew blueish again, improving my mood. There were not docks in the traditional sense, places where ships could dock. A fine construction of raised paths intertwined around a series of circles.

Nursery pools for the fish stretched as far as I could see.

A couple of Gwythienians peered straight down into one of the pools in the distance. One of them noticed us and nodded a greeting as he strode to the nearest raised path and followed it to us.

As he neared, it became apparent that he and Gaedyen knew each other—they stiffened and glared. But Gaedyen spoke to him as he had to Nurshiel, explaining the situation and imparting the importance of his cooperation. In the end, he agreed to what Gaedyen asked.

From there, Gaedyen flew us to another part of Odan Terridor, a large place with a dirt floor that slanted down toward what could be a stone stage.

"This is where the Ceremonies have all been held in the past. We need to clean the place up a bit, but it will be presentable. What do you think, Enzi?"

I slid off him to get a closer look at the stage. Huge and granite, it was whiteish-beige with slightly darker swirls running through it, like a fancy countertop. Above and slightly behind it, four smaller sections were erected with high pillars. Where future Possessors would sit?

"So the old Possessors would stand there, on the big stage, and the new ones would be up high on those things?"

Gaedyen nodded. "That is correct."

"How exactly does the power transfer? I mean, since no-one is the first person to touch it after the last Possessor dies."

"I do not know. I do not understand it, but hopefully we will find out soon."

Surveying the overgrown plants around the base of the stage and throughout the vast area where the audience would watch from, I heaved a sigh. "This is going to take a while. How about I start with these little weeds at the base of the stage, and you tackle that big mess on the left side?"

Tiredness swept over Gaedyen's face as he took in the task. Heaving a long breath through his nostrils, he faced me. "I could not do this without you, Enzi. Thank you. For everything."

"Just think." I said as I dug my fingers into the dirt at the roots of a weed. "In a few weeks this will all be over, and we can take a day off."

"I am living for that right now." He gave me a tender smile.

Returning his grin, I ripped the weed out by the roots and started on the next.

# CHAPTER SIXTEEN

After a week of extensive landscaping, haggling over lodgings for an unknown number of guests from each of the realms, and dealing with Nurshiel and the other food suppliers, we were back in my world.

I stood on the pot-holey road I'd driven down looking for the necklace I'd dropped months ago, before all this began. Facing the apartment building Mom and I had spent the last several years in, my stomach suddenly changed its mind about this whole thing.

Gaedyen brushed an invisible shoulder against me. "Are you nervous?"

Nervous was an understatement. The slight breeze cooling my face helped my worry a little. "Yeah. I hope this is the right thing to do. I don't think there's any other way for me to get into the hospital, much less for me to get him out. I just don't know how well she'll take it. I'm about to turn her world upside down."

"It sounds to me like she has already experienced that a few times. Maybe her world is turned just so that this bit of rocking will knock it back into place."

I smiled. "Hopefully something like that."

"Are you ready?"

"Nope."

He placed his huge hand on my shoulder for an instant, then stepped off the road. "I will be right here."

He would wait for me to bring her here, where he could safely reveal his dragon face to her if all went well.

I squared my shoulders, took a deep breath, and headed toward the place that had once been home.

There was the street where I first met Gaedyen in human form. When he'd insulted Carlie and Jillian. I smiled. That was one of the best moments of my life, seeing the looks on their faces.

I walked down the street and took in the familiar but distant view: our shabby row of apartments. The streetlight with the broken bulb. The parking lot full of potholes, the faded parking spot lines all but gone now. A few unfamiliar cars scattered around.

The door to number seven.

I swallowed. *Knock, knock, knock.*

Footsteps.

The familiar creak of the door.

Mom's face. Older. Tired. The bags under her eyes a little darker. Several more gray hairs.

And then I was in her arms, and she was crying my name. I wrapped my arms around her, ashamed of how much grief I'd caused her by staying away so long.

"Enzi, I am so sorry. So, so sorry. I should have told you about your father. It was just the timing—you already had so much to deal with. You were so young…"

She grabbed my shoulders and held me at arm's length, giving me a good once-over. "You look great! Oh my gosh. Where have you been? No, I don't want to know. I'm so glad to see you, Enzi. You have no idea how sorry I am. Are you back for good?"

I took another deep breath and gave her a smile. "I'm glad to see you too, Mom. I'm sorry I haven't been better about letting you know I'm okay. It's just, well…it's kind of hard to believe."

Her face fell slightly. "Why have you been gone so long, without staying in touch?"

"That's a long story, Mom. It's just…"

I looked into her eyes. How to say it right? What if I explained it all wrong, and she thought I was crazy? How could I be sure she would believe me?"

"Mom, what if I could tell you what actually happened to Dad. And that he isn't crazy. Or at least, he wasn't when he was committed."

Her eyes narrowed as one brow rose above the other. She didn't answer. Well, why not plow through and get it over with?

"And what if I could tell you I know why you're afraid of water. And how that and what happened to Dad are related?" I winced, hoping I hadn't worded it all wrong.

She started to say something but couldn't get it out. Then she reached out a shaking hand and said, "Why don't you come inside and tell me what in the world has been going on."

"Actually"—I took her hand—"I need you to take a walk with me. There's something I have to show you."

"Oh, okay." She stepped carefully through the doorway, never taking her eyes off me. "Start with the part about your father. Please." She twisted the lock on the inside knob and let the door slam closed.

I took a long step over a pothole as we started across the parking lot toward the road.

"Okay. So you know the part about how he thinks he was attacked by dragons?"

"Yes."

"Well, he wasn't wrong about that. Those creatures are real. They're called Gwythienians. Most of them are good, but some aren't. Dad got in the middle of a fight between the bad ones. Everything he said they did…it's actually true."

I sneaked a glance in her direction. She was watching the road beneath us, wary of its unevenness. "And the part about him accidentally taking the rock from the dragons?"

"Yes. The rock belongs to them. It's…um…valuable." No reason to throw in more magic than necessary on top of everything else I was unloading on her. "It had been dropped there by accident. He picked it up and accidentally got involved. But do you know why he picked it up in the first place?"

"Uh, no."

"Because when he saw it, he thought of you. He thought it was something you'd like. He planned to bring it back for you as a surprise."

Her mouth trembled, and she crossed her arms, continuing to stare at the ground.

"Now for the really weird part…"

She blew out a puff of air. "That wasn't the weird part?"

"Unfortunately, no. These dragons have a few special abilities. They can turn invisible, and they can see through water into other places. A few of them can change forms and turn into humans. Over a hundred years ago, one of them discovered he had this unusual ability and…well…he is our ancestor. He was one of the Gwythienians whose gifts were strong, and I guess because of that, some of his descendants carry the ability, even though we can't change forms. That's why you can see things in the water, Mom. You've never been crazy."

"I've never told another soul about that, besides your father," she whispered. "But I guess I wasn't hiding it as well as I thought."

She ran her hand through her brown-and-gray hair. "This is a lot to take in." She huffed an awkward laugh.

I smiled slightly as I stepped over a pothole in the road. "Yeah. I thought I was crazy at first too."

"Gosh. Does this mean I was wrong to allow him to stay in that place all this time, getting all sorts of drugs and treatments for a problem he doesn't actually have? And he was telling the truth the whole time. I feel like a horrible wife. No wonder none of the drugs ever worked. So, um, how did all of this start?" She followed me to the woodsy side of the street.

"That's a long story. I promise to tell you one day, but there is something much more important we need to do."

"Okay. What's that?"

"We're going to save Dad."

She whirled on me, eyes bright. "What? How?"

"With a little help from a dragon."

"Mom, this is Gaedyen. He's a Gwythienian—which is basically a dragon. Though he'd describe it otherwise."

I smiled wryly at him, amused by the memory of how serious he'd been about explaining the difference between himself and a fire-breathing dragon when we first met.

Gaedyen turned visible for a moment and nodded respectfully at Mom before quickly disappearing again. "It is wonderful to meet you, Mrs. Montgomery," he said.

"Um," Mom peered around as if perhaps she'd lost sight of him by looking at the wrong angle.

"Oh, right. Mom, Gaedyen has to stay invisible right now." I glanced at him, gesturing toward Mom. "Gaedyen, this is my mom."

"It's, uh, great to meet you, Gaedyen." She looked concerned she might actually be going crazy. She'd see soon, though.

"All right, so, Mom—Dad thinks the Gwythienians who attacked him for the rock all those years ago are still after him for it. We think if we give Dad the opportunity to return this rock to *a* Gwythienian—Gaedyen in this case—it could help him get past the fear and start healing."

I searched her face, hoping she would agree or at least be willing to go along with it.

Eyebrows raised, she nodded.

"So the only problem is getting Dad and Gaedyen in the same room." I watched Mom's face, hoping she'd believe us. "I don't think there's any way we could get Gaedyen into his room in the ward. That leaves one option. Do you have any idea how we can get him out of the ward?"

Mom swallowed, slowly regarding me and then glancing toward the space where Gaedyen sat. She glanced back at me. "Well, I'm allowed to take him for a walk in the gardens outside the building."

I frowned. "I don't remember gardens there."

She smiled sheepishly. "They call the bit of grass a garden. It's really just some space behind the building. But he likes the fresh air. No one would think anything strange of me signing him out for a walk."

Brightening, I thought through the layout of the ward and wondered how we'd sneak Gaedyen there. "Great! Is there a place where Gaedyen could be hidden from most people but visible to Dad?"

Her eyebrows scrunched together. "No, not really. It's pretty open."

"Hmm…could we sneak Dad into the car, take him somewhere Gaedyen can safely wait, and then get him back before anyone comes looking for him?"

"I'm only allowed to sign him out for half an hour at a time, so it would be close, but it could work." Her smile touched her eyes this time.

Was she finally starting to let herself hope?

I smiled back. "It's a plan, then." Now for getting to the ward in the first place. "So, Mom, the fastest way to get there is by—

um—flying. Do you think you could handle that? Or would you rather drive?"

She went faintly green in the face and barely stopped herself from peering at Gaedyen's space again. "I think I've had enough magicky stuff for one day. Driving the car would be a nice, normal thing to do to help me take it all in."

"That sounds like a good idea to me," said Gaedyen. "Enzi, how about you drive your mom, since she has a lot of new information to take in? I will fly ahead to the meeting-place we discussed."

"Perfect. See you there." I smiled goodbye in his general direction.

His heavy footfalls faded as he ran for takeoff. "Now, Mom, you're going to need the brightest, most noticeable outfit you own."

The receptionist's manicured nails clacked away on a keyboard at the front desk. "How can I help you?" She glanced up and recognized Mom. "Oh, Mrs. Montgomery. I could hardly recognize you in those clothes."

I eyed Mom's bright orange sweats and clashing red dress shirt and winced. It was pretty bad. But memorable for sure.

The receptionist squinted at me. "Alright. You and one guest are all checked in. Go ahead up. Visiting hours are until noon, then start back at two. You've got a little time before lunch but not much."

She was just going to let us pass?

With a nod and a smile Mom led the way to an elevator, and I followed.

Not being in stealth mode really made getting to his room a whole lot easier.

We knocked, then went inside.

"Mac." Mom opened her arms to him. He was sitting in one of the easy chairs, reading a newspaper.

A slow ceiling fan rustled the corners of the papers strewn over the wall. All with that symbol from the helicopter that had crashed in Odan Terridor. It was so strange when my two worlds overlapped.

"Lisa!" A huge grin brightened his face as he stood and hugged her with one arm.

Tears pricked my eyes. Despite it all, they still loved each other. If only this would work! Then they could be like this forever. How beautiful. I had to make this happen.

"And, Enzi? Is that you?"

"You know me?" I squeaked.

"Yes, of course! I'm so sorry I didn't recognize you that day you came. They're always messing with my medications. If I remember correctly, it was a bad day. I'm so sorry if I screamed at you. I'm afraid I tend to do that sometimes. I don't know when I'm all there or not."

"Mac." Tears trailed down Mom's cheek as she squeaked out, "Mac, I was wrong. You haven't ever been crazy. I should've trusted you, and instead I made you stay here, for almost eight years."

"What do you mean?" He touched her shoulder.

"Dad, the dragons are real. I've seen them. And the ones you met were in a big fight. The other ones never act like that. One of the nice ones is actually waiting to take the rock back. Right now."

His eyes bugged out of his head, and he sank back into the chair, hyperventilating.

I reached toward him, unsure how to calm him down. "No, Dad, listen. He has no interest in hurting you. Look at this." I pulled the fake Gwythienian rock—one of the purple ones from Tukailaan's lair—out of my pocket. "This is the rock. I found it, and if you give it back, they won't haunt you anymore.

They will know you returned it, and you never have to worry about them ever again. Okay? Do you think you can do that?"

"Yes, but how will I get out? I'm locked in; there are cameras. You two will have to get clearance to open the door, and they'll watch who leaves."

"That's okay, Mac." Mom put her hands on his shoulders and grinned at me. "We have a plan.

Mom helped Dad into his wheelchair and tucked an extra set of his white clothes behind him.

She pushed him toward the door, pressed a red button on the wall, and smiled up at a camera in the corner above the door. A moment later, the door buzzed, and Mom pulled it open without a problem.

Following her out, I eyed the camera. So that must've been how I'd been caught when I was here before. I must've been too terrified and shocked to notice the button.

The door closed firmly behind us, and we walked through a few sterile hallways and traveled down the elevator until we reached the front desk. Mom smiled at the receptionist like nothing in the world was wrong. She was doing a pretty good job playing it up.

A right turn and another hallway later, we spilled out into the garden.

Rich, manicured grass covered the small piece of land between the building and the parking lot. A stone fountain spurted water from three different tiers in the middle of the plot, and well-groomed shrubs made a little border around it all.

"It is kind of a garden, I guess," I said. Not many flowers, though. My great-great-great-grandmother might have been able to help with that.

We wheeled Dad next to a bench backed by shrubs and facing away from the building.

I spoke as I looked around me. "Okay. Mom, you go stand by the fountain for a minute. Be as active as you can, swinging your arms or reaching for the fountain—whatever you can think of to keep the attention of anyone watching us from the inside. Dad, I'm going to wheel you around really slowly as if we're just talking and looking at the shrubs. When we reach the tall shrubs by the car, Mom, you need to be extra distracting for a few seconds so we can slip behind them. Then you'll wait here and try to look normal until we get back. Okay? Maybe calling over to where we're supposed to be with a cheerful wave once or twice would be good?" Looking back and forth between them, I hoped they would agree with my idea.

Mom reached over to me. "I am *so* proud of you, Enzi."

Dad smiled at me too, a glisten in his eyes. "It's great to finally meet you."

"You too." I smiled, tears coming to my eyes too. But we didn't have time for that just yet. "All right, Mom, whenever you're ready."

She stood and waltzed toward the fountain, dramatically taking in the scenery around her.

I grabbed the handles of Dad's wheelchair. "Here we go." We made it to the far side of the shrubs, and I hoped they were tall enough to conceal us.

"You guys still have this same car?" Dad beamed at the faded blueish Oldsmobile with one bright orange fender and about one and a half functional headlights. "My old *Tin Can!*"

"You know this car? Wow, I didn't realize it was *that* old."

"We've known each other for ten minutes, and you're already making fun of me for being old?"

I looked askance at him, afraid I'd offended him. But he smiled, opened the passenger door, and pulled himself from the wheelchair into the car.

I folded up the chair and put it in the backseat, then opened the driver's door. Wind whooshed above me, and I glanced up, smiling at where I guessed Gaedyen to be. I watched the sky for a moment, wondering if I would catch a glimpse of him. Air whooshed above me again. I guessed he was circling, waiting for me to start driving.

So I dropped into the driver's seat and cranked the key. "We're just going a little ways away, somewhere with cover. We'll meet my friend there."

"Your friend? I thought it was a dragon?"

"He is…a creature who looks like a dragon. He claims to be different, even though he looks like one."

He watched the ward shrink in the rearview mirror. "It sounds like you know him."

I checked for traffic and turned out of the parking lot. "I do." Was that too clipped a reply? I certainly didn't want to get into that right now.

"And this dragon…he's not dangerous?"

Should I lie? No, if I wanted Gaedyen to stop lying, I couldn't go around lying all the time. "He could be dangerous if he wanted to be, but he's not dangerous to us. We'll be fine, Dad, don't worry. Here." I handed him the stone. "Take this. You have to be the one to give it to him, okay? Then everything you have been worrying about will be over."

I gripped the steering wheel.

He exhaled. "How different our lives would be if I'd never touched this thing."

It was true. His simple act of touching that rock had changed the future of our whole family. But now, I don't think I would have it any other way. This was how it was meant to be.

"I think it must've happened for a reason. Some things that happened aren't good, but some of them are. I think everything must happen for a reason, even if we don't see it at the time."

"Hmm. Sounds like you're awfully wise for your age." He grinned at me again. "I'm proud of you, Enzi."

This was not the time to get choked up. I blinked back tears and swallowed hard. "We're getting close."

All the leaves in the trees ahead of us rustled, but the branches in the rearview mirror didn't move. That couldn't just be wind, could it? Gaedyen should have already landed in the clearing.

I hunched over the wheel to get a better look. If he was doing that, was it a warning not to come? But if it wasn't him… could Meleena have found us? Was she going after him?

Surely not…but I *didn't* know for sure. She'd somehow known things—when we would be at Susan's house, that we would be there at all. When we'd returned to Geneva and Bricriu. But there hadn't been enough water around for her to be watching us through it, had there?

*Kymri's seeing crystal! Meleena stole a Cathawyr seeing crystal when she stole the rock of healing ages ago. If she's still alive, she could easily know where we are right now. Where Gaedyen is. Alone.*

Suddenly all the swirling leaves ceased. I pulled over and parked. If I drove down this road, we would reach the clearing where Gaedyen was waiting for us. And what if it was more than just him? What if he needed help? I couldn't take my dad into that.

And the arkencain…

"Um, Dad, wait here a second. I need to make sure everything is ready."

I slid out of the car and closed my door as quietly as I could. Not wanting to unsettle him, I swiftly pulled out the bow and arrows and held them in front of me so he couldn't see them. I walked slowly over the ditch and into the trees before breaking into a run.

# CHAPTER SEVENTEEN

Heavy scuffling sounds disturbed the leaflitter and shook a few trees up ahead. I shoved leaves and thorns out of the way as I raced toward Gaedyen.

So Meleena had found us, and they were fighting invisibly. Again. *Do they always have to fight invisibly? How am I supposed to help when I can't tell who's who?*

My toe struck something, and I fell. It was a rymakri, sticking out of the ground at an angle. I grabbed it and shoved myself to my feet, flailing to keep my balance.

"Gaedyen?" I announced my presence—if the fumbling around hadn't already done it. I needed to know which invisible thrashing was him.

Gaedyen flickered to visibility, then vanished. His eyes looked strained with worry before disappearing.

And then he flickered again just in time for me to see him kick Meleena off.

Her body soared through the air and she twisted, landing a few feet in front of me. I wasted no time in launching myself toward her and driving the rymakri toward her heart.

But she squirmed to one side, and I stabbed her forearm instead. "Crap!"

I ripped the rymakri free and raised it to stab her again, but she kicked my legs out from under me and I hit the ground hard. I struggled to pull in a breath as she pushed herself up and leaned over me.

"I still do not understand. Why would a Gwythienian ever fall for a puny human like you?" She brought down the arkencain.

A wet squelch sounded, and Meleena was flung away from me, roaring. I glanced around wildly. Gaedyen flickered into view, holding a thick branch out between me and the deadly weapon's blow.

"Thank you." I breathed hard, reaching up to take his hand.

"Thank *you*, Enzi," he replied, pulling me to my feet. "She almost had me."

Meleena rolled over with a hiss and bounded away. We launched after her, Gaedyen grabbing some branches and biting rymakri as we ran.

Suddenly I lurched forward as something struck me from behind. "Ahh!" I broke my fall with the rymakri, then heaved myself back to my feet.

"Are you okay?" Gaedyen asked, looking frantically above us for where Meleena might be lurking invisibly after pushing me over.

"Yeah. Where'd she go?"

He stared around us, ears flicking this way and that. "I do not know."

"There's something wrong with any Gwythienian who would desire to be human and be with a human." Meleena's voice floated around us, Gaedyen's earflaps flickering to find her location. He growled, stepping closer to me.

"I am going to end Tukailaan's line today. Rid the world of the embarrassing phenomenon of his strange human-loving propensities."

Nocking a rymakri into place on the bow, I glanced at Gaedyen. Our eyes met as his lip curled into another snarl.

"And I will not be stopping there. I shall end Batran's whole line. Both the descendants of Tukailaan and those of Padraig. Just to ensure I have wiped out any trace of whatever causes you strange Gwythienians to behave so unnaturally."

With a sound like the wind racing through the trees, Meleena's eerie voice vanished.

We waited a few beats for her next move, but nothing happened.

"The descendants of Tukailaan." I faced Gaedyen. "Mom."

"Do we have time to finish what we came here to do for your father?"

My heart raced. We might not be able to get him out again, not if we're caught after this. And Meleena couldn't grab Mom from the garden without being seen, so she would have to wait. Maybe until we got home later. "Yes. Let's be quick. Come to the edge of the woods by the road. I don't want to waste time and energy pushing him all the way to the clearing."

He nodded grimly and we sprinted back to the *Tin Can*.

Gaedyen paused a few steps inside the tree line. I trudged on, the glint of the sun on the car windows visible through the trees, when a big, warm hand clasped my shoulder and brought me to a halt. I spun with a frown, and found Gaedyen's eyes on me with such a look of concern that for a moment, I forgot everything else. "Gaedyen?"

"Just…" He bent and kissed my forehead. "Be careful."

I nodded, ignoring the sting behind my eyes. I whispered a kiss toward him, then raced for the *Tin Can*.

Heaving for breath, I struggled to focus on my dad and what we came here to do rather than on Mom and what peril she might be in soon, or how much Gaedyen was worrying about me, which was sweet, but I didn't have time to think about it right now.

We had to finish this first. Then we could deal with whatever came next.

Pulling the driver's side door open, I called, "Everything's ready!" without bending my head low enough for him to see my face. After I slid the bow and arrow into the back and retrieved the wheelchair, my dad pulled himself into it, and I pushed it over the rough, uneven ground. His hand intermittently squeezed the rock or fiddled with it. He dropped it on his lap once and practically dove for it, as if it might disappear as soon as it was out of his hand.

I sure hoped this would work. Mom and Dad might be able to be together again, to be happy like they were supposed to be.

If they both survived the day.

"It's just us. We're coming. It would be best not to surprise him."

I hoped he'd get what I was saying. That he should already be visible so we could approach him, rather than him popping up from invisibility with no warning. I didn't know how easily my dad might snap after everything he'd gone through.

There he was, lying on his stomach squished between a few trees too close together. Not good if Meleena came back. But hopefully it would work for a few minutes just to get this done. *Good thinking, Gaedyen, lying down. That'll make you look a little less huge and dangerous.*

The moment Mac caught a glimpse of him, he froze, eyes popping.

I grabbed his arm. "It's okay. Don't freak out. He just wants you to give the rock back, then he will leave and you will never have to see another one of them again. Okay? This is a good thing. It's a chance for you to prove you've been right all along."

He didn't respond, but he let me continue to push him forward. When we reached Gaedyen, he nodded at me, then at Mac, who bowed at the waist.

"I understand you have something of mine, human." Gaedyen looked down his nose at Mac, playing the part well.

And maybe having a little too much fun with it considering the gravity of the situation. Had he actually made his voice deeper?

My dad straightened, still looking down, and held out the rock. "I am sorry I ever touched this rock. I didn't know it was yours, and I never would've touched it if I'd known. I give it back to you now, in the hopes you will tell your people I did so, that I may live without fear of being pursued for the rock. Is that something you can do?" He tentatively raised his eyes to Gaedyen's.

Gaedyen reached toward him and held his huge, cupped hand underneath Mac's. Mac tilted the rock into it.

"Thank you, human, for the safe return of my rock. You may rest assured I will inform everyone else you are to be left alone for the rest of your life. No one will bother you. No one will even know where to look for you."

Mac let out a long, relieved sigh. "Thank you, Your Majesty."

I had to hold in a laugh. I'd be giving Gaedyen crap for that later for sure.

"Go in peace, humans. I will leave you now." And he vanished.

Mac let out another huge breath. "I can't believe that's all it took. I am so glad it's over!" He turned to me. "Enzi, how in the world did you find the rock? And arrange this meeting with the *dragon*?"

I hauled his wheelchair around and pushed toward the car. If I told him it was in his uniform pocket and we'd had it all this time, would he be angry for us not bringing it to him? I'm sure he'd asked Mom about it many times, just as he'd asked me that day. Maybe he would be better off without one more instance of our not trusting him. But I wouldn't lie to him. I'd just see how long I could get away without hurting him with the truth.

"It's a really long story. And we need to get you back before they find out I drove off with you. That could get us in big trouble. Especially Mom." And there was plenty worse trouble to deal with besides that.

He frowned. "I wish I didn't have to go back there."

"I know." After I helped him back in and stowed the wheelchair, I tore my door open and hopped in. "For what it's worth, I wanted to bust you out and hide you or something. But there's too much government stuff involved. We have to get you out the right way, or else you'll be looking over your shoulder for the rest of your life. Wouldn't you rather have the best shot possible at a normal life?"

He deliberated as he fastened his seatbelt. "Yes, I guess I would. But for what it's worth"—he grinned—"thanks for wanting to bust me out."

I stepped on the gas and whirled the car around to speed back the way we came. "You're welcome. Dad."

# CHAPTER EIGHTEEN

*I* peered around the garden for Mom as we approached, my heart racing with fear that I'd made the wrong decision about going ahead with that while Meleena could be heading for Mom. But she stood in front of the shrubs, a hospital security member on either side of her.

*Oh fan-freaking-tastic.*

Sluggishly I put the car in park and faced Dad. He returned my worried look but kept silent.

I unfolded his wheelchair, and he hauled himself into it by the time our greeting party reached us.

Turns out the ward has rules about taking a patient away in a vehicle for any length of time. Mom feigned ignorance, and I went with actual ignorance about their rules. We got in trouble and lost our freedom to visit Dad without a chaperone. From now until we got him free, Mom would have to have an escort into his room and to take him out for fresh air. That was obnoxious, but hopefully it wouldn't be for long.

"How long do you think it will take to get him out permanently?" I glanced at Mom in the passenger seat.

She leaned back, rubbing her tired eyes. "Oh, I don't know. Probably a year or so. There will be a lot of red tape. And scientists don't like things they can't explain. We'd better hope they come up with a good reason for what actually happened real quick, otherwise they'll waste a lot of time on tests and who knows what to confirm he really is cured of all the things they—we—thought he might have had."

"Hmm." I didn't like the idea of him having to be there *that* long.

"Will you be coming home tonight? I wish I could invite, er—what's his name?"

I smiled. "Gaedyen."

"I wish I could invite Gaedyen to spend the night, but I'm afraid he wouldn't fit in our apartment." She frowned. "Hey, you did say that he can turn human, didn't you? If he would do that, he could come in." She made a sort of smile-wince, and my heart went out to her for trying so hard to accept something so outlandish for my sake.

"Well, he used to be able to, but that ability is currently stuck. He had a bad injury and now isn't able to change forms. And thank you for the offer, but we have to get back to Odan Terridor for some, um, important events."

Her face fell. "Oh. When will I see you again?"

Wincing, I kept my eyes on the road. "I don't know exactly. But it won't be as long as last time."

She nodded. "That's good. I missed you. And you know, I wanted to tell you something."

I flicked a glance her way. "It's okay, Mom. I'm not mad about you keeping Dad a secret anymore. I'm just glad he's okay and anxious to get him out."

"You still need to know. It's true they told me he was dead before you were born. I thought for years he was. When I found out he was alive, after going to see him to confirm his identity, I went straight to your room to tell you. That was when I found you…after it happened. I forgot all about him being alive, when

I found you and realized what you had been through. It was so…ugh.”

So not all of the story had been a lie. That was a relief. And I had to admit it made sense not to want to spring something so huge on a little kid after she'd just escaped being abused by an older boy. I wished I would have known these details before.

She closed her eyes, tears sliding silently over her grimace. "You were in the hospital for a couple of days, then resting at home, and that was enough for you to handle. Then you went back to school, and your friends turned into jerks. I didn't want to spring anything on you then. You didn't need another insane person in your life. After that, things just kept coming up that made your life harder. I wanted to give you an easier life than the one I had. So often I felt I must've failed as a mother, not being able to save you. If only I would have done something differently."

"Mom…"

She held up a finger. "Hang on a second. I'm almost done. When they started him on some new therapies a few years ago, I hoped they'd cure him. I was planning to tell you about him once he was more stable, so you wouldn't have to go through seeing him like I had. I was supposed to hear back about the final results by your birthday a few months ago. But it didn't go as planned—obviously, since it turns out there wasn't an actual condition to treat. And you were the one to find the news. It wasn't even supposed to be sent to that address. It was supposed to go to work. And they screwed it up."

She threw her hands up toward the *Tin Can's* droopy ceiling. "And the reason the money never added up was because of insurance. There was a whole fiasco with insurance when they found him and found the facility to place him in near us. Once he was there, we couldn't move him. That's why we didn't move after it happened. I'm so sorry, Enzi."

She took a deep breath.

"Despite everything I tried to do, you still had to get a job too young to help me pay bills, not even for your own fun money. I feel guilty every day for everything, Enzi. But I did what I could. There was nothing I could fix, or I would have."

I slowed to a stop in front of the sleepy red light around the corner from the apartment. My voice came out quiet. "I'm sorry I blamed you for so much when you were doing the best you could. I didn't know. I was selfish."

"I'm sorry I never told you about your father. I wanted to, but I didn't want to upset your world any more than it was already."

I hugged her. "Thank you for everything you did for me growing up. All the little things I didn't even know about. I'll make it up to you someday."

She hugged me back. "Enzi, you don't have to make anything up to me. That's my job as a parent, and I wasn't a very good one. Just don't go too long without giving me a call again, okay?"

"I promise. And you weren't a bad parent. You were the best mom I could've had."

She smiled and turned away, swiping at tears. Her weepy smile contorted into wide-eyed horror as she stared out the windshield. Before I could react, we were upside down, soaring through the air, screeching to a halt with roof against pavement.

Was that a fallen tree across the road…? My vision blurred as Mom's scream pierced my eardrums.

"Mom, are you okay?"

I recognized Gaedyen's roar from somewhere close. "Gaedyen?"

A piece of the *Tin Can* blurred past us, and another roar joined Gaedyen's. *Meleena. Crap!*

I couldn't see past the shoulder of the road—I needed out. Feeling around for the seatbelt buckle, I glanced at Mom again. She'd stopped screaming.

"Enzi, are you okay?" Mom hissed frantically.

I met her wild eyes. "Yeah, I think so. I don't feel any pain—" Just then my thumb found the button, dropping me face-first on the upside-down ceiling of *Tin Can*. "Ouch. Okay, now I feel pain. Are you okay?"

She undid her seatbelt and landed next to me with a bit more finesse. "I think I'm okay, but something's going on out there." She peered out the window.

I followed her gaze and winced at the blood already dappling the pavement. With a quick glance at Mom to be sure none was hers, I shifted to kick the door out.

"Yeah, it's another Gwythienian. A bad one, if you couldn't tell." I leaned on my back and kicked the door.

It didn't budge.

Mom wrenched me back. "What're you doing? They'll hear you!"

I pulled away from her as gently as I could and readied to kick again. "I know. That's what I'm counting on."

I kicked again with more success and awkwardly climbed out of the opening.

"Stay here, Mom. Like, seriously. You can't help and would only get us all in more trouble, okay?" Peering through the back seat window, I debated wrenching the door or crawling back through to retrieve the bow and arrows. But the quiver lay under a bent piece of metal reaching out from under the back seats, the few carved rymakri dispersed throughout. I couldn't see the bow. *Crap.*

I pushed myself up and ran toward Gaedyen without wasting time finding and digging the bow out. I needed to help him now.

But something was wrong. I jogged toward the end of the blood where I thought I'd heard the roaring. But that was it— the roaring had stopped.

Gaedyen flickered back into visibility, lying on the ground.

Horror froze me to the spot.

Meleena appeared over him, arkencain held high, leering.

I was helpless. Worthless. Too far away and with no weapons. There wasn't a thing I could do about what was about to happen.

She let her foreleg fall, the arkencain's point racing toward Gaedyen's neck.

I shot into a sprint, knowing I'd be too late.

Something whirled from my peripheral vision into Meleena's face, causing her to flinch.

Another step and I took advantage of her distraction and lunged for the arkencain, knocking it out of her grip and causing it to skitter across the pavement.

An orange piece of the *Tin Can* dropped between Gaedyen and Meleena, and there was Mom, standing several paces back with her arm still outstretched from hurling the piece of metal like a giant Frisbee. *Well, nice job, Mom!*

Meleena spun, knocking Mom to the ground with her tail as she raced for the arkencain.

"Mom!" She didn't move.

Meleena skidded to the arkencain, caught it up in one hand, and flung it at us.

"No!" I threw myself over Gaedyen, but I wasn't fast enough. The arkencain shrieked as it lodged itself between Gaedyen's side and the pavement.

I blinked, staring down at the deadly weapon from where I was draped over Gaedyen's back. Had it scratched him, or missed him?

Meleena snarled and raced back toward us. I shoved myself all the way over Gaedyen's back, landing on the hard pavement and tearing the arkencain up from the ground. Meleena pounced, and I shifted to aim the arkencain at her. She twisted in the air when she saw it, but the motion gave me access to the fine scales on the underside of her tail. I shoved the arkencain upwards and felt a satisfying tear as it cut through her scales and tore a long gash in her flesh. Her tail flicked to the side, yanking the arkencain out of my hand. It seemed to be lodged in her flesh still.

I stared in shock at the piece of poisoned rock protruding from her tail. Would we finally be safe from her?

She roared and rolled sloppily over the street. Holding up her tail, she shook the arkencain loose and examined the deep scratch that started about two thirds of the way down.

I smiled grimly at her, standing between her and my loved ones and hefting the arkencain. Hot blood dripped from her wound and plinked to the ground.

She roared right at me, and then turned and vanished. I waited for a surprise attack to come from the sky. Listening for the sound of Gwythienian winds, I picked up the sound of Gaedyen's wheezing breaths. Had he been stabbed? And Mom…I whirled to face Mom, laying face down on the pavement.

*Crap!*

Since I knew Gaedyen was breathing, I left his side to check on Mom.

*Please be okay, please be okay.*

I rolled her over gently and she blinked up at me.

My shoulders sagged in relief as I hugged her. "Thank freaking goodness you're alright! I mean, are you alright? Does anything hurt?"

"Where's the mean dragon?" she asked, turning to glance around for her.

"I think I finally finished her off. I got in a good hit at least. She left."

"And Gaedyen?"

I glanced back at him. "I'm not sure. He's alive but I think he's knocked out. Can you sit up?"

Mom twisted around to her knees. "I can stand. I'm okay."

She pushed herself to her feet and glanced between the downed *Tin Can* and Gaedyen.

Relieved that she was okay, I shoved off the ground and sprinted for Gaedyen.

Gaedyen came to after several minutes of me freaking out. He had several small scratches, but nothing to cause as much blood loss as there was on the road. I guessed he'd gotten in some good strikes on Meleena, and they'd healed enough to stop bleeding by the time she took off.

There was something like road rash all over his back and sides from where he'd skidded over the pavement, but as best I could tell, there was no arkencain strike. I'd nearly cried with relief when I couldn't see a stab wound.

He was mostly back to normal now, if a bit dazed. He'd rolled the *Tin Can* back over and to my surprise, it still ran. I glanced at the trees I'd left him in on the other side of the road from Mom's apartment. I didn't like leaving him there, but he was too weak to maintain invisibility.

"Thanks for that, earlier." I tried to keep my lips from trembling as I reached out to hug Mom. "That was really impressive, I have to say. And I'm sorry about the *Tin Can* getting a bit smashed."

"That thing won't ever stop running." She let out a little laugh, then her lips trembled as she said, "Enzi, why don't you just stay here and away from all that? Please. It terrifies me to know that's what you're dealing with."

I stepped back, taking a deep breath. "This is something I have to do. It's bigger than me. It's important. And hard to explain. But on the bright side, Meleena thinks you're dead, so you don't need to worry about her finding you again."

Her eyes glistened. "Please stay."

"I can't," I whispered, blinking a tear free.

She glanced behind me to roughly where Gaedyen was hiding in the trees. "I hope he takes as good of care of you as you do of him."

I smiled. "He does."

She squeezed me once more, then let go and ducked through the door. She never did like to let me see her cry.

"Goodnight, Mom. I'll see you soon."

"Goodnight, Enzi. I love you."

"Love you too."

The door creaked to a close, and I was alone out front. I heaved a sigh. What a day. I wanted Gaedyen. I needed his familiar steadiness. I might need to cry just from all the emotions zooming around today. I wasn't sure yet. I felt a bit numb. Like when you scrape your knee and there's a moment before it really hurts, but you know the feeling is about to come. There was just too much to cope with all at once.

I turned to head toward the street, and there he was, standing tall and proud and completely visible right in the middle of the road. He was crazy. But he knew I needed him.

I took a step toward him, and the next thing I knew, I was running. I slammed into his neck, wrapping my arms around him as he wrapped a huge hand around me.

"Enzi, it is okay. I am okay. Your parents are okay. And we did what we planned to do for your father."

"I'm so glad you're okay. And they're okay. Thank you for all you did. Really. So much."

"Do you not wish to sleep on a real bed tonight?"

"No. I *wish* to sleep next to you on the ground like usual."

A light rumble of satisfaction emanated from his core. "I love you."

"I love you too."

"Shall we be off?"

I let go, avoiding his eyes—maybe the embarrassed-of-crying thing was hereditary—and heaved myself over his back.

# CHAPTER NINETEEN

"So here's a little nuance." It had come to my mind the day after seeing my parents, as Gaedyen and I flew toward Ofwen Dwir, the home of the Rubandors and our first stop on the journey to call all the chosen next Possessors for the Ceremony.

Lying on the dirt and leaf-litter, I crossed my arms over my face to block the dappled sunlight while I considered the issue. A rymakri rested in my hand, freshly made and ready for me to spend some time practicing.

"Didn't you say you needed to transform into your human form in order to get through a small hole into Ofwen Dwir?"

Gaedyen stopped stoking the fire. "Yes, I am afraid I do. I fear I will have to tear through their wall to make the hole bigger. I do not see any other way."

I uncovered my eyes and sat up, watching him. "Or…I could do it."

He studied me for a long moment. "I cannot just throw you into the Rubandors' waters all by yourself. Besides, you would not be able to hold your breath long enough to reach it." He resumed stoking the fire with more ferocity than was necessary.

"You can carry me down, then I can crawl through. You said the Rubandors are right outside, right? They'll take me to the atmosphere chamber so I can breathe, and I'll invite them to Odan Terridor."

"I do not care for that idea at all."

I frowned. "All right, then. What do you propose? You really think their wall will be destructible? I'm pretty sure you would've gotten through it that way the first time, if it were really possible."

Annoyance rumbled in my stomach, but I kept it down. Reminding myself he was like this because he cared about me, I continued.

"If we don't get each realm to the ceremony, it won't happen. Then Veri will…we won't be able to save him. We have to convince each realm to participate in the ceremony. We can't skip the Rubandors, and you can't fit or break through their wall. I'm our only option."

His stoking stick burst into splinters as he pounded it a bit too hard into the ground. "I cannot let you do that. What if you do not make it? What if something horrible happens to you and I lose you?"

"Gaedyen, I have to go. It's not a matter of you letting me. This is my choice."

He growled, avoiding my eyes.

I picked up a blunt stick and threw it lightly at his shoulder, frowning. "Wasn't my willingness to risk myself for the wellbeing of others what made you start caring about me in the first place?"

He whirled on me, teeth grinding together. "Do not twist my words! I refuse to be manipulated into taking you down there." His eyes flamed as he scowled at me.

I stumbled backward, fear pricking my chest for the first time in months. I raised my rymakri at him, for the first time ever. I had no idea he would react that way.

The anger melted off his face when he saw my fear. "Enzi, I am sorry. I did not mean to startle you. It is just that—"

I pushed myself to my feet and held up my pointer finger. Very calmly, I said, "Gaedyen, nobody screams at me. I don't tolerate being treated that way. Not anymore. And I never expected it to come from you. Don't *ever* do that again."

I turned and walked into the trees. Leaves crumpled under his feet as he rose to follow me.

I called over my shoulder, "I need some time, Gaedyen. Don't follow me."

I stood next to Gaedyen on the same ledge overlooking the ocean where Gaedyen had left me with two rymakri and a breaking heart as he dove for the Rubandors' realm a few months ago. The same place where Tony had appeared and turned into Tukailaan and nearly killed me.

My heart grew a little more tender toward Gaedyen at the memory, despite our argument from the day before. We'd barely spoken since he'd yelled at me. I'd gone out with the rymakri and brought back a couple of rabbits for us to share, and then we'd gone to sleep in silence.

I didn't like the silence, or the hard feelings. I intended to say something to lighten things between us before diving, just to be on the safe side, but I struggled to find the words.

"You know, believing in me wouldn't kill you. I'm not the weakling human I was when we first met."

"I know. Just…be careful, Enzi. I cannot…" His voice choked, and he looked away without finishing his sentence. "Please do not do this, Enzi."

I threw my hands up, exasperated. "Then what do you want me to do?"

"Stay here with me."

I crossed my arms. Of course I would rather be with him. But there were more important things to worry about right now. "That's not going to help us save Veri."

Gaedyen stared me down in silence.

"Fine. If you're determined to be upset about me doing something you can't, that's your choice. I'm going down there. I'll be back as soon as I can."

I slid down the sloping edge, pulled off my shoes and socks, and dipped my feet into the ocean.

The water chilled me immediately, sending an uncomfortable shiver through my skin. I walked out farther, soaking my clothes and shivering, until I had to tread water to keep my head up. I could still see land clearly, so I knew from the liryk Aven had given us that I wasn't far enough out yet to be over the entrance. I paddled farther and farther, feeling lonelier and lonelier.

At last I lost sight of land. I took a deep breath, dove toward the dark below, and started kicking.

A light appeared ahead, and a few seconds later, I could make out the circular stone opening into Ofwen Dwir. I strained toward it, knowing they would notice me soon based on Gaedyen's warning.

No sooner was I through the hole than flashes of red appeared and disappeared. I moved slowly, hopefully communicating I wasn't a threat. But my lungs were burning.

One of them bumped me, and I stretched out Aven's rock, hoping they would recognize it.

It was too dark to make out their expressions, but they must've understood, because I was suddenly being escorted somewhere else. Hopefully to the atmosphere chamber Gaedyen had been taken to before.

Things I couldn't see in the dim light brushed my arms, but my lungs were screaming so badly I barely noticed.

My body convulsed and forced me to breathe in water. My lungs were on fire.

Where was the freaking atmosphere chamber?

# CHAPTER TWENTY

At last I broke through some kind of invisible barrier and took an enormous, heaving breath of air. Collapsing to my knees, I coughed up salty water between frantic breaths.

"You do realize this is not the Rubandor rock, human?" A strange, deep voice rumbled.

My arms shook as I pushed myself up to see the speaker.

The strange mottled-gray creature had a huge, salamander-ish head, tiny black eyes, and a mouth that stretched all the way around the front of its face. A tangle of what looked like soaking wet red hair hung from either side of its head, though it was bald on top. It had two arms with dumpy fingers on each hand but no back legs. Its body morphed into a thick, finned tail. Altogether he was about ten feet long.

There were several more like him watching from just outside the atmosphere chamber. Reddish hair floated around the other one's faces. Was that the fire-water the lyric was talking about?

"Uh, yeah." I put one fist to my mouth as I coughed more ocean from my chest. "I am aware that this is the Adarborian rock, but we do have yours as well."

Each of the onlookers jumped back, their wide mouths hanging open and their wispy red hair waving in front of them and then slowly floating back into place.

The one speaking to me seemed to frown, though his unusual face was hard to read. "And how has that come to be?"

"A human came here to discuss the rocks with you several weeks ago. He called himself Shaun or Gaedyen."

He nodded.

"Tukailaan, the Gwythienian that human told you about, buried it before he died, and we uncovered it."

"Tukailaan is dead? So our rock is not Possessed then?" Hopefulness rang in his voice, though his little black eyes remained expressionless.

"Tukailaan *is* dead, but no, the person who picked it up accidentally took Possession of it."

A collective groan and angry splashing came from the onlookers.

"But!" I got to my feet, each breath still burning my aching lungs. "There will be a Possessorship Ceremony in Odan Terridor in ten days! Possession of each rock will be transferred to each realms' desired Possessor. If you send your next Possessor and a few delegates immediately, you will get there in time."

He stared at me. Had he never once blinked the whole time we spoke?

"Why have they sent a human to tell us these things?"

"Because the Gwythienian I'm traveling with can't fit through the entrance into your realm. Why the huge dome anyway?"

"To protect us from worse things than you can imagine."

I raised an eyebrow. "Okay. So will you come to the ceremony and reclaim Possession of your rock?"

"I will confer with my people. We do not have a true leader now, without our rock or our last Possessor, so deliberation may take some time."

I nodded and folded my legs to sit. "Okay. I'll wait here for your answer."

Something that might have been a smile crossed his huge, strange face. "No, human. You will not. It is time for you to leave. If we decide to come, you will see us there."

I opened my mouth to argue, but several of the creatures burst into the atmosphere chamber and hauled me to my feet, barely granting me time to take a breath before plunging me into the water to exit their realm.

When at last I broke the surface and swiped water from my eyes, I searched the ledge for Gaedyen, ecstatic and maybe a little smug about my success with reaching the Rubandors, and hopefully convincing them to come. We needed to secure the Odan Terridor liryk from the Crivabanians so the Rubandors could get there.

I beamed at the ledge, but no one was there.

*He must be a little farther back, hidden in the trees.*

But I paddled closer, and still there wasn't the slightest hint of red anywhere. I pulled myself onto land and climbed up to the ledge, my heart sinking further and further. Where was he? Maybe just invisible?

"Gaedyen?"

Dirt clods freckled the grass in places—the few places grass remained. Was this evidence of a fight? A fight that resulted in Gaedyen being taken away somewhere against his will?

My heart raced. Had Meleena found us? But Gaedyen hadn't smelled her at all on the way here. I knelt and traced a track in the dirt with two fingers. No, not a track. Lots of little tracks together. Made by lots of little feet.

The words of an old Crivabanian poem recited by one of Veri's people came back to me.

*One alone not mighty, together a force unified.*

Last time we'd been here, Veri and I had accidentally pissed off all the other Crivabanians. And they'd never liked Gwythienians to begin with. And that one really annoying one—Prince Something?—had nearly taken Gaedyen down with his friends when we'd escaped.

Had they found him alone and taken this opportunity to capture him?

Focusing on the disturbed ground again, I followed the pulled-up grass as it turned into tracks.

"I'm coming for you, Gaedyen."

# CHAPTER TWENTY-ONE

*I* stumbled around in the redwood forest for ages, shivering from my wet clothes. Finally I felt a strong feeling I shouldn't go to the left, and remembering Veri's explanation about how the barrier of the realm works, focused on going exactly where my head told me not to. Aven had said that there were plenty of secret entrances into Maisius Arborii. Maybe it was the same in Sequoia Cadryl.

When I felt so much resistance it made me nearly sick, I almost gave up. But then I saw it: gentle light glowing from the inside of one of the biggest redwood trees in the whole forest. I crept inside, fighting what felt like a physical barrier pushing against every point on my skin. And then I was through. The resistance vanished. I breathed deeply, then scoured the ground for clear tracks.

Willing myself invisible, I parted the ferns and watched as several Crivabanians scampered past me, all heading in the same direction. Fearing invisibility wouldn't be enough to hide me if several of them ran into me, I carefully followed their path from a distance.

A Crivabanian was speaking loudly up ahead. His voice sounded familiar. And my gut roiled with instant ire for it. How did I know this Crivabanian voice?

"Not *only* did this monster kidnap our own Veritamyk from us, but he also destroyed one of the entrances into our realm, and several innocent trees along with it."

*Well at least I know I'm in the right place.* I crept closer, slowed by the thickening ranks of observing Crivabanians ahead of me. I peered around a ginormous tree trunk, and there he was.

Gaedyen's forelegs were bound in front of him with green rope that looked similar to the material my Crivabanian clothes had been made from. More ropes of the same material bound each back leg to a tree trunk behind him, and there were even ropes around his shoulders, lifting his wings at what had to be an uncomfortable angle. I winced at the pain it must be causing him.

"Since I am Dyn Meddy's spokesperson during this time of ill health for him, I will take your request to him myself."

A few Crivabanians shot their little hands into the air and shouted, "Prinspur!"

That was the little devil's name. Prinspur. But spokesperson for *Dyn Meddy*? Dyn Meddy was dead—I knew that because Veri had taken Possession of his rock. What was Prinspur up to?

"I think I can speak for all of us present when I say we want this monster killed for his crimes!"

*Excuse me? Oh, I am so putting a stop to this right now.*

I crept around the gathered squirrel people, careful not to make a sound or accidentally touch one of them. It was really difficult. Why wasn't *floating* a Gwythienian ability?

A Crivabanian in front of me shivered and turned toward me. Had I touched her tail with my shoe? I held my breath, hoping she'd think it was wind or a bug.

She turned back to Prinspur, her hands fisted and planted on her hips just like Veri's so often were. "I'm not convinced he needs to die, Prinspur. That's kind of dramatic, don't you think?"

Startled by her bravery, I held my frozen pose and watched for Prinspur's reaction.

His features morphed into a scowl. "Dylnora, of course we can count on you to be difficult." He scrubbed his hands over his face. "If no one *else* objects, then I will take our decision to Dyn Meddy and—"

Dylnora made a high-pitch smirking sound in the back of her throat and inspected the prim black claws on one forefoot. "I'm telling you right now, Prinspur, Dyn Meddy isn't going to go for that."

*Yeah, because he's dead and Prinspur is using everyone's ignorance of that fact to his advantage.*

Hoping this argument would buy me more time and some cover noise, I continued to creep toward Gaedyen, carefully dragging a good-size branch along the ground behind me. Carrying it would be a clear giveaway, but I hoped if it was low enough, it might be easier to miss in the midst of the mounting argument.

I was almost to him. How could I get his attention without anyone else noticing? Remembering an old nickname of mine for Gaedyen, I smiled and opened my mouth to whisper. "Captain."

His earflaps flicked, but nothing more. Too subtle.

"Hey, Gaedyen." I hissed.

His eyes bulged, and his earflaps stood straight up.

"Shh!" I glanced around, hoping no one noticed his reaction. "I'm going to lift a branch to your mouth, okay? Bite down, and I will draw it out to make a rymakri. Go as slow as you can, and maybe they will be too distracted to notice."

Gaedyen seemed to force himself to relax again, his eyelids drooping and his shoulders loose. But his earflaps flicked minutely with every drag of the limb against the leaf-litter.

Carefully, I lifted the stick, hoping it would blend into the background of trees and leaves behind me. I lifted it to Gaedyen's mouth and tried to place it in between the right teeth. He pushed the branch with his tongue a bit farther to one side, then clamped down on it. Someone screamed.

Prinspur pointed at Gaedyen, eyes wide. "He's making a rymakri! Someone grab that stick from him!"

*Okay, then.* I flung away the invisibility and threw all my weight into yanking the rymakri through Gaedyen's specially shaped molars. Brandishing the sharpened, Gwythienian saliva-strengthened weapon, I leaped in front of Gaedyen.

"Prinspur is lying to you! Dyn Meddy is dead!" I shouted, backing against Gaedyen's bound forefeet and subtly searching for the knot with my other hand.

A murmur spread through the crowd, but accusing eyes remained on me.

"I'm telling you the truth! I saw someone else become Possessor of the rock shortly after his death at the hand of Tukailaan's arkencain. Prinspur is trying to use Dyn Meddy's authority to manipulate you all. Don't let him!"

My fingers slipped on the strange tie that defied my every attempt to get undone.

"Prinspur?" Dylnora asked, standing on her tiptoes to watch him over the rising crowd. "Is this true?"

"Of course not! Don't listen to these foreigners."

Dylnora crossed her arms and glared at Prinspur as the knot finally gave a little.

"Prove it!" she demanded, just as I freed Gaedyen's hands.

He roared and stumbled around to undo his back feet. He seemed weaker than he should have, off-balance. How long had those ties been probably cutting off blood flow to his feet?

"Stop them!" Prinspur shouted.

I winced, fearing the onslaught of little teeth and claws tearing at my skin and overtaking me, just as they had Gaedyen.

No one obeyed his order.

I launched myself onto Gaedyen's back and cut through the ropes around his wings with the rymakri. I nearly fell off as he shook off the torn ropes, but then he righted himself and I found myself sitting at the base of his neck, scowling down at Prinspur.

"Prove to all of us that Dyn Meddy is alive," I said. "If he is, then we will deliver our message to him. If he's not, then we'll deliver the message to you. Come on, Prinspur. Where is Dyn Meddy?"

He stared in shock at Gaedyen and me, and I struggled to hold back my victorious grin.

Prinspur crossed his arms like a petulant child. "I don't have to do anything you demand, human. I don't take orders from your kind *or* Gwythienians."

"So no one in your realm is interested in the whereabouts of your rock, or the approaching Possessorship Ceremony that will allow a chosen dignitary from your realm to become the Possessor of your rock again?"

Dylnora stared at me, then raised her fists at Prinspur. "You'd better do what she says right now, Prinspur! We can't afford to ignore this information. Take us all to Dyn Meddy."

Prinspur glowered between Gaedyen and me and Dylnora. His shoulders slumped in defeat, and I expected him to confess. But instead he waved us after him and stomped off into the trees.

Gaedyen and I glanced at each other, then followed him.

"Just let the Gwythienian go first and avoid getting trampled, you guys. Seriously." Dylnora grumbled, pouncing to the lead but being careful to avoid Gaedyen's feet.

A short walk through giant trees and thick green ferns later, we arrived at the infirmary tree, where Gaedyen in human form and I had spent most of our previous visit here.

Prinspur paused before the door, then turned toward us. "We really shouldn't disturb his rest. He's very ill. He needs to avoid stress."

"Please, Prinspur," Gaedyen rumbled. "Do you expect us to believe that? How could you expect us to trust that you are simply protecting a sick Dyn Meddy when you could so easily be protecting a lie to further your own agenda?"

Prinspur glowered at Gaedyen again, then sighed and pushed open the door.

A fire danced on the wall within, and I remembered when I'd first woken there weeks before. So much had changed since then.

I wondered what Prinspur would bring out. An imposter dressed as Dyn Meddy with convenient facial bandages? Or maybe he'd pretend Dyn Meddy was sleeping and couldn't be disturbed, or that he'd somehow disappeared from the infirmary and we should send a search party after him.

I rolled my eyes. How long was this charade going to take? We still had to get the Liryk for the Rubandors, then fly all the way to Maisius Arborii in South America before we could go home and finish preparing for the ceremony. We *so* did not have time for this.

Prinspur appeared in the doorway again, supporting another figure.

How far would he go to keep this up?

Dappled sunlight, dripping between leaves hundreds of feet above us, reached the other Crivabanian's face, and I gasped. Gaedyen twitched back half a step.

It *was* Dyn Meddy.

And he was very much alive.

# CHAPTER TWENTY-TWO

"Dyn Meddy?" Gaedyen asked, shocked.

My mouth hung open. I couldn't believe it.

Prinspur lowered Dyn Meddy to sit on the top stair leading into the infirmary. He got clumsily down, heaved a big sigh, and faced us.

"Yes, it's me. But let's not waste time on that. How fares Veritamyk? And what is this about our rock and a Possessorship Ceremony? Does this mean all the rocks have been found?"

My hesitation was probably small enough only Gaedyen noticed. I hoped. Where in the world would we find the other two rocks? If we didn't find them before the ceremony, everyone's efforts and travel and hopes would be for nothing. But it would be hypocritical for me to outright lie about the rocks, after how much I'd been hurt by Gaedyen and Mom lying to me. What could I say that would be true and still convince them to come?

I pulled out the Rubandors' rock for proof. "Here is evidence the rocks have been found." Well, at least several rocks had been found. "The rest will be at Odan Terridor for the Possessorship Ceremony."

I glanced at Gaedyen to do the actual inviting, since it was his realm.

He said, "We would like to invite dignitaries and your chosen Possessor to participate and retrieve your rock, restoring balance to your realm along with the others."

Dyn Meddy coughed into his little hand, the black fur there freckled with silver. "That is excellent news, Gaedyen. Thank you for coming all this way to share it with us. Of course we will participate. But I fear my ability to travel is poor at the moment."

"Dyn Meddy," I asked, "how are you still alive? We saw someone else gain Possession of your rock. We've been grieving your death for weeks. I'm so glad to see you're alive, but how can that be?"

He heaved another sigh, blinking slowly. "I do not know, Enzi. I am very sick, perhaps at death's door. Maybe getting close enough to dying releases Possession as well as death. I do not know. But tell me, how is Veri? Why is he not here with you?"

"He wishes he were here," I answered, "and he would be so delighted to see you're still alive, but there was something else he really needed to do. It would mean so much to him if you could come to the ceremony."

"I will consider it, Enzi. I do not know if I can survive the travel, but my days are numbered as it is."

Gaedyen cleared his throat. "We heard you had been struck by an arkencain, Dyn Meddy. But that must not be true, since you are still alive?"

"Unfortunately, that is what happened. I've been able to eke by a little longer because of a special tincture I take every day to stave off the poison. But I still grow weak and approach death. You didn't happen to find that rock of healing, did you?" He coughed into his hand.

"Is it true the rock of healing can heal even an arkencain wound?" I asked, hoping to evade his question.

"I've never seen it myself, but that's what I've heard. It sure would be nice if it were true. I could really use it right now."

"And the stress of being interrogated only speeds the poison's effect, I'm afraid, Dyn Meddy," Prinspur said, glaring at Gaedyen and me.

"Of course we do not want to exhaust him," Gaedyen said, nodding to Prinspur. "Thank you for speaking with us, Dyn Meddy."

Dyn Meddy nodded back. "Of course. Dylnora, Prinspur, see that Gaedyen and Enzi are given a meal and proper lodgings for sleep. They need rest. And after you send them off with the utmost respect tomorrow, you two will prepare to leave for Odan Terridor."

Reeling from the shock of finding Dyn Meddy was, in fact, alive, despite Veri becoming the Possessor of the Crivabanians' rock, Gaedyen and I followed Prinspur and Dylnora away from the infirmary tree.

Brushing a hand over Gaedyen's shoulder, I asked, "I wonder if because Veri had another rock that was ready to be Possessed…maybe the one influenced the other, and that's how he became Possessor even though Dyn Meddy wasn't actually dead?"

"Perhaps, though it seems unlikely." Gaedyen watched the Crivabanians ahead of us closely while he spoke. Was he avoiding my eyes?

"Gaedyen, what's up with you?"

He hesitated for a long while, but I was prepared to wait him out.

"Enzi, I am so sorry I ever doubted your abilities. I see now what an idiot I was. Can you ever forgive me?"

Crossing my arms, I eyed him with mock severity and tried not to let on how terribly relieved I was that he was okay. "I'll think about it."

He gave me a small smile. "Thank you."

I nodded and kept my arms crossed. No reason to let him off too easily.

He tripped over apparently nothing and stumbled.

"Gaedyen! Are you okay?" I reached to steady him, unsure how to help when I was so much smaller.

"Yes, I am all right. Still getting the feeling back after being tied up, I suppose."

I watched him closely for several seconds, paying especially close attention to his back leg with the old injury Prinspur had taken advantage of when we were last here. He didn't appear to be limping on it.

He caught me watching him and rolled his eyes. "I am fine, Enzi. Really."

"I hope so."

We followed our escorts in silence for a while, a gentle breeze whistling through the leaves far above us.

Gaedyen caught his forefoot on something and paused to regain his balance.

"Really, Gaedyen—"

He cut me off with a smile. "You know, I was afraid being rescued would feel demeaning. That I would feel less of a Gwythienian. But actually, what you did was rather...*sexy*. I enjoyed being rescued by you, Enzi." He grinned at me slyly.

I couldn't repress a smile. "Is that so?"

He nodded and planted a kiss on my forehead with his big dragon face. I shivered at his closeness, again worried and a bit curious about his becoming human again.

"Odd to see the two of you so lovey-dovey." Prinspur's haughty voice broke the pleasant moment.

I glowered at him. "You don't get to have an opinion about us. Not one that matters, anyway."

He snickered. "I just meant it's kind of weird to see the offspring of two beings who hated each other and fought to the death being all mushy with each other."

Hearing about our fathers fighting somewhat to the death did dampen the mood a bit. "Were you there? Did you see what happened?"

"I know enough." He smirked.

"Enough for what purpose?" I snapped at him.

"Here we are!" Dylnora trilled as we reached a little table with food spread over it.

Prinspur leaped over the table and sat next to Dylnora, immediately dragging bits of food to his place.

Dylnora rolled her eyes and approached Gaedyen and me. "Please have a seat wherever you are comfortable. Additional platters are being brought as we speak."

"Could we also bother you to provide us with a small vial of that tincture for arkencain strikes? In case we should encounter Meleena again soon?" Gaedyen asked Dylnora.

She nodded. "Of course. I'm sure Dyn Meddy will agree to part with some before you leave."

Glaring at Prinspur and his obnoxious secretiveness, I sat on the ground and eyed the approaching platters, hoping at least one of them contained some Crivabanian blue fruit.

# CHAPTER TWENTY-THREE

After landing somewhere between Sequoia Cadryl and Odan Terridor for the night, I checked on the rocks where they were stored in my pack before curling next to Gaedyen. A vile of black liquid sat next to them, mostly full.

Scrunching my nose at the nasty-looking stuff, I held it toward Gaedyen. "Is this that tincture for arkencain wounds?"

He nodded. "Yes."

"That was a brilliant idea, asking for some of it. I mean, I hope Meleena is dead, I just hope we won't end up needing it." I stuck it back in the bag and lay down next to Gaedyen.

He draped his wing over me and lay his head on the ground. His steady breathing soothed me—I loved listening to him breathe. I loved feeling his skin against my back. I loved knowing he was someone I could trust like no one else.

The possibilities of our fathers being the cause of each other's bad endings weighed on me. But it wasn't *either* of our fault. It was in the past, and it wasn't because of us.

It still pulled tension tight in the air. I'd felt Gaedyen's stiffness all day. He was bothered by it, too.

But tonight, we needed rest. We still had to convince the Adarborians to come to Odan Terridor. Last time we'd seen

Annwyl, who was probably their leader now, Gaedyen had chosen the life of his dying mother, who'd stolen from all the realms, over the life of Aven, the Possessor of their rock and Annwyl's own mother.

Not something Annwyl was likely to forgive easily. Or ever.

"Gaedyen?"

"Hmm?"

"I love you."

"I love you too, Enzi."

Something sounded off in his voice. Maybe he was just tired. Or maybe it was just how tired I was.

It was probably nothing.

When I checked on the rocks the next morning, I could have sworn the little bottle of tincture wasn't as full. I pulled it and the rocks out and felt around the bottom for a spill. If that thing was leaking precious medicine, we needed to find a new container before doing anything else.

But I didn't feel anything in the bottom of the bag. Holding it up to the sun, I didn't see any stains, either. *Hmm.*

I replaced the items and decided it must've been shadows from the fire making me think it was fuller than it was.

We took off toward Maisius Arborii quickly, heading for the Amolryn tree from the Adarborian Liryk. Gaedyen flew more slowly than the urgency of our situation seemed to require. "Can't we go any faster?" I shouted against the wind.

"I am flying my best. I will get us there as quickly as I possibly can."

I frowned. Why did he sound so tired? We'd barely been flying for an hour, and he hardly ever showed weariness. "Are you sure you're okay to fly? You sound like you're coming down with something. Do you feel sick?"

"Just too tired to talk *and* fly at the same time, Enzi."

His voice sounded wheezy. As soon as we reached Maisius Arborii, I'd have Parva, the Adarborian healer who had helped us last time we were there, take a look at him.

Hours later, we passed the Amolryn tree at barely a mosquito's pace. The not-so-welcoming welcoming committee would be on its way soon, but I worried most about Gaedyen's sudden exhaustion. Flying long distances could be tiring, I knew, but he never showed it like this.

Something caught my eyes, and I glanced up to see the many flickering colors of the Adarborians' wings approaching on the horizon.

I tapped Gaedyen's shoulder reassuringly. "Here we go."

Annwyl was, as always, in the lead. And in a bad mood. Her vibrant green wings contrasted beautifully against her dark skin, but her bright eyes gleamed with murder. The purple-feathered curvy line that flowed down the front of her dress flickered, reflecting dazzling bits of sunlight.

She sped past her entourage and hovered in front of Gaedyen's face, brandishing one of their blow-dart weapons. "How dare you two show your faces here after choosing to let my mother—my peoples' leader—die?" Annwyl growled through clenched teeth. Rage rolled off her in waves.

"Your hesitation, Gwythienian, will go down in history as one of the greatest mistakes ever made by one of the realms. Your name will live in infamy for what you did!"

I couldn't see Gaedyen's face, but something felt wrong. He was struggling to keep us aloft and hovering on the same level as Annwyl. His wings shuddered. Surely he wasn't intimidated by Annwyl's words? Sure, she wasn't someone to brush off, but to be so visibly affected was not like him.

"Gaedyen?" I leaned forward, peering at the side of his head. "Gaedyen, look at me."

He stiffly turned his head, his heavy eyes barely meeting mine before rolling back into his head. His wings slowed, then stilled.

And then we were falling.

"Gaedyen!" I scrabbled for a better hold, squeezing my knees around his neck as hard as I could, desperate not to be separated from him.

Gaedyen couldn't die.

His people needed him. All the realms did. We had to finish this. He couldn't die, especially not now.

Had they shot him with a blow dart? Had I missed the pop of breath, the whoosh and stick of a dart flying and finding its mark?

Gaedyen's useless wings rippled like loose sails on a stormy sea, the air of our falling whistling past my ears.

I gripped the sack holding the rocks and the arkencain treatment, hoping none of them had fallen out.

*The arkencain treatment.*

Gaedyen getting slower as our journey progressed…the uncharacteristic weariness…how easily he let himself be captured by the Crivabanians…his strong interest in securing the arkencain antidote…

The arkencain hadn't pierced Gaedyen's skin, but it had brushed across the exposed skin that had been damaged when he skidded over the asphalt. My heart dropped to my toes even faster than we were falling from the sky.

Had Gaedyen been dying for days?

# CHAPTER TWENTY-FOUR

The impact numbed me to the shock and terror before it could sink in.

We had crashed.

But no pain screamed at me.

No broken bones…not even a scratch.

I strained against the distraction of what had happened to Gaedyen to cause this and forced my eyes to focus on our surroundings. What had cushioned our fall?

The trees sank around us, as if we were rising.

I leaned over, peering under Gaedyen. Five Adarborians, including Annwyl, supported Gaedyen on their arms and shoulders from below. They were lifting him, their feathery wings straining under his weight. Had they all grown a bit? Maybe they were all Cadoumai—able to change size like Veri now could because of their rock.

*What is going on?*

I pressed my hands over Gaedyen's neck, feeling for a pulse.

His heart was still beating. Relief washed over me and then washed away my energy. I slumped over him, taking deep breaths, struggling to think of what I should do or say next.

"What did you do to him?" I shouted at Annwyl as we tilted into the leafy front entrance into Maisius Arborii.

Annwyl snarled. "We did nothing, human. He seems—well, it remains to be seen."

Remembering the medicine, I dove into the pouch and pulled out the bottle. I was certain I was right about it being lower than it had been the night before.

"Annwyl."

She glared up at me.

"I think he might have been struck by an arkencain."

"Obviously." She rolled her eyes and shifted slightly so that Gaedyen's limp forearm obscured my line of sight to her face.

Obviously? How could I have missed it before? It must've been a shallow wound to take so long to affect him. Like just the poisoned edge making slight contact with his injured skin.

When we reached the elevated treehouse we'd stayed in before, I stumbled off Gaedyen to help slide him off the Adarborians' backs and onto the floor.

He breathed just a bit too quickly for sleep. Kind of like he was in a nightmare.

I fumbled with the container, wondering whether I should drop a little in his mouth or on his wound. Which of the road rash scratches was the one the arkencain had made contact with?

*Oh, Gaedyen. I'm so sorry I didn't see.* Tears pricked my eyes as the horror began sinking in. *Why didn't you tell me? Why would you keep this a secret?*

Parva fluttered into the treehouse the size of a tiny doll, then promptly grew taller than I was and knelt next to Gaedyen. "What happened? Did one of us shoot him with a dart?"

"No." My voice broke. "I think he was stabbed with an arkencain."

Parva spun to stare wide eyed at me. "But…"

"I know. Not exactly stabbed, but it made contact with his skin where it had already been injured. Can you do anything for him?" I held up the tincture, careful not to reveal I had their missing rock. "Could this help him? We just got it from Dyn Meddy. It's been helping him get by since he was stabbed with the same arkencain."

She took it from me, unstoppered the vial, and sniffed. "This should help. The Crivabanians are good with their healing, I must say." She set it on the wood floor next to her bag, then opened the flap and pulled out a few more things. "Do you know where the arkencain made contact?"

"On his lower back, sort of to the side. You can see the injured area still." I pointed to the thickened, red skin where the scales had been rubbed off. "Somewhere within this area."

She laid her hands gingerly over the wounded area and lightly felt around, starting closer to his tail and moving up toward his head. "Ah. There it is."

Frowning, I peered at the spot she'd indicated. How had I not seen it before?

"See how it's got a straight edge there? That must be from where the arkencain's edge touched his open skin. Can you see the greenish tinge?"

Nodding, I blinked back tears. It was closer to his heart than I'd thought. The skin she indicated was slightly puffier than the rest of the wound. Like it was infected. I winced.

Parva met my gaze. "He should not be exhausting himself with flying right now."

I scrubbed my hands over my eyes. "I know. But we both have to be back in Odan Terridor in a couple of days. His best chance of being healed will be there."

She eyed me. "What do you think will be able to heal him from an arkencain wound in Odan Terridor?"

"I can't tell you."

Her face hardened. "Very well. If you are determined to move him, we must find a way to do it safely. I must warn you, however, that I strongly recommend keeping him here. And how you will convince Annwyl to help, I cannot imagine."

Eyes watering, I watched her apply a salve and bandage to Gaedyen's wound, then pull his lower lip down slightly and drip a few drops of the precious tincture into his mouth.

This just couldn't be real. We were so close. But now, Gaedyen was dying.

Annwyl crossed her arms and glared at me. "I cannot forgive that oaf for choosing his mother, the criminal, over mine, the Possessor. A criminal and absent mother over a Possessor and leader of a realm." She threw her hands in the air and turned away from me.

I needed her to stop hating us. Just a little. Gaedyen and Veri's lives and peace between all the realms depended on it. Geneva's new power might be our only hope for healing Gaedyen, but if Annwyl didn't come to the ceremony, Veri would still be lost.

I had a hunch. There was that name Aven had whispered as she died in my arms. Someone important to her. Asking Anwyll about the name now could soften her toward us or enrage her further. Was it worth the risk?

"Who was Falbane?"

Her eyes tightened. "How do you know that name?

"Aven's last words were 'Falbane, at last,' like she was going home to someone she'd lost a long time ago. Someone important to her. Like maybe…the father of her daughter?"

Annwyl's eyes flicked toward the setting sun. "Falbane was not my father. He was a human and my mother's lover before she accepted Possessorship and became an important public figure. She only spoke of him once. She suffered too many losses because of her Possessorship."

Well, my plan to align Gaedyen's desire to know his mother with my assumption of Annwyl's desire to know her father wouldn't work. *Shoot.*

"I see," I said lamely.

"It should not surprise me that she spoke of Falbane rather than my father. My father was a useful political thinker for my mother, but he was a stern father and a severe husband. I cannot think my mother was happy with him. No passion existed between them, other than to argue over my mother's decisions. He was right sometimes, but so distasteful about it that it did not endear him to either of us."

She gazed at the sky for a long moment. "Eventually—after, well, far too much—I stood up to him and convinced Aven to be rid of him and his poisonous manner. He was banished and, thank goodness, has not had the gall to return."

I stared at her wide eyed. "That was so brave of you. I wish I could do something like that."

She glanced sidelong at me. "You have someone you need to get rid of?"

"Sort of. Someone from the past." Resistance rose against letting this rude, impossible woman into my deepest innermost thoughts and fears. But maybe that would bring her around to our side. "I haven't seen him in years, but I…I have nightmares about what he did to me. They happen less often now, but they're still there. I wonder if standing up to him somehow in real life might make them finally stop. But I can't imagine how that could possibly go well."

Annwyl kept her gaze on the sunset. "I spent many nights wishing to save Aven and myself from my father. When I finally stood up to him, it was not because I finally felt brave enough. It was because I decided I would not take any more of his anger on myself or on my mother. I decided enough was enough and took action."

I considered her words. Did feeling brave really not have anything to do with it?

"How did you finally know enough was enough?"

"It had been enough all along. We should not have endured his rages. It wasn't a matter of how much was enough. It was deciding I would not endure anymore." She looked up sharply, suspicion on her face. "I should not have told you so much."

I persisted, genuinely curious and also hoping that this connection between us might help our case somehow. "Did you ever wish you would've grown up with Falbane instead? Ever wonder if maybe he was your real father?"

"He couldn't have been. I would not be Cadoumai if my father were human."

My thought whirled around Geneva's story of how humans came to be. "Annwyl, correct me if I'm wrong, but it wasn't the first generation of kids with parents of different races that were stuck as humans, right? It was further down the line, if those kids also had kids with people of other races. So technically, it would be possible."

She faced straight ahead, stoic as a Gwythienian. "Highly unlikely."

I thought about the carvings on the quiver Aven had gifted to me. An Adarborian and a Gwythienian. Arrows were not the common weapon among Adarborians—blow darts were.

"What if Falbane were a Gwythienian Shimbator? It would not be impossible…" I mused.

She cut me off. "What do you really want, human?"

I pursed my lips, annoyed at being referred to by *what* I was rather than *who* I was yet again. "Do you want to follow in Aven's footsteps and be the next Possessor?"

She stared at the sky. "I would spend my life striving to live up to her magnificence as a leader and an individual."

I nodded, staring forward, trying not to annoy her with my gaze. "Do you think you're the best choice for your people?"

"Yes."

"Do you have their support?"

"Yes. I believe I do."

"Then you need to know your rock has been found, and a Possessorship Ceremony will be held in Odan Terridor soon. The only way to become the next Possessor is to come to Odan Terridor and—"

"I do not wish to spend any more time in the presence of the Gwythienian who chose to let my mother die and a human who insists on prying into my personal life."

"Annwyl, would you give up the leadership of your people—leadership that is your peoples' wish, I might add, since you have their support—for the sake of a grudge?"

She glared at me, getting a little taller as her eyes shot daggers toward mine.

"Besides, the Cathawyrs are real, and Kymri, their leader, will be present at the Ceremony. She is very knowledgeable about the past. I bet she'd know the truth about Falbane."

She blinked, her expression startled. "Kymri, the Cathawyr leader, will really be there? Are you sure?"

"One hundred percent sure. She will be there, and she will be able to answer your questions."

She shrank back down to her smaller size and crossed her arms. "I dislike you, Enzi. You make too much sense."

# CHAPTER TWENTY-FIVE

Kneeling beside Gaedyen's sleeping form, I waited for his eyes to open. Parva said it should be any time now. I brushed my fingers lightly over the softer scales of his face. We had to get him back to Odan Terridor pronto, and Kymri had better get herself and Geneva and Veri there ASAP. Gaedyen needed the rock of healing. It was the only thing strong enough to fight the arkencain's poison. My heart had shattered at Parva's words. But I had to keep it together to give him the best chance of getting well again.

Of surviving.

But Meleena had survived it. So the rock of healing had to be able to help.

He blinked and squinted at me, then opened one eye. His pupil retracted as it adjusted to the dim light pouring through the trees into our little treehouse room.

My chest ached with relief and pain, watching him wake so slowly. "Hey, Gaedyen. You scared me to death, you know."

He let out a rumbling sigh and shifted his weight stiffly, as if he were sore. "I am sorry, Enzi. I thought I could remain strong long enough to get us here and back to Odan Terridor.

Especially once we got the arkencain tincture from Dyn Meddy. But I am weaker than I thought."

Pausing to swallow back the tears in my voice, I lightly stroked his face again. "The only thing you did wrong was not tell me about it."

"But you did not ask if I was struck with an arkencain, so technically I did not lie."

I frowned. "Good relationships aren't built on *technicalities*, Gaedyen. You should've told me."

His eye closed. "I was planning to tell you once we got back. I thought it would be best not to weigh you down with the information when you could not do anything about it anyway."

Irritation twisted in my gut with my fear for his life, and I opted to change the subject. "I convinced Annwyl to come to Odan Terridor. We will be leaving soon."

His brow rose. "I am highly impressed you managed to convince her to come, despite her opinion of me." Gaedyen stretched his wings toward the moon, then rested them back in place.

"Yeah. She and I had a sort of bonding moment almost. Dare I say, she might not think all humans are garbage now. Maybe."

Gaedyen closed his eyes and smiled. "Well done."

"Thank you." I brushed a hand over his head. "Parva thinks you should rest for another day before leaving for Odan Terridor. And that even when you leave, you will have to be escorted by Cadoumai Adarborians to ensure you're able to make it."

His brow furrowed. "But that puts us far too behind."

"I know. That's why I think…I think I need to go on ahead. With Aven. For the ceremony. For Veri."

My heart squeezed painfully at the thought of leaving him behind. But Veri's life was in danger, too. Why couldn't it just be my life, instead of the lives of two people I couldn't live without?

"I do not like the idea of being separated. But I agree that you and Annwyl should get there as quickly as possible. You are a Possessor and her realm has chosen her to be their next Possessor. The ceremony cannot take place without the two of you there. I am not necessary."

"Yes, you are. You are extremely necessary." My voice went hard with fear. Was he giving up?

He smiled at me, lifting one huge hand to rest against my cheek. "Maybe to you. But not to saving Veri's life. You could do that without me if you needed to. Then you could welcome me home with the good news when I arrive."

He tilted my chin up so I had to meet his eyes. "You can do this. And I will be right behind you. Please. For Veri. Do not delay."

I bowed my head to lean it against his. "Thank you for your support and confidence, Gaedyen."

"You deserve them both. And more."

I closed my eyes and whispered, "I'll see you again soon." A tear drop landed on his skin, darkening the scale it spread over.

He wiped away a tear with one finger and then placed his hand back on the ground. "I will see you again, Enzi. We will be reunited in Odan Terridor and Geneva will heal me and everything will be okay."

Lips quivering, I nodded and did my best to smile.

"I will always love you, Enzi."

I laid my other hand over his and squeezed the three fingers mine could wrap around. "I will always love you, too."

Aven and I and a few other Adarborians left a few hours later. Gaedyen would leave with his accompaniment the next day after he'd had more time to rest.

Saying goodbye to him was the hardest thing I'd ever done. I had to trust we would see each other again soon, and that Geneva would be able to save him as soon as he reached Odan Terridor.

Flying with the Adarborians was much less fun than flying with Gaedyen. They couldn't turn invisible, so they flew so high that it was hard to breathe comfortably. And on top of that, I couldn't ride on one of their backs. I had to be *carried*—by the biggest Adarborian man who flew with us. It made me feel fat, and it made me uncomfortable. Being carried meant someone else touching me. Someone else's arms and hands holding me up.

It pissed me off.

At last, we finally called it a night and drifted lower to make camp. The haze surrounding my brain all day finally faded with the increased oxygen, and the discomfort I felt at being carried increased.

"Annwyl. I need to speak to you. In private," I informed her as soon as we landed. Moonlight shimmered through the trees, dappling the shadows on the ground.

Stoic as ever, Annwyl nodded and followed me a few feet away from the others.

Crossing my arms, I spun to glower at her. "You took action when enough was enough. So am I."

She frowned, waiting for me to continue.

"I don't like…I mean, I'm not comfortable with being…"

I dropped my face into my hands. Why was it still so hard to say?

I tried again. "Annwyl, I get that my inability to fly is an issue that has to be overcome." I paused, unsure how to continue.

"Yes, thank you for stating the obvious. Why is this a matter for private discussion?"

"There's someone I need to stand up to and banish from my life, and I'm trying to build up the confidence for that. But being carried by a man is making it worse."

She blinked, then her eyes softened a bit. I hoped that meant she understood and wouldn't need further explanations.

"I see. Would it help if a woman carried you instead?"

"Yes." I sighed in relief. "Thank you."

She nodded. "The new arrangements will go into effect first thing tomorrow." Eyeing my quiver, empty except for the bow, she tossed me a small folding knife. "Sharpen some sticks about the size of a rymakri. You never know when you might need them. It is good to fight with a partner, but one may not always be available. Get yourself prepared."

"Wait, *you're* carrying me the rest of the way?" I asked Annwyl the next morning.

She just eyed me, as if annoyed. "Yes. Are you ready?"

"Why would you take on the burden of carrying me when you're the leader and could easily pawn me off on anyone else?"

"Because I am the leader. And a leader does not give anyone a job they are not willing to do themselves. A leader must be strongest in order to win their people's trust. And that does not just pertain to winning battles."

I blinked at her.

The other Adarborians took to the sky and hovered above us. The next thing I knew, Annwyl had scooped me up and was flying to meet them.

"We need to have a conversation, Enzi."

*She just called me by my name! What's that about?*

"This person you need to banish—do they live near Odan Terridor?"

I frowned. "Yes…why?"

"You should know. It is not a matter of building up enough confidence. You will never truly feel ready. It is better done and over with than haunting you forever. And if you choose to deal with them today, I will go with you. Support you. If you wish."

I stared at her, shocked. "What? Today? But Veri, Gaedyen—the ceremony! Those things are way more important. We don't have time to deal with him before taking care of all that."

"If he lives near Odan Terridor, that is no excuse. Gaedyen will still be a few days behind us. The rest of my people will fly ahead to let Soroco know what has happened and that you are on your way."

I could barely come up with a response. "But I have no idea what to do."

"Healing is a process. All you have to do is start."

A start. Hmm. This had all started in the barn, where all the nightmares took place. Anytime I found myself in a similar place, I felt like I was back there, paralyzed and terrified.

Could I face the barn? It would be strange and uncomfortable, but less horrific than facing him.

"If I think of a way to start, will you get off my case about it?"

"I am not getting on your case about it, Enzi. I am not forcing you to do anything. I am only warning you that there will never be a right time. You will never feel ready. I am telling you what worked for me and letting you know I will give you my help if you want it."

My head spun with the insanity of seeking him out to… what? Deal with him? Somehow? What would I actually do?

A shiver went through me and I clutched my bow and quiver tighter. Taking a slow breath, I closed my eyes and imagined how dealing with this now might make being around Gaedyen in human form easier. Since he *would* be surviving and he *would* be going through with his ridiculous plan to confine himself to his human form for the rest of eternity, maybe this wasn't such an outlandish idea after all.

Shoving down the repulsion, I opened my eyes. "All right. I know where we can start."

# CHAPTER TWENTY-SIX

There it was. The crumbling old barn I'd run into almost eight years ago when I'd heard the barn cat had a new litter of kittens, only to find something much worse inside.

"That's it." I gestured toward the wilting gray structure, and Annwyl's wings slowed slightly as she lowered us toward it.

The moon glowed brightly above us, casting a dark shadow from the far side of the barn. Annwyl set me down in that deepest cover of darkness and shrank to the size of a hummingbird. She hovered over my shoulder, glancing around for danger.

I stepped toward the barn and reached for the door.

Annwyl lightly touched my arm. "You can do this, Enzi."

I gave her a small smile. "Thanks, Annwyl. I don't feel ready, but like you said, I don't think I'll ever find the right time. So I want facing it to be over. I want to prove to myself I can do it."

She nodded grimly.

I pushed on the collapsing door and stepped inside. Moonlight glowed in elongated strips on the floor wherever planks from the crumbling walls were missing.

Like the sun beams that day.

No dust moats floated around this time. Now nothing stirred up the dust on the floor.

A flash of memory zipped through my mind.

"This place, what happened here, it doesn't define me," I said to the moonbeams. "I am more than that. I'm a fighter. A rymakri thrower. A girl who flies with dragons. And a darn good cook."

The blood and knife were gone, as was any evidence of the dead cat and kittens. Of course it all was by now.

"I'm a lover of music. The daughter of Mac and Lisa Montgomery, neither of whom were actually crazy after all. A friend of Veritamyk. A girl with a dragon for a boyfriend. A girl who refuses to be too afraid to let someone good love her."

Tears slid down my cheeks as I spoke these words and realized I actually believed every single one of them.

"I am no longer Enzi of the ruined life, or Enzi of regrets. I'm Enzi of dragons and flying and songs and true friends."

It felt a little silly speaking out loud to the empty building, and it was embarrassing that Annwyl was hearing it all. But it was all true and it was kind of nice not to be alone.

I breathed in the air of that place one last time, then turned my back on it and walked out into the summer night breeze.

Annwyl grew back to her normal size, still remaining in the shadows. "How do you feel?"

"I'm not sure. I feel…like I needed to say those things. More for myself than anything else. And I think it was the right thing to do, coming to tell this place it has no hold over me anymore. I guess I feel good, but maybe it will take some time to get used to."

Nodding, Annwyl surveyed the stars. "Are you ready to carry on to Odan Terridor?"

Facing her, I nodded. "Yes."

She scooped me up, and her wings carried us upward, leaving the barn behind. There was Jillian's house, her gigantic mansion, amidst the trees ahead. It looked like we would fly over it as we made our way to Odan Terridor.

So I watched as the glint of the blue-tinged windows grew from a tiny white speck to something larger. One window was open, and there was movement inside—maybe Jillian trying on clothes from a recent shopping trip? Shadows shivered over the floor too, some of the shapes probably belonging to Carlie. As we got closer, so did their shadows. Were they hugging? Dancing to the radio, maybe?

A wave of nausea washed over me as I understood.

The other shadow was Caleb's. How she could ever date him…after everything. Plus, he had to be a horrible boyfriend. *Ugh*. We were nearly to the house, about to pass over, when Jillian pushed Caleb away. He bellowed at her.

I cringed away from his voice. I'd never wanted to hear that again. But they were fighting? He threw her to the ground just as we passed over her window. Was he abusing her like he'd abused me? I rolled out of Annwyl's arms, bringing the bow and my carved rymakri-like projectiles with me.

Landing on the other side of the roof, I hesitated. I didn't owe Jillian anything, but nobody deserved to be treated the way Caleb treated people. I hoped I was wrong. Maybe something different was going on. But as I crept across the shingles, over the peak of the roof, toward her window, I heard enough.

Jillian hissed a scream. "No, Caleb. I'm not in the mood."

"Do I look like I care?" he shouted.

I couldn't let this happen to anyone again. Not if I could help it. I leaped in front of the window, nocking a rymakri and aiming at Caleb's hideous silhouette.

Their shocked faces snapped toward me—Caleb lying over Jillian on the floor, bits of clothing strewn around. Annoyance shadowed Caleb's face. Fear painted Jillian's.

I waited for them to recognize me, but I realized with the moon behind me, I must be too backlit to be recognizable. I stood facing the two people who'd hurt me more than anyone else in the world. Yet—knowing they couldn't actually see me even though I was perfectly visible was somehow amusing.

Did I have the guts to send this arrow at Caleb? And where would I aim? I still wasn't that great a shot, but Caleb was less than fifteen feet away from me, so there was a good chance I would hit my mark.

"What do you want? Can't you see I'm a little busy?" Caleb rolled off Jillian, revealing more of himself than I cared to ever see. Jillian scrambled away, but Caleb stepped on her stomach to stop her escape. It disgusted me, the way he treated her. Maybe she deserved some vengeance for how she'd treated me, but not this. Nothing like this.

I could stop it. Should I shoot to kill? Probably no one could ever link his murder to me. I barely lived in the real world anymore anyway. Mom hadn't seen the bow or the rymakri, though my DNA would be on it…

*Too bad this isn't a real rymakri that would disintegrate.*

Caleb moved faster than I could see and sent an object from Jillian's dresser at my face. I dodged it and wondered why it never made a clattering sound against the roof. I raised my bow.

Caleb frowned at me and stepped closer, keeping his other foot on Julian. "Why are you here? Who are you?"

What could I say? Should I tell the truth? What would he do? Well, the truth wasn't just what he'd done to me anymore. There was a lot more to my truth now. I would tell him all of it, then.

"I am someone who isn't going to let you get away with this again." Clarity on where to aim hit me with such certainty, I didn't even question it. I wouldn't end his life. I would make it a miserable life for him. One he couldn't use the way he had up to this point. "And you're the piece of shit boy who's done treating girls this way." I let the arrow fly.

Caleb screamed, his hands flying to the rymakri now protruding from his crotch.

He fell off Jillian and into her dresser. Jillian scampered back on all fours, cowering against the wall. Footsteps finally came from somewhere in the house. Good. Her parents, hopefully. They'd deal with this.

I turned to leave and the moon hit my face as I glanced back at Jillian. I didn't want to leave someone alone like I'd been after what happened to me. But I'd done what I could. It was time to go.

Her eyes met mine as I slid out the window. I looked for Annwyl and saw her holding the thing Caleb had tried to chuck in my face. Something heavy. She leaned on the other side of the window casually, holding up the object like it didn't weigh anything.

Eyes on me with a quirky grin, she pitched it back through the window and pushed away from the roof. A crack and a groan followed, and I knew she'd hit Caleb squarely on the head.

I chuckled, then we jumped off the roof and flew toward my house.

# CHAPTER TWENTY-SEVEN

We reached Odan Terridor at the same time as the Crivabanian delegation. Annwyl set me on my feet and then launched into a political discussion with one of the other Adarborians. Still shocked and a little giddy over what I'd done, I turned away from the politics to see the Crivabanians arriving.

Dyn Meddy sat on a sort of gurney supported at each corner by another Crivabanian. He was sitting up, at least, but he looked even skinnier than he'd been a few days before.

He wheezed. "Enzi. It's good to see you again."

"Thank you for coming, Dyn Meddy. I hope the journey wasn't terribly rough on you."

The Crivabanians carrying his chair set him down and followed Prinspur and Dylnora farther into Odan Terridor.

"The truth is"—he leaned toward me, whispering—"I'm hoping to see Veri. How is he?"

I explained about Veri becoming a double and then triple Possessor, and how he was with Geneva, who Possessed the rock of healing, and that Kymri the Cathawyr would be coming soon.

"He's been mourning you ever since he became the Possessor of your rock and assumed you'd died. He'll be so happy to see you."

Dyn Meddy frowned. "Perhaps I shouldn't have come."

"What?" My eyebrows rose with my voice. "Why would you say that? He'll be so happy to see you. He's missed you so much."

"But he will only have a short time with me before the arkencain poison finishes me off. He'll have to go through all that misery again. He takes losses awfully hard, you know. His older sister died when she was about his age now. He'd idolized her and depended on her, and it broke him. I think that's what gave him the desire to become a healer. The trouble with that is, no matter how brilliant of a healer you are, you still can't save everyone."

I frowned. "I hadn't thought of Veri having to go through losing you all over again. Poor guy."

Dyn Meddy pulled a vial of dark liquid from somewhere and took a small swig.

My stomach sank further. Arkencain antidote. And Gaedyen, who wasn't here yet. "Um, Dyn Meddy? Do you have more of that tincture?"

"Yes, we do. I brought extra in case anyone needed it. These are terribly dangerous times."

I sighed, scrubbing a hand over my face. "Yeah. Gaedyen will need it."

His eyes went wide. "No! Tell me he wasn't struck."

I nodded, blinking tears from my eyes. "Since Geneva is the Possessor of the rock of healing, we're hoping she may be able to heal him—and maybe you, too—but we could use more of your tincture until then."

He closed his eyes and nodded slowly. "You'll have access my entire supply."

I gave him a weak smile. "Thank you. Now, please, let me show you to your quarters."

It was finally time for the Possessorship Ceremony. Crowds were already beginning to head toward the stage, and nerves were fluttering in my belly. Gaedyen finally arriving an hour ago helped a lot, but now it was time to see if all our plans would work. And Kymri, Veri, and Geneva had still not arrived.

Gaedyen took a deep breath and looked down at me. "Ready?"

He always used to say that when we were about to fly. He loved flying so much. Would he ever be healthy enough to fly again?

"Ready" was all I could say.

I walked next to Gaedyen through the rows of Gwythienians, Rubandors, Adarborians, and Crivabanians and onto the stage. The Crivabanian future Possessor, Dylnora, sat on the first pedestal. Next to her sat Annwyl, followed by Nurshiel and his obnoxious smirk. On the other side, Gwelendel, the Rubandor future Possessor, sat in the pool of clear-bluish water.

The future Possessors would be displeased if Veri, the Possessor of three of their rocks, didn't show. They would also be less than thrilled to discover we still didn't have the Rubandors' rock or the Gwythienians' rock. We were counting on Kymri's plan to get them herself. Had she been able to?

If that didn't work, tensions would surpass anything even Gaedyen could manage.

I followed Gaedyen's gaze over the crowd. All these people who disliked him and mistrusted him based on things that had happened outside of his control when he was a hatchling, people for whom he'd done so much—they all frowned like he was inconveniencing them with his presence.

He'd once told me he wished he could see a Possessorship Ceremony. To see members of every realm gathered in peace, laughing together, not suspecting each other. They were together and peaceful, for the moment, but certainly not looking happy about it. Gaedyen was finally getting to see it, but it wasn't what he'd wished it would be.

A few decades ago, Aven, Gwaltmar, Dyn Meddy, and Padraig were standing up there, awaiting their destiny. What would they think of the people chosen now?

But where in the world was Veri? Kymri said he would arrive safely here just in time. Was there a problem? What if, in spite of her and Geneva's help, he wasn't healthy enough to travel?

I bit my lip, looking at my toes to avoid the questioning eyes of the crowd. A shocked intake of breath came from the back of the room, and I glanced up in time to see not only Veri, but also a practically glowing Kymri accompanied by five regal Cathawyr and a very calm Geneva.

Gasps rippled through the crowd. Several seconds went by before anyone could take their eyes off Kymri long enough to notice Geneva. But then someone did.

"Betrayer of the realms! Curse you!"

Geneva's eyes flickered toward the male Gwythienian who spoke, and Gaedyen took an automatic—though wobbly—step forward.

"Wait." The clear, ringing tone of Kymri's voice echoed though the cavern. All eyes went to her. "There are parts of your story you do not know, people of the four realms. You would do well to hear me out before taking actions you may regret."

Everyone fell silent.

Kymri began walking down the center aisle, followed by Geneva and Veri, then the other Cathawyr.

Kymri's eyes sparked at the uproar. Baring her teeth, she let out a deep, rumbling growl that echoed off the cavern and shushed the crowd. "Ferrox and Geneva lost their lives because they attempted to save the realms, not to take the rocks for themselves!"

She glowered at the crowd for a long moment. "They risked their lives and lost so much to save Padraig and the lives of yourselves and your loved ones."

Her pale fur stood out against the dark stone of the stage as she paced. "You would have been right to fear Tukailaan's rage and trickery many years ago. It was ever in his heart to rule, and he spent decades scheming how to do it. Seventeen years ago, he connived a false plan to be overheard by his nephew, Ferrox, and Ferrox's Committed, Geneva. He'd learned where the rocks were kept, and he let slip he was going to steal them and start the Possessor assassinations with Padraig. Ferrox and Geneva knew that Tukailaan would abstain from murdering the current Possessors if he did not have the rocks in hand, because he would not know who would become Possessor next. So they went to the hiding place and stole the rocks to protect Padraig and the others."

Gaedyen and I watched the crowd murmuring as they regarded Kymri. Would they believe the truth now that they were hearing it from her? That Ferrox and Geneva had only been trying to sabotage Tukailaan's ruse?

"But Tukailaan and his son, Bricriu, were awaiting their retreat. Bricriu attacked the first to emerge, thinking it would be Ferrox, whom he hated for winning the heart of his beloved. When he realized he had attacked Geneva, he was horrified and carried her off to heal her. Ferrox had the rocks, and when Geneva called to him that she was all right and to fly on to protect them, he did, though he didn't want to. She insisted."

Geneva's eyes shone as she kept her gaze on Kymri.

"But Tukailaan went after him. Struggling through exhaustion, after days of fighting and fleeing, Ferrox dropped one rock. Then two more when Tukailaan attacked him again. Then the last one when Tukailaan ripped him from the sky. They continued to fight, accidentally bringing a human," she gestured toward me, "this human girl's father, into the mix. The rock found its way to him and thus to her."

That's the part the Crivabanians witnessed. Tukailaan and Ferrox fighting over the rock my dad accidentally picked up.

"Ferrox and Geneva are two of your greatest heroes, and their memory and their son have been greatly mistreated all these years. No one, other than Padraig, has ever sacrificed so much for all four realms as the three of them."

# CHAPTER TWENTY-EIGHT

*I* met Gaedyen's astonished gaze as murmurs broke out among the crowd.

Kymri continued in her calm voice. "Tell me, is the son of the heroes of the realms not the one you want Keeping the rocks that hold your power safe from now on? Is the Gwythienian who dared take a chance and risk his life flying to each of your realms to find out what he could for you not the person you want as your leader? Is the Gwythienian willing to give up his wings for the one he loves, give up his homeland for you all, without explaining how in the wrong you've always been, not the one you want Possessing your rock?"

Several pairs of Gwythienian and Adarborian wings rose into the air as they chanted "Gaedyen! Gaedyen!" Crivabanians leaped into the air and pumped their fists, Rubandors splashed their tails in the water. "Gaedyen! Gaedyen!"

Gaedyen turned wide eyes on me, his expression a whirl of emotions: relief, fear, appreciation, shock…

He turned to Nurshiel and looked even more surprised. I followed his gaze. Nurshiel was folding his wings after landing in front of the stage, his place with the other future Possessors vacated. His eyes were on Gaedyen, and though his face betrayed no emotion, he jerked his head toward the podium he'd just left. "You belong there." Nurshiel nodded once before striding into the crowd.

Gaedyen glanced back at the crowd, then at me.

"It's your choice, Gaedyen." I grinned at him, pressing a hand to his shoulder. "But for what it's worth, there's no one I would rather surrender my Possession to."

This way everyone would be even more invested in him getting medical care for the arkencain wound as soon as possible.

He glanced at me once more, completely dumfounded.

I laughed. "Gaedyen, look at those people. They are your people, and they do want you. You dreamed of a day when you would see this. Well, it looks like today is finally that day." I beamed at him as he swung his gaze to the open Gwythienian pedestal.

Shouts of his name rose up again. With a final nervous glance at me, he stepped into his new place.

I stooped to pick up Veri and carried him to his place before the pedestals. He was so light. I could almost see his skeleton through his fur, and darker circles hung under his eyes. I was ready for that part of the journey to be over. The sooner he gave up his triple Possession, the sooner he could start healing and get back to normal.

He smiled at me. "Let's do this." He pulled all four rocks from his pouch and placed the purple one in my hand.

We reached up together, facing the pedestals. I held my rock, and Gaedyen enclosed my hand and the rock in his. Curled in Veri's tail was the Rubandors' rock. His tail stretched down toward Gwelendel, and she prepared to take it from him.

Veri held the Adarborian rock up toward Annwyl with his one hand and the Crivabanian rock toward Dylnora with his other. For one instant, each of the realms was connected.

It was beautiful.

"Possessors"—Kymri's clear voice rang out over the crowd—"release your rocks into the hands of those who are to take Possession."

We all obeyed, and Gaedyen smiled gratefully at me. He knew how much I wanted to keep it, though he was the first person I'd be willing to give it to. I'd expected to feel something whoosh out of me, to feel the loss of the power the rock gave me. But I didn't feel anything change. It had come quietly, and it left quietly. I took a deep breath, trying not to think of how much I would miss it.

The new Possessors admired their rocks and grinned in awe at each other. Gaedyen smiled at me.

"Well, now they've got all the power. How do you feel about giving it up, Veri?" I glanced down at him.

He was slumped on his stool.

My vision tunneled as my heart dropped, it's frantic beat thudding in my ears.

"Veri!" Scooping him up, I looked to see if he were breathing. He was, but just barely. "Kymri!" I shrieked. "Something's wrong with Veri!"

Her sapphire eyes flashed with concern. "Bring him here."

I cradled his limp body and raced down the stage to where Kymri and Geneva sat. "Veri's dying! Heal him!"

Geneva placed both her Gwythienian hands over Veri's body and closed her eyes, concentrating hard.

Nothing was happening. I wanted to shout my frustration, but I tried to keep it together and trust she was doing all she could. Interrupting wouldn't help Veri.

I stared at Veri's barely moving chest.

Geneva barely breathed in front of me, her hands trembling. A tear splashed over her fingers and seeped between them.

A gasp came from his dry lips, and air rushed back into him. He breathed more deeply, sat up, and rubbed his eyes. Peering at us as if we were coming back into focus, he gazed around the room. "The rocks…they're all gone. The abilities aren't there anymore. I feel empty without them."

Kymri blinked at him. "It will take time to adjust, Veritamyk, but you will not feel so empty soon."

"What a pity you started without me," a chilling voice rang from the entryway.

We all turned toward the entrance, and a collective gasp rippled through the crowd. A Gwythienian stood there, grinning darkly.

"Meleena?" Geneva asked, her voice an octave higher than usual. "You're still alive?"

"It is a relief to find all three rocks stolen from me in one place." She grinned menacingly at Geneva. "It is intriguing how close the little Crivabanian got. But he missed one of the details." She stepped forward and I gasped at the sight of her nub tail. She'd cut off half of it—the part I had gotten the arkencain into. That was how she survived. Removing the damaged part before the poison could travel through her blood to the rest of her body. Should I have cut off some of Gaedyen's skin? Would that have helped him? Was it too late now?

Gaedyen and I glanced at each other, unsure of what she meant about Veri missing a detail. A detail about what?

Meleena sauntered toward the stage, apparently enjoying the attention. She flaunted the arkencain in one hand, and everyone shuffled back. Her grin widened, and she swaggered even closer.

Kymri's whiskers twitched, like she smelled something bad but was trying to control her face.

"You see," Meleena continued, "the secret is you have to take Possession of all of them at once. If you take only a few at a time, the strain becomes more than your body can handle, especially a body as small as yours, little creature. Once you have taken Possession, it cannot be undone except by death. It was tricky for you, Crivabanian, to give up Possession of three. I am surprised you managed to survive it. Too bad your survival will be so short lived."

She lunged at Veri, brandishing the arkencain.

# CHAPTER TWENTY-NINE

"*I* don't think so!" I nocked one of my carved rymakri as Gaedyen launched himself in front of Veri, and Kymri leaped toward Meleena, flames in her sapphire eyes.

Meleena roared and scraped her claws over Kymri's face before shoving her headfirst into the ground. With her other hand, she drove the arkencain toward Veri and Gaedyen.

I let my rymakri fly and nocked another as a sickening wet sound squelched from Gaedyen's chest.

"Gaedyen!" I shrieked. He'd already survived an arkencain wound longer than he should have. His body couldn't take another!

He grunted and fell, Veri scrambling and struggling to get out of the way without his ability to change size or increase strength. Veri made a high-pitched yelp as Gaedyen's shoulder landed on his foot, pinning him to the ground.

I pressed down the terror and let a third arrow fly, begging it to strike Meleena anywhere that would count. One stuck out from her back, apparently not deep enough to do any damage. The second appeared to have missed, but the third hit her chest. She roared, and I nearly screamed in triumph and frustration at not being able to check on Gaedyen.

I wanted to call his name, but I didn't want to draw her attention back to him. I caught Veri's eye and nodded harshly at Gaedyen, hoping he'd be able to check on him even while his foot was stuck.

Geneva roared back at Meleena, but louder and even more fiercely. Fire blazed in her eyes as she dove over Gaedyen, Veri, and me and knocked Meleena down, Meleena's stump tail flailing strangely.

A couple Gwythienians emerged from the crowd, running at Meleena with fierce snarls. But she kicked one aside and threw the other back into the crowd.

I took the opportunity to drop next to Gaedyen's head and hiss in a strained whisper, "Gaedyen! Gaedyen, are you okay?"

He didn't respond. The gash in his chest leaked bright red blood all around me, and I struggled to keep down my panic.

"Gaedyen…" I touched his Gwythienian cheek, hoping against hope he would somehow survive. *But it had been an arkencain a second time…*

"He's still breathing." Veri huffed from behind Gaedyen.

"Veri!" I hurried around and heaved gently against Gaedyen's wing shoulder so Veri could wrench his foot free. He backed up, holding his injured foot up gingerly and wincing.

I went back to Gaedyen's face, hoping his eyes would be open.

"Gaedyen?" I touched his cheek again, tears spilling down mine when his eyes remained shut.

Roaring and slashing came from Meleena and Geneva, but it sounded like it was coming from far away. My world was melting into gray around me. Nothing mattered but Gaedyen. And he was dying right before my eyes now.

Kymri might have twitched somewhere behind Gaedyen, but he was all I saw.

"Gaedyen." I sobbed. Then coming to my senses, I shrieked, "Veri! Veri, do something! Even if the arkencain is a…a death sentence, if we stop the bleeding, he could still live a lot longer, right? Where's Dyn Meddy? We need his arkencain tincture!"

Veri tried to push himself to his feet. He balanced on one, barely putting weight on the other, and stumbled back to his hands and knees. "Enzi, we need to distract Meleena so Geneva can heal him. That's his only chance."

"That's not good enough!" I shouted.

"Enzi, none of the plants I need grow here. I'm so weak and my mind is so fuzzy I can't even remember all the ingredients I'd need. I'm so sorry!"

I whirled away from him, trying to focus through my blurry vision.

Meleena was on Geneva; she could make a death blow at any moment. A handful of Crivabanians jumped from head to head in the crowd, coming to our aid. But their delegation was small, and this piece of it was hardly enough to sway the battle in our favor.

I pressed my palm against Gaedyen's skin. "I love you, Gaedyen. Veri, stay with him." I ripped the bow from the ground and tore across the stage toward the battling Gwythienians.

Geneva hissed as Meleena leaned forward, her Gwythienian hands over Geneva's neck.

*Her hands are there…then where's the arkencain?*

I searched frantically for where she may have dropped it.

It gleamed from the ground far on the other side of where they fought.

*Fantastic.*

I zoomed toward them, leaped over Geneva's tail, and bent to retrieve the arkencain.

Something slammed into me, throwing me forward and somersaulting me over the weapon.

*No!*

My vision trembled, but Meleena was stalking toward me, her head bent low and a grin on her face.

"I will never understand a Gwythienian's fascination with a human. What weak, killable creatures you are."

She slapped me with her huge arm, tossing me over the arkencain once more.

I strained toward it, my fingers groping for the poisonous weapon. Careful to grab the correct end, I closed my fingers around it. *Should I throw it to Geneva for her to use on Meleena, or use it myself?*

It was better in anyone else's hands than Meleena's, and she was closing in on me.

"Geneva!" As I bellowed her name, I prepared to throw it, but my sweaty hand slipped.

Meleena flung me down before I could throw it.

"Do you think you are better than me, human? More attractive, more desirable? More dangerous?" Her smile was replaced with menace.

"Hardly!" I snarled. "I don't know why Gaedyen chose me. I'm not a hot choice among my own species, either. But for the record, I would rather be me with all my imperfections than a cold-hearted bitch like you." I strained to think past the pounding in my head to come up with more words to distract her while my fingers strained toward the arkencain.

She tossed her head and tore a Crivabanian off her neck. She pitched the poor thing back into the crowd, then removed another while pacing in a half circle around me, one eye on Geneva.

"Do the two of you think you will ambush me? Do you think you can take me by surprise? Me, Meleena, the chosen committed of the great Tukailaan, who beat even him in the end?" She growled.

"Enzi!" Veri shouted from behind Gaedyen, pointing to the side. I followed his finger and saw Geneva's wide eyes staring at me.

Something moved behind Geneva.

Kymri was back up! She regarded me with her bright eyes, then glanced at the arkencain, then herself, just like Gaedyen had the first time he wanted me to toss him a stick to bite into a rymakri.

I understood.

She leaned forward, her shoulders undulating as she prepared to leap toward us off the platform…

I'd been staring at her too long. Meleena followed my gaze just as Kymri leaped into the air to soar over Geneva.

I threw the arkencain.

Her huge white paws reached for it.

Meleena brandished her wing claws over her head and into Kymri's abdomen—and blood streamed from Kymri's stomach.

# CHAPTER THIRTY

Kymri curled into an awkward shape and hit the ground as the arkencain traced a thin red line over her back.

"No!" I reached toward her, too far away to be any good. "Kymri!"

Meleena shoved Kymri over onto her back. "It was me, you know, cat, who killed your daughter, Caranyla. That was how I got Possession of the rock of healing. You were right all along. Too bad you can do nothing about it now." Her grin opened her mouth wide, displaying sharp teeth and the specially shaped teeth in the back for making rymakri.

Then her jaws closed over Kymri's white neck just as her paw closed over the handle of the arkencain.

"No!" I shouted, stumbling forward, knowing I was too late.

And then Geneva barreled into Meleena, rymakri raised to strike. She howled and plunged the sharp branch toward Meleena's chest.

Meleena rolled out of the way, sliding Kymri onto Geneva's thrust at the last instant.

The rymakri pierced Kymri's chest before Geneva could change course. She roared in shock and horror as Meleena laughed, gained her feet, and lunged at Geneva's throat.

The arkencain went flying from Kymri's weak grip. I dove for it again.

I wrenched it out of the air and stumbled toward the fighting dragons. Were they trampling Kymri beneath them? There wasn't anything I could do for her now.

End Meleena, and Gaedyen might have a chance.

End Meleena, and Geneva could heal him.

End Meleena.

End Meleena.

My thoughts felt as blurry as my teary vision. If only I could still turn invisible! But I'd given that up for Gaedyen to become Possessor. I'd just have to do what I could without the safety of invisibility. It was our only chance.

Hefting the bow in one hand and the arkencain in the other, I ran as fast as my rubbery legs could go.

Using the bow like a baseball bat, I threw all my momentum into an upward strike under Meleena's throat. The bow struck her chin, flinging her head up.

Here was my one chance.

I dove forward, the arkencain in front of me, aiming for her chest. With a wet squelch, it pierced her thick skin and kept going.

Meleena roared and threw herself backward.

I tried to keep hold of the arkencain, but it was suddenly out of my grasp. Where did it go?

Meleena writhed on her back, hissing and spitting all sorts of curses.

I searched for the arkencain, then focused on the blood in case it was covered in it.

Geneva heaved a breath beside me. "It remains in her chest, Enzi. There!"

I stared at Meleena's chest, noticing for the first time how much blood there really was. It wasn't stopping and healing itself. The little Possession she had over the rock of healing wasn't doing the trick anymore. Had the arkencain's poison interfered with her Possession?

With a great, heaving breath, Meleena went still at last.

Geneva and I stared at her, unwilling to believe it was true. Then Kymri heaved a sigh that struck us both into focus.

"Gaedyen!" I shouted as Geneva lifted Kymri in one arm and limped after me on three legs.

I hit the ground on my knees and slid to him. "Veri! Are you okay? How's Gaedyen?"

"Still breathing but getting weaker. Blood loss and poison— there's nothing I can do. Geneva…" Veri's voice trailed off as he stared up at Geneva. Veri sat next to Gaedyen and rested one little black forepaw on Gaedyen's foreleg.

Geneva laid Kymri, still breathing, next to Gaedyen and dropped down beside them, one Gwythienian hand on Kymri and one on Gaedyen.

"Veri, come here and sit next to me. I will help your foot heal."

"Geneva, they're way worse off and need all your focus—" Veri objected.

"Come now!" she commanded in a quiet but firm voice.

Surprise and confusion crossed his face, but he limp-crawled to her and sat next to her. After several minutes, Gaedyen's breaths grew deeper, like he was sleeping instead of…of dying. I glanced at Kymri and noticed the same thing.

"I think it's working!" I whispered, ecstatic.

Veri kept his eyes on Geneva, looking more miserable than he should've if things really were working.

"Gaedyen?" I returned my focus to him, brushing my fingers over his head, hoping desperately for a flicker of his eyelids, a creasing of his brow, anything.

"Enzi?" he whispered.

I nearly jumped to my feet with relief but restrained myself and leaned closer to him instead. "Yes! Gaedyen, I'm here. Geneva's healing you. You and Kymri were hit with an arkencain, but Geneva's healing you, and it's working!"

Gaedyen winced, still not fully opening his eyes. "Veri?"

I glanced at Veri again. Why wasn't he more excited about Gaedyen and Kymri making a full recovery?

"He's fine. He hurt his foot, but he'll be okay. No arkencain." And no need to tell Gaedyen it was his fault Veri's foot was crushed.

A weeping sniffle came from Veri, and we all turned to him.

He leaned against Geneva, whose head rested on the ground, her eyes closed. Veri's little arms were wrapped around Geneva's huge arm, and tears flowed from his closed eyes.

"Veri," I whispered. "Veri, it's all right. Gaedyen and Kymri are coming around. Even their arkencain wounds are healing!"

I beamed at him, but he turned his face away, into Geneva's arm.

I frowned. "Geneva, what's upsetting him…Geneva? Geneva!"

Her chest had stilled, her hands withdrawn from those whose lives she'd just saved to rest in front of Veri. Her eyes closed forever.

Tears welled in my eyes as I faced Gaedyen.

"She…she's dead?" Gaedyen's face hurt to look at.

*She can't be dead! Gaedyen only just met her.* They needed more time. A sob escaped my throat. It was too soon. Much too soon.

Kymri's voice was weak and husky. "I am sorry, Enzi and Gaedyen, for your loss. She wished she could stay longer, but now she is at rest and reunited with Ferrox at last. This was the choice she wanted to make."

I leaned against Gaedyen's quivering form, longing to comfort him, unsure how. Too much had just happened in the space of a few minutes. His tears welled and spilled over, dripping to the dirt floor. He took one deep breath and then another, blinking away the tears.

I laid my hand on his shoulder. "It's okay to cry, Gaedyen. You don't have to be strong all the time."

Kymri's eyes closed, but her mouth opened. "Gaedyen, your Keeper speech."

I glared at her. He was expected to make a speech as the leader, but how could she be worried about that right now? Especially when there had been hardly any help from the crowd just now? "Gaedyen, I'll speak to them for you. I'll think of something."

I turned to approach the stage, but he caught my tiny human hand in his huge Gwythienian one and held tight. I looked back at him. He smiled softly, though a tear rolled down his face.

"Thank you, Enzi. That is most considerate of you, and I greatly appreciate it. But this is something I have to do. Geneva's memory has only begun to heal, and today she is dead. She has done a great deed twice now, and only just been recognized for one. I will see that she is remembered for her actions." He stood and turned to go. "Though I would appreciate your company on stage."

I was so proud of him and so glad to be with him. I followed him to the stage.

"Members of the four realms." His voice boomed over the crowd. Their chattering quieted as they beheld their Keeper. "Geneva, the last hero of the realms, has just passed on to the next life."

A soft rumble of surprise rippled across the audience.

"She died restoring my health so I can serve you to the utmost of my ability. She died minutes after hearing how she and her beloved Ferrox were fleeing to save us, not to destroy us, that night seventeen years ago. She died without hearing a kind word from any of us, thanking her for what she did or apologizing for what we thought she did."

He took in a shuddering breath. "Let us make it up to her as best we can. Let us remember her for her bravery, her self-sacrifice, and her love for others. Let us remember that when she was not able to save us the first time, she succeeded in bringing it about the second time. Let us remember her as the good person she was."

The four realms roared, the three Possessors behind us cheered, and Kymri and her company nodded in our direction.

# CHAPTER THIRTY-ONE

Three days later, after Kymri and the new Possessors finally returned to their own realms, Gaedyen and I made our way out of Odan Terridor for a few minutes alone. As we strolled through the trees now thick with summer foliage, I breathed in the scent of honeysuckle on the air. That was nice. But I was nervous, and I had a feeling he was too.

I eyed his wings, his earflaps, the beautiful deep crimson color of his scales. "Gaedyen, how are you feeling?"

"I feel better. More like myself, now that the poison is gone and the older wounds have also been healed. But I do not know that it was worth the loss."

I laid a hand on his shoulder. "Geneva thought it was. And I would have too. I do. But that wasn't what I meant."

He sat on his haunches and looked down at me. "What did you mean?"

"I mean, how do you feel about this—about permanently changing into a human?"

He breathed in slowly, looking up at the stars. "Comfortable with my decision as far as I am concerned myself, but worried that you are less comfortable with it. Are you sure you will still love me when I am no longer a majestic creature?"

He was trying to lighten the mood. Despite thinking I had gotten over this guilt, it came roaring back at his words. And judging by the way he looked at me now, it showed on my face.

But instead of revisiting that old discussion, I smiled. "Yes, Gaedyen, of course I'll still love you."

He smiled back, and it warmed my heart. My eyes brimmed over with emotion.

"I am ready, Enzi. Are you?"

I nodded, unable to speak. He stared into my eyes for one long moment. Then he closed his and bent in on himself. His wings and tail were sucked into a whirlwind of red and bronze, which quickly turned darker and then materialized into his human form. The guy I had known as Shaun. He grinned, shaking his long hair out of his eyes.

And he was naked. My heart skipped a beat as I beheld his beautiful dark skin. His broad shoulders extended into long arms thick with sculpted muscles. I think my heart must have skipped a couple more beats as I took in the rest of him. *Wow.*

But he was not just Shaun, not the person I'd thought Shaun was. He was still Gaedyen. It was hard to wrap my mind around, but he was. I'd just watched him change into this form from the one I knew so well.

But how could all *this* really be mine?

When my wandering eyes finally roved up to his face again, he was grinning even more.

Heat rushed into my face. I thrust the clothes at him and faced the opposite direction while he dressed.

Soft laughter met my ears along with the sound of rustling fabric as he shrugged on the pants and shirt. I thought I was relieved I'd brought him a change of clothes. But if I was being honest, I was a little annoyed at myself. I secretly wished I hadn't.

And that surprised me. I never thought I would feel attracted to someone that way. But maybe…maybe even that could change.

"Enzi." His breath tickled my ear, and my heart raced at his nearness. I hadn't even heard him approach. "Do you remember the story I told you about my journey to Ofwen Dwir?"

"Yes." My face heated.

"That is how I feel right now." His hands found my waist and rested there ever so slightly, almost hovering right above my T-shirt.

And it felt. So. Good. Not uncomfortable or reminiscent of anything bad from the past. It was so different.

Was that just me, or was he trembling too?

"Is this okay, Enzi?" he whispered into my ear.

In answer I slammed my hands over his and pressed them hard against my waist.

The action surprised me, as much as it probably did him. But I needed him there. I just needed him to hold me *right there*. I had never felt something like that before, but it came over me so powerfully and in such a rush, I just had to.

His breathing was ragged. Why was he so far away? He was right there. Why couldn't I feel him against my back?

Squeezing his hands in place, since I absolutely could not bear for them to move, I stepped back into him and stretched up onto my toes to be as against him as was physically possible.

His breath caught, and he tightened his grip. It was a glorious feeling. For the first time, I truly believed him. I felt in my heart and in my gut how desperately he needed me. How he wanted me. Me, of all people.

But it was impossibly clear in the way he held so tightly to me. So firmly yet so gently.

Why was I not kissing him? What was the fastest way to be kissing him?

I whirled around to face him. Fear showed on his face, fear that he had done something wrong and scared me. But what he had done was so indescribably the opposite of that, it would have taken too long to explain, and we *so* did not have time for that.

My arms encircled his neck and desperately pulled his head to my level.

My lips found his. Soft. Warm. Perfect. Exactly as they should be.

An instant later, his arms wrapped around me and sent thrills all over. I couldn't help the sigh that escaped my lips, and I didn't have time to be embarrassed by it. It made him hold me tighter.

As my blood churned, longing for him with every cell in my body, I was overwhelmed by the rightness of this. This, this was how things were meant to be.

A bit of cool night air chilled my side as one of his arms left me. I broke the kiss to find out what was wrong. It needed to be there, why had he moved it?

Before I could ask, his hand found its way over my hip just barely underneath my T-shirt. His fingers slid slowly over my skin. Chills broke out everywhere as it found my waist and rested there. So warm, so human.

I thought nothing could feel so amazing as his hands on my waist, but that feeling was impossibly outmatched by his hand on my waist without the stupid shirt in the way.

His other hand needed to be on my skin. Curse this shirt. Curse all clothes that kept us apart! Hadn't we been apart enough?

With one hand I gripped his neck and pressed his lips harder on mine. Forcing my other hand underneath his, I pulled the insolent fabric out of the way and pressed his other hand against my skin. His thumb traced over my hip, and I savored it.

One of his hands slid around to my back and pressed me harder against him.

"Gaedyen." I whispered his name, unable to think of anything else but him. "Gaedyen."

"Yes?" He paused, his voice tickling my ear.

"You're wonderful."

He wrapped his arms even more tightly around me. "So are you."

# EPILOGUE

"So…you and this dragon, huh?" Mom raised an eyebrow at me, a smile tugging at the corners of her mouth as she leaned over the kitchen counter, her hands wrapped around a warm mug.

I rolled my eyes, hiding my grin as I sipped steaming coffee from my own mug. Mom's grin grew as I sat the mug on the counter and shifted on my stool. It was weird, talking with her like this. We had joked about boys when I was young, but not for years now. It was nice to have her teasing me like this, even though I pretended to be annoyed. "Yeah. Remember how I told you he is able to turn into a human?"

"But he is currently stuck in his dragon form? I feel a little crazy having this conversation right now, you know."

I laughed. "Yeah, he was then, but not anymore."

Thinking of Geneva's sacrifice to save him sent a cloud of gloom over my happiness. I would miss her. I wished Mom could have met her. I think they would have liked each other, despite their species differences.

"Oh? How did that get fixed?" She brought her coffee mug to her lips and sipped, never taking her teasing, smiling eyes from mine.

I winced. "That's kind of a long story. I think it would be better if I tell you that one sometime in the future."

She rolled her eyes. "Okay, if you say so. I mean, there *is* only so much of the bizarre and other-worldly I can handle. In one day."

Despite her moderate reaction, my refusal made her sad. It hurt her feelings that I didn't confide in her as I once had. But some of this was too much for her, and some of it was just too much for me to relive so soon. I did have one bit of good news for her, though.

"So you sort of got to meet him in dragon form, but would you like to meet him in his human form? Without any impending kidnappings?"

She paused. "You serious?"

"Yep. He's on his way right now. Should be here any minute."

"Ahh!" She practically threw her coffee at the poor countertop and ran around to bury me in a bear hug.

"All right, all right," I laughed, holding my sloshing mug out of the way. "Gotta breathe, here."

She pulled away slightly. "Sorry! I'm just so excited to get to know him. I only spoke about two words to him when we first met. Oh my gosh, I should clean. Can't have my daughter's boyfriend thinking I'm a slob!" With a huge grin, she leaped off me and two steps later was fluffing the cushions in the living room.

"Mom, really, you don't have to do that. He won't care. This will probably be the first time he's ever been in a human house. He won't notice."

She attacked the dirty plates and bowls in the sink next, ignoring me.

"Have they said when they'll let Dad out yet?"

She rolled her eyes. "'A few months.' Whatever that means." She took a deep breath and stared at the soapy plate in her hand. "It will be incredible to have him home again."

"I'm so happy you'll be together again, Mom. Now that I have someone…I'm beginning to understand how rough it would be to be without them. And raising a child on your own, too. I don't think I've ever told you how much I appreciate all you did for me."

Tears welled up in her eyes. "Thanks for that, sweetie."

Searching for a topic to break the awkwardness, I remembered something she'd started to tell me earlier. "Hey, Mom, what were you saying about insurance?"

"Oh! Yes!" She laid the clean plate on a towel on the counter. "Somehow it worked out so I can take a three month leave of absence to stay home with your father while he gets used to things outside the ward." She was practically glowing with excitement.

"That's fantastic news, Mom! Wow. I'm so glad you guys get that time together. Also, while we're on the subject of Dad… what do you think about keeping Gaedyen's real identity a secret from him? Just to be safe?"

Her smile slackened into a look of seriousness. "I think you're right, Enzi. It would be best not to risk…reminding him of all that."

I nodded, taking another sip of coffee and glad we were in agreement on this.

There was a knock at the door. I turned automatically, my heart thrilling. It was him!

I slid off the chair to answer, but Mom beat me to the door. She yanked it open. "Hi, Gaedyen, right?" Her voice trilled with a beaming smile. "It's so nice to see you again! Please come in." She held out a hand and practically latched on to his, dragging him past me into the living room.

"Um, hello?" He smiled at me as she dragged him past. Grinning, I rolled my eyes and followed, taking a seat next to him on the couch.

"Can I get you anything? Coffee?" Mom asked.

"No, thank you, Mrs. Montgomery. I am fine."

Mom shot me a look and flicked a hand toward Gaedyen. "Such manners! Enzi, you snagged a good one."

I laced my fingers through his and smiled at him.

"But really, Gaedyen, you can call me Lisa."

There was a lot of smiling and laughing, and it was all genuine, if a bit awkward when Mom asked him if he planned to marry young. She didn't need to know we were already more than married by his culture's standards. It would hurt her feelings not to have been to the ceremony. But that was okay.

As soon as we were older and it wouldn't be weird for us to get married human style, we would have a nice little ceremony Mom could plan entirely herself, if she wanted.

Two hours later, Gaedyen rose to leave. I stood with him, hugging a still-hyper Mom.

"Oh, but when will you be back again?" her eyes searched mine.

"I don't know for sure, Mom. But it won't be as long as last time."

She smiled, eyes brimming with mixed emotions. "Okay."

I hugged her again, then took Gaedyen's hand and led him out the creaky old front door. Hand in hand, we walked toward the parking lot on our long journey back to the entrance to Odan Terridor, when a tall blonde figure stepped out of a car and interrupted us.

I blinked. It was so strange to see her face here of all places, with Gaedyen by my side and thoughts of Odan Terridor in my head, that it took me a moment to recognize her. "Jillian?"

She rubbed a bandage on her arm, her eyes focused on her shoes. "Um, hi." She looked up at me, wincing a little. "Did…did I see you the other night?"

I hesitated, then said, "Yeah." So she *had* recognized me. What would she think about me knowing what had happened? And that I had been on her roof shooting arrows at her abuser on top of that?

Gaedyen watched me, then Jillian, his hand squeezing mine a bit tighter.

"Yeah. Well, thank you. I only got with him because it was cool to date someone in college, and he'd been popular at school before. But it turned out…he's actually a really horrible person. That wasn't the first…well, maybe you weren't lying about what he did to you." She shoved a tear from under her eye, still avoiding mine. "I guess…I'm sorry for not believing you. And thank you for helping me anyway."

She lifted her eyes to mine for the briefest of moments before she swept around and sank back into the car. Then she sped away without a backward glance.

A strange feeling almost like sisterhood came over me. Maybe that wasn't the right word, but she believed me now. I no longer needed it like I once had, but it was nice. And it turned out she hadn't had the perfect, easy life I'd always thought—she had suffered through some of the same things I had. I didn't hate her anymore.

"What was that all about?" Gaedyen stepped in front of me, searching my eyes. "That was one of the girls who tried to steal the necklace when we first met, was it not? You did not tell me you had seen her recently."

"Oh, sorry, Gaedyen." I finally pulled my eyes from Jillian's retreating form and focused on his concerned gaze. "I actually saved her from Caleb. Annwyl and I—we flew over Jillian's house on the way to Odan Terridor. Caleb was in her room, and…and she didn't want him to be. I, uh, shot him with a rymakri. Between the legs."

Gaedyen's dark eyebrows rose nearly into his hair. He winced. "Oh. Well…good."

I laughed a little hysterically and pulled Gaedyen toward the road. "Yeah. It was." I gave Gaedyen a more detailed retelling of the events, and soon dirt and leaves replaced the potholed road as we entered the woods.

Gaedyen smiled. "I wish I could have seen the bastard's face when the arrow found its mark. Good shot, Enzi. May it plague him forever."

"I guess I didn't really want murder on my hands, even if he did deserve it. But I didn't want him to hurt me or anyone else ever again. Not even Jillian. It seemed the best option."

He chuckled, that deep rumble I loved sounding just the same from his human chest.

"Surprise, surprise!" A shout came from behind us, and I jumped, landing in a crouch and wishing to be able to turn invisible. Gaedyen reached for a tree branch and jumped surprisingly high, no doubt forgetting he couldn't bite it into a rymakri as he'd once been able to.

A shadow rustled through the branches where we'd just been standing. My heart thudded in my ears. Gaedyen's breaths came quick and deep.

Veri's mischievous grin and swoosh of bangs appeared between the leaves. "I have a surprise for you guys! Wait till you hear..." He glanced around. "Gaedyen? I thought you weren't supposed to be able to use your Gwythienian form anymore?" His quirked eyebrow disappeared under his bangs as his words got through my adrenaline-filled brain.

Gwythienian form?

I turned to face Gaedyen, and there he was in all his brilliant red glory—a twenty-foot-long dragon, staring at me with as much shock as I must be showing.

"Gaedyen? How'd you do that?" I asked, mystified.

"How did *you* do *that*?" he countered.

"Do what?"

He gestured toward me, and I looked down. Dirt and leaves filled my vision where my torso, legs, and feet should have been. I dropped my hands to touch my legs, my stomach.

Yes, I was definitely right there. But..."I'm invisible?"

"Yes," they said together.

"But how...Gaedyen, I could've believed becoming Possessor of the Gwythienians' rock could give you the ability to transform again—maybe. But if I'm not the Possessor anymore, why can I turn invisible?"

"I have no idea." Gaedyen stared at his altered limbs. "But the rock has nothing to do with Shimbator abilities. It makes any Gwythienian have the skills of the best Cadoumai, which covers turning invisible and seeing through water into other places, not shifting into another form. Becoming a Possessor should not have affected me in this way."

"Can you change back?" Now that I'd had time to get used to his human form, I was interested in getting it back again, as much as I also admired this form.

He closed his eyes and bent in on himself, and a moment later, he stood before me in human form, naked again.

"Oh, uh…" He glanced at Veri, who covered his eyes with one hand and made a show of parting his fingers and giggling.

"Well, that's a relief." I tramped over to him and searched for bits of probably-ruined clothes. I found enough of his T-shirt for him to tie around his waist and was glad I was invisible so no one could see my face.

"So I can change back and forth at will now?" He grabbed his shoulder and pulled it forward, attempting to see what his mark looked like.

"It looks…the same, really. Slightly more healed, maybe. But mostly the same, with scars running through it from the fall."

"Then how…?"

"I have an idea," Veri said, much more gravely than he usually spoke.

We stared at him, worried by his tone.

"I came to tell you the good news—which did not at all deserve the overreaction you two threw at me, I might add— that Dyn Meddy is healed."

"What? Really?" I asked, shocked and delighted.

"Yes. The arkencain poison is gone from his system."

Gaedyen asked, "Was it that tincture after all? It was stronger than he thought?"

"No, Gaedyen, I think it was your mother," said Veri.

"Huh?" I looked askance at him. "What are you talking about?"

"Just listen and I'll tell you! Enzi, you surrendered Possession to Gaedyen at the ceremony, and Gaedyen, you became

Possessor as far as we knew, even though you were succumbing to an arkencain wound. Right?"

"Yes."

"Yeah."

"Well, you know how I gained Possession from Dyn Meddy after he was struck? I thought it was because he'd died, because that's how Possession transfers. But he hadn't died. The poison was introduced into his system, which without the rock of healing, equaled imminent death."

He looked expectantly at us.

I frowned. "So you're saying because Gaedyen had arkencain poison in him during the ceremony, he didn't actually take Possession of the rock from me. I kept it the whole time?"

"Yes! And you, Gaedyen, and Dyn Meddy are both alive now because Geneva sacrificed herself to save you and Kymri from the poison, and I think when she did, it covered others who'd been poisoned. Meleena might've been saved too, if that rymakri hadn't gone through her heart."

"Okay," said Gaedyen. "But then how am I able to change forms when my mark was ruined beyond repair?"

Veri's signature smirk came over his face.

"Veri! Tell us. What is it?" I begged, turning visible again.

Veri dropped to the ground and stepped toward us. "Maybe Kymri was wrong and your wound wasn't as damaged as we thought." Veri dropped from his branch and hung suspended by his knees like a trapeze artist. "Or maybe Geneva also healed your mark when she healed everyone from the arkencain poison."

He flipped to the ground, landing on his feet, and continued. "Or maybe Geneva passed on Possession of the rock of healing to the last person she touched, and that person was me. And I've been healing your wound every second for the last few days so you could still have your wings and take Enzi flying. And so Enzi could stop feeling guilty for you choosing to be human forever for her. And to get that idiot Nurshiel off your back. And so that we could all go flying again together, which is the most fun I've ever had and not something I'm willing to let you deprive me of."

"Veri!" I knelt in front of him and hugged his little neck.

Gaedyen wrapped his human arms around us for a big group hug, and I couldn't imagine being happier.

"All right!" Veri announced, pushing free of us. "That's enough of that. As the Possessor of the rock of healing, I've got things to do. I'll catch you two later." He backed into the trees, wiggling his eyebrows at us.

I rolled my eyes and pushed myself to my feet. Gaedyen rose and stood behind me, wrapping his arms around my waist and resting his head on my shoulder. "So…you're still Possessor, then."

"I guess so." I grinned, delighted.

"How about a celebratory moonlight flight, since we still get to do those now?"

I beamed at him, and soon, we were flying. Veri was safe and an even better healer now. Dad would be home with Mom soon. Gaedyen loved me back.

And so the human and the dragon lived happily ever after.


# THE END

Connect with Savannah!
@savannahjgoins

Instagram | Goodreads | YouTube | Twitter | Facebook

Visit Savannah's website for writing tips and story updates!
savannahjgoins.com

Did you enjoy this book?
If you have a minute, a review would be greatly appreciated!

# ACKNOWLEDGEMENTS

I wrote the first draft of this book during NaNoWriMo in 2017, but I didn't touch it again until spring of 2020. Revising this book during the Covid nightmare was a challenge. But I'm so grateful for all the blessings that came my way and helped me turn this horrendous first draft into something book-shaped.

Firstly I thank God for infusing my soul with this love of writing and enabling me to find and enjoy so many opportunities to improve my craft. And for the many great failures in my life that seemed insurmountable at the time, but all served to point me down this path I'm now on.

I can't thank the creators of Zoom and Facebook video calling enough for the ability to continue meeting with my local writers group and keep in touch with my fellow writers during the pandemic. I'm thankful for living in a time of technological advancement that allowed me so much access to the joy and comradery and encouragement of my writer friends despite going so long without seeing each other in person.

To my husband Ben, thank you for supporting me through a second career that often leaves me falling asleep standing up. I'm so grateful to get to do life with you, and your support of my writerly dreams means the world to me!

To Missy, thank you for reading this book through more drafts than any other person besides myself. Your enthusiasm for even my roughest drafts means more than I can ever say, and I am so grateful to have your unconditional support. And thank you to Bill, Jenny, Fronzy, and Austin for cheering me on!

To my parents, Gregg and Jenny Glass, thank you for your support and encouragement along the way. And to my sister and brother-in-law Tori and Ashish Cherian, thank you guys for supporting me from my very first book signing and through many since! Thank you to my grandparents, Grams and Pop, and Noni and Papa Glass, for your ceaseless declaration of my awesomeness to all your friends and possibly some random strangers. Thank you for your unconditional love.

To my critique partners Stephanie Mirro, Renee Dugan, Alicia Grumley, Heather VenKat, and Holly Hanson, thank you girls for reading this book when it was in terrible shape and I had no idea what to do with it. I couldn't have gotten this far without your thoughtful suggestions and soul-lifting encouragements.

To my Writer's Business Mastermind, Brittany Wang, Holly Hanson, and Alicia Grumley, I'm so glad that our Mastermind has been around for over two years now, and I treasure your professional feedback on business pursuits and your casual check-ins and cheering sessions. It is an honor to walk this journey alongside you three!

To the Dream Big Writers Group, I am so blessed to get to see your faces every week. Sometimes several times a week since we also get to meet on zoom in between writing sessions now. Cam Steiman, Alicia Grumley, Cy Wyss, Tina Chase, Lauren Bronstein, Chris Beckman, Ruth Williams, Janeen Jarrell, Karen Beidelman, Abby Normal and many more, thank you for welcoming me to the group back in 2017. You have become some of my most dearly treasured friends. And to think I almost didn't go to that first meeting! You have all had a tremendous impact on my life, and I couldn't be more grateful for your unconditional love and support through the good times and bad. I am so pumped to get to meet in person again!

To Michele Harper, one of the very first writers I met way back in the beginning. If not for your generous welcome to the

Heartland Christian Writers Group all those years ago, I don't know if I would have ever found the audacity to believe I could become a writer. Thank you, thank you, thank you for your mentorship, friendship, and the many adventures we've shared and are still scheming up for the future!

To the Snack Pack, Alicia Grumley, Annie Sullivan, Michele Harper, Kristen Ungerect, Mackenzie Lauka, and Rachelle Wood, thank you for being such a fun and uplifting group of fellow writers to hang out with!

To my many new writer friends since The Crivabanian was published, Tabatha Reid, Sarah Babbs, Lisa Hopwood, Abbi Burns-Cappel, Jeff Hackett, Amber Marie, Kaitlynn McShea, Lillian Harshaw, and Stephanie Cain, I'm so glad to have met you through local writer events and can't wait to see the exciting writerly things you do next.

To my many fellow local authors, Allison Bliss, Mike DeCamp, Victor Prince, Jenny Medenwald, Sarah J. Schmitt, Laura VanArendonk-Bough, Teresa Beasley, Michelle Gambs, Julie Johnson, Steve Craig, Russ Eberhart, and Kaylin R. Boyd, I'm so grateful for the author events we've gotten to participate in together in the past, and I hope for many more in the future!

To my wonderful Street Team, Heather Sokol, Alicia Grumley, Annie Sullivan, MaryAlice Peoples, Holly Hanson, Kahla Leighton, Jill Hackman, Brittany Wang, Kimberly Paterson, Heather VenKat, Jenna Streety, Teresa Beasley, Missy Goins, Stephanie Mirro, Kristin Ungerecht, Dominique Nieves, Katie Nellis, Jessi Elliot, Jessica Bullard, Stephanie Marie, and Morgan Cain, who have encouraged me along the way and gotten excited about my books with me, thank you all so much!

To my incredible day job team, particularly Jennifer Sickles, Carynne Carter, Beth Skiles, Suz Hewitt, Nancy Annes, Dawn Hobson, Marji Yeoman, Samantha King, Nancy Johnston, and Lori Calvert, thank you all for tolerating my nerdiness and for squealing with me over the exciting book news. It's no secret

I'm working towards writing fulltime, but until then, there's no team I'd rather be a part of.

To my first and most priceless editor, Nadine Brandes, thank you so much for combing through a hopelessly deplorable draft of The Gwythienian. You taught me more than any other individual about writing, and it's only because of you that The Gwythienian wasn't a horrible embarrassment. You taught me about info dumping and repetitive writing and pointed out my bad writing habits with the sincerest kindness. You guided toward innumerable improvements. If it wasn't for your ceaseless encouragements in between all the red marks, I might not have made it this far.

To my editing and proofreading team, Michele Harper and Kathleen Collyer, thank you for your invaluable efforts in cleaning this mess up and making it shine.

To my chapter heading illustrator, Rob Costacorta, thank you for making a breathtakingly beautiful illustration of the Cathawyr Mountains! I'm so glad to have found you and been blessed with your incredible artwork throughout the entire series.

To my formatter Jeffrey Collyer, thank you for doing a lovely job refining and formatting this book on a crunch schedule.

To my character artist and the designer of all three of the new series covers, Ingrid Nordli, thank you for making my characters real and for creating the most incredible covers I've ever seen. I can't wait to work on the next series with you!

To the designer of the silhouette style cover for The Cathawyr, thank you for matching the style of the original series so that this one could match. It was a pleasure to work with you!

To all my readers, thank you for taking the time to go on this adventure with me. Whatever that thing is that you don't think you can do, go try. And as long as it brings you joy, keep trying though the failures. It's been a bumpy ride for me, full of mistakes and lessons learned. But I have no regrets over my many failures and embarrassments because through each of them I've learned and grown and met the most amazing people and even managed a few successes along the way. Whatever it is that you want to do, I believe you can do it. Don't let your next chance go by. Take action to make your dreams come true. You got this.

# VOCABULARY

Adarborian (Ah-dar-bore-E-an)—a humanoid creature with hummingbird-like wings capable of dramatically growing and shrinking.

Amolryn (Am-ole-wren)—a great South American tree that produces a variety of colored flowers, and according to legend birthed the first Adarborians from its blossoms.

Annwyl (Ann-will)—an Adarborian leader, daughter of the great Possessor, Aven.

Arkencain (Ark-in-cane)—a dangerous magical weapon created by the Arkensilvers. Capable of slowly poisoning its target to death over several days.

Arkensilver (Ark-in-silver)—an extinct race of magical creatures capable of intensely weaponized magic.

Arunca Rymakri (Are-un-kah Rim-ak-ree)—the art of knife- and spear-throwing, according to the Gwythienians' traditions.

Aven (A-vin)—an Adarborian, Possessor of their rock, mother of Annwyl.

Bricriu (Brick-ree-oo)—a rogue Gwythienian, whose identity and intentions are currently unknown.

Cadoumai (Cad-oo-my)—any member of one of the four realms whose gift is very strong.

Cathawyr (Cath-ah-we're)—the fabled race of great cats about whom the realms have many legends.

Crivabanian (Cree-va-bane-E-an)—a creature like a large flying squirrel with hidden depths of physical strength.

Coranyla (Cora-ny-lah)—a Cathawyr and the creator of the rock of healing.

Divinado Legendelor (Dee-vin-a-dough Leg-an-dell-or)—a special night of storytelling among the Crivabanians.

Ferrox (Fare-ox)—a Gwythienian, father of Gaedyen and son of the great Padraig, husband of Geneva. One of the Betrayers of the Realms.

Gaedyen (Gay-dee-yen)—a Gwythienian, son of the Betrayers of the Realms, Ferrox and Geneva, and grandson of the Keeper, Padraig.

Geneva (Gin-E-va)—a Gwythienian, mother of Gaedyen, wife of Ferrox. One of the Betrayers of the Realms.

Gwaltmar (G-walt-mar)—a Rubandor, the Possessor of their rock, friend of Padraig.

Gwythienian (G-why-thin-E-an)—a dragon-like creature with the ability to see through water into other places and to turn invisible.

Kimry (Kim-ree)—The leader of the Cathawyr race and the creator of the orange rock. The only Cathawyr to have lost her natural color.

Liryk (Lie-rick)—the directions to one other realm given in the form of a poem from one realm to another many years ago.

Malwoden (Mal-woe-den)—giant snails, found only in Odan Terridor. The favorite food of the Gwythienians.

Masius Arborii (Maze-E-us Are-bore-E)—one of the four realms, home of the Adarborians, located in the jungles of South America.

Ofwen Dwir (Oaf-when D-we're)—one of the four realms, home of the Rubandors, located under water off the coast of California.

Rubandor (Roo-band-or)—a creature like a giant axolotl who can sense their surroundings with sonar-like abilities.

Odan Terridor (O-dan Tare-i-door)—one of the four realms, home of the Gwythienians, located under Tennessee and the surrounding states.

Padraig (Pah-j-rig)—a Gwythienian, the Possessor of their rock and the Keeper of all the rocks, father of Ferrox and grandfather of Gaedyen.

Parva (Par-vah)—an Adarborian healer.

Sequoia Cadryl (Sec-oi-ya Ca-drill)—one of the four realms, home of the Crivabanians, located within the redwoods of California.

Soroca (Sore-oh-kah)—Gaedyen's aunt on Geneva's side.

Tukailaan (Too-ky-lahn)—a Gwythienian, brother of Padraig and one who wishes to steal his place as Possessor and Keeper and to gain Possession of all four rocks.

Rymakri (Rim-ak-ree)—the wooden knives and spears made by the Gwythienians. They do not last long and must be used immediately.

Shimbator (Shim-bah-tore)—a legendary type of Gwythienian, one who is able to transform into a human and back into a Gwythienian at will.

Veritamyk (Very-tam-eek)—a Crivabanian creature who befriends Enzi on her journey.

Vorbiaquam (Vore-bee-ak-wam)—a cavern in Odan Terridor with walls of waterfalls and pools of water on either side of the strip of land within, a place for Gwythienians to look into the water for other places.

9 780999 864558